Contents

ADULT MATURINGS

LIFELONG LESSONS

DEATH'S VICTORY

FOREWORD

I've always enjoyed well-written short stories. Through the years, when I found an exceptional one by a Christian author, I would make a copy and file it away. This volume is the result of all those years of collecting.

While story collections have grown in popularity recently, and there are a number in the bookstores, I didn't want to churn out yet another volume of stories with varied quality and readability. The stories in this book were chosen carefully and thoughtfully.

There were several books I read that were too lengthy in published form but were just too good to ignore. I used excerpts out of books such as C. S. Lewis's *The Lion, the Witch, and the Wardrobe* and Keith Miller's *Habitation of Dragons,* and I contemporized a segment of John Bunyan's *Pilgrim's Progress.* I also condensed the books *A Man Called Norman, The Best Christmas Pageant Ever,* and *The Pineapple Story.*

It may be surprising to some, but even acquiring permissions for the use of each piece in a compilation can be quite tedious and time-consuming. But it is all worth the effort if the volume benefits readers. I would like to thank Jeanette Thomason, special projects editor at Baker, for her suggestions and improvements to the project.

I wish for you, the reader, to be captivated as I have been by the enchantment of these stories. May they encourage and challenge you in the quest to know God better and to become more like him.

CHILDHOOD SIMPLICITIES

The Lion, the Witch, and the Wardrobe

C. S. Lewis

In one of Oxford professor C. S. Lewis's most popular tales, four young siblings get lost in a wardrobe and end up in another world. A strange wonderland with unearthly creatures, it is a bleak place of perpetual winter, where a witch—the White Witch—has placed a wicked spell so that spring can never come. She's also turned into stone many of those who oppose her. A majestic lion named Aslan is the only one who can free the land from her spell. As the story progresses the witch encounters Edmund, one of the four children, and beguiles him with an irresistible delicacy called Turkish Delight. The following excerpt tells of the horrible lengths to which Aslan is willing to go in order to buy back Edmund from the witch's evil clutches—a reminder of the lengths to which Christ went to redeem humanity.

The moonlight was bright and everything was quite still except for the noise of the river chattering over the stones. Then Susan suddenly caught Lucy's arm and said, "Look!" On the far side of the camping ground, just where the trees began, they saw the Lion slowly walking away from them into the wood. Without a word they both followed him.

He led them up the steep slope out of the river valley and then slightly to the left—apparently by the very same route which they had used that afternoon in coming from the Hill of the Stone Table. On and on he led them, into dark shadows and out into pale moonlight, getting their feet wet with the heavy dew. He looked somehow different from the Aslan they knew. His tail and head hung low and he walked slowly as if he were very, very tired. Then, when they were crossing a wide open place where there were no shadows for them to hide in, he stopped and looked round. It was no good trying to run away so they came towards him.

When they were closer he said, "Oh, children, children, why are you following me?"

"We couldn't sleep," said Lucy—and then felt sure that she need say no more and that Aslan knew all they had been thinking.

"Please, may we come with you, wherever you're going?" said Susan.

"Well—" said Aslan, who paused, it seemed, to think. Then he said, "I should be glad of company tonight. Yes, you may come, if you will promise to stop when I tell you, and after that leave me to go on alone."

"Oh, thank you, thank you. And we will," said the two girls.

Forward they went again, one girl walking on each side of the Lion. But how slowly he walked! And his great, royal head drooped so that his nose nearly touched the grass. Presently he stumbled and gave a low moan.

"Aslan, dear Aslan!" said Lucy. "What is wrong? Can't you tell us?"

"Are you ill, dear Aslan?" asked Susan.

"No," he answered. "I am sad and lonely. Lay your hands on my mane so that I can feel you are there and let us walk like that."

The girls did what they would never have dared to do without his permission but what they had longed to do ever since they first saw him—bury their cold hands into Aslan's beautiful sea of fur and stroke it. In so doing, they continued to walk with him.

Presently they saw that they were going with him up the slope of the hill on which the Stone Table stood. They went up the side where the trees came furthest, and when they got to the last tree (one that had some bushes about it), Aslan stopped and said, "Oh, children, children. Here you must stop. And whatever happens, do not let yourselves be seen. Farewell."

Both the girls cried bitterly (though they hardly knew why) and clung to the Lion. They kissed his mane and nose, his paws, and his great, sad eyes. Then he turned from them and walked onto the top of the hill. Lucy and Susan, crouching in the bushes, looked after him and this is what they saw.

A great crowd of people were standing all round the Stone Table, and though the moon was shining many of them carried torches which burned with evil-looking red flames and black smoke. But such people! Ogres with monstrous teeth; wolves, bullheaded men, spirits of evil trees and poisonous plants, and other creatures whom I won't describe because if I did the grown-ups probably would not let you read this book—Cruels and Hags and Incubuses, Wraiths, Horrors, Efreets, Sprites, Orknies, Wooses, and Ettins. In fact here were all those who were on the White Witch's side and whom the Wolf had summoned at her command. And right in the middle, standing by the Table, was the Witch herself.

A howl and a gibber of dismay went up from the creatures when they first saw the great Lion pacing towards them, and for a moment the Witch herself seemed to be struck with fear. Then she recovered herself and gave a wild, fierce laugh.

"The Fool!" she cried. "The Fool has come. Bind him fast."

Lucy and Susan held their breath waiting for Aslan's roar and his spring upon his enemies. But it never came. Four Hags, grinning and leering, yet also (at first) hanging back, half afraid of what they had to do, had approached him.

"Bind him, I say!" repeated the White Witch.

The Hags made a dart at him and shrieked with triumph when they found that he made no resistance at all. Then others—evil dwarfs and apes—rushed in to help them and between them they rolled the huge Lion round on his back and tied all his four paws together, shouting and cheering as if they had done something brave, though, had the Lion chosen, one of those paws could have been the death of them all. But he made no noise, even when the enemies, straining and tugging, pulled the cords so tight that they cut into his flesh. Then they began to drag him towards the Stone Table.

"Stop!" said the Witch. "Let him first be shaved."

Another roar of mean laughter went up from her followers as an Ogre with a pair of shears came forward and squatted down by Aslan's head. Snip-snip-snip went the shears and masses of curling gold began to fall to the ground. Then the Ogre stood back and the children, watching from their hiding place, could see the face of Aslan looking all small and different without its mane. The enemies also saw the difference.

"Why, he's only a great cat after all!" cried one.

"Is that what we were afraid of?" said another.

And they surged round Aslan jeering at him, saying things like "Puss, Puss! Poor Pussy," and "How many mice have you caught today, Cat?" and "Would you like a saucer of milk, Pussums?"

"Oh, how can they?" cried Lucy, tears streaming down her cheeks. "The brutes, the brutes!" Now that the first shock was over, the shorn face of Aslan looked to her braver, more beautiful, and more patient than ever.

"Muzzle him!" said the Witch.

Even as her minions worked about Aslan's face, putting on the muzzle, one bite from his jaws would have cost two or three of them their hands. But he never moved. This seemed to enrage all that rabble. Everyone was at him now. Those who had been afraid to come near him even after he was bound began to find their courage, and for a few minutes the two girls could not even see him—so thickly was he surrounded by the whole crowd of creatures kicking him, hitting, spitting on him, jeering.

At last the rabble had enough of this and began to drag the bound and muzzled Aslan to the Stone Table, some pulling and some pushing. He was so huge that even when they got him there it took all their efforts to hoist him onto the surface of it. Then there was more tying and tightening of cords.

"The cowards! The cowards!" sobbed Susan. "Are they still afraid of him, even now?"

Once Aslan had been tied (and tied so that he was really a mass of cords) on the flat stone, a hush fell on the crowd. Four Hags, holding four torches, stood at the corners of the Table. The Witch bared her arms as she had bared them the previous night when it had been Edmund instead of Aslan. Then she bent to whet her knife. It looked to the children, when the gleam of the torchlight fell on it, as if the knife were made of stone not of steel and it was of a strange and evil shape.

At last she drew near. She stood by Aslan's head. Her face was working and twitching with passion, but his looked up at the sky, still quiet, neither angry nor afraid, but a little sad. Then, just before she gave the blow, she stooped down and said in a quivering voice, "And now, who has won? Fool, did you think that by all this you would save the human traitor? Now I will kill you instead of him as our pact was and so the Deep Magic will be appeased. But when you are dead what will prevent me from killing him as well? And who will take him out of my hand then? Understand that you have given me Narnia forever; you have lost your own life and you have not saved his. In that knowledge, despair and die."

The children did not see the actual moment of the killing. They couldn't bear to look and covered their eyes. While the two girls still crouched in the bushes with their hands over their faces, they heard the voice of the Witch calling out.

"Now! Follow me all and we will set about what remains of this war! It will not take us long to crush the human vermin and the traitors now that the great Fool, the great Cat, lies dead."

At this moment the children were for a few seconds in very great danger. For with wild cries and a noise of skirling pipes and shrill horns blowing, the whole of that vile rabble came sweeping off the hilltop and down the slope right past their hiding place. They felt the Spectres go by them like a cold wind and they felt the ground shake beneath them under the galloping feet of the Minotaurs. Overhead there went a flurry of foul wings and a blackness of vultures and giant bats. At any other time they would have trembled with fear, but now the sadness, shame, and horror of Aslan's death so filled their minds that they hardly thought of it.

As soon as the wood was silent again Susan and Lucy crept out onto the open hilltop. The moon was getting low and thin clouds were passing across, but still they could see the shape of the great Lion lying dead in his bonds. Down they both knelt in the wet grass to kiss Aslan's cold face, stroke his beautiful fur—what was left of it—and cry till they could cry no more. Then they looked at each other and held each other's hands for mere loneliness and cried again; and then again were silent.

At last Lucy said, "I can't bear the look of that horrible muzzle. I wonder, could we take it off?"

So they tried. After a lot of working at it (for their fingers were cold and it was now the darkest part of the night), they succeeded. When they saw Aslan's face without the muzzle, they burst out crying again and kissed him and fondled him and wiped away the blood and foam as well as they could. And it was all more lonely and hopeless and horrid than I know how to describe.

"I wonder, could we untie him as well?" said Susan presently. But the enemies, out of pure spitefulness, had drawn the cords so tight that the girls could make nothing of the knots.

15

I hope no one who reads this book has been quite as miserable as Susan and Lucy were that night. But if you have been—if you've been up all night and cried till you have no more tears left in you—you will know that there comes in the end a sort of quietness. You feel as if nothing is ever going to happen again. At any rate that was how it felt to these two.

Hours and hours seemed to go by in this dead calm, and they hardly noticed that they were getting colder and colder. At last Lucy noticed two other things. One was that the sky on the East side of the hill was a little less dark than it had been an hour ago. The other was some tiny movement going on in the grass at her feet. At first she took no interest in this. What did it matter? Nothing mattered now. Then she saw that whatever it was had begun to move up the upright stones of the Table. Now the movement was about on Aslan's body. Lucy peered closer. The motion came from little grey things.

"Ugh!" said Susan from the other side of the Table. "How beastly! There are horrid little mice crawling over Aslan.

"Go away, you little beasts." She raised her hand to frighten them away.

"Wait!" said Lucy who had been looking at them more closely still. "Can you see what they're doing?"

Both girls bent down and stared.

"I do believe . . . ," said Susan, "but how queer . . . they're nibbling away at the cords!"

"That's what I thought," said Lucy. "I think they're friendly mice. Poor little things. They don't realize he's dead. They think it'll do some good untying him."

It was definitely lighter by now. Each of the girls noticed for the first time the white face of the other. They could see the mice nibbling away, dozens and dozens, even hundreds, of the field mice. And at last, one by one, the ropes were all gnawed through.

The sky in the East was whitish by now and the stars were getting fainter—all except one very big one low down on the Eastern horizon. They felt colder than they had been all night. The mice crept away again.

The girls cleared away the remains of the gnawed ropes. Aslan looked more like himself without them. Every moment his dead face looked nobler, as the light grew and they could see it better.

In the wood behind them a bird gave a chuckling sound, startling them. It had been so still for hours and hours. Then another bird answered. Soon there were birds singing all over the place.

It was definitely early morning now, not late night.

"I'm so cold," said Lucy.

"So am I," said Susan. "Let's walk about a bit."

They walked to the Eastern edge of the hill and looked down. The one big star had almost disappeared. The country all looked dark grey, but beyond, at the very end of the world, the sea showed pale. The sky began to turn red. They walked to and fro more times than they could count between the dead Aslan and the Eastern ridge, trying to keep warm. Oh, how tired their legs felt. Then at last, as they stood for a moment looking out towards the sea and Cair Paravel (which they could now just make out) the red turned to gold along the line where the sea and the sky met and very slowly up came the edge of the sun. At that moment they heard from behind them a loud noise—a great cracking, deafening noise as if a giant had broken a giant's plate.

"What's that?" said Lucy, clutching Susan's arm.

"I—I feel afraid to turn round," said Susan. "Something awful is happening."

"They're doing something worse to him," said Lucy. "Come on!" She turned, pulling Susan round with her.

The rising of the sun had made everything look so different—all the colors and shadows were changed—that for a moment they didn't see the important thing. Then they did. The Stone Table was broken into two pieces by a great crack that ran from end to end, and there was no Aslan.

"Oh, oh, oh!" cried the two girls rushing back to the Table.

"Oh, it's too bad," sobbed Lucy. "They might have left the body alone."

"Who's done it?" cried Susan. "What does it mean? Is it more magic?"

"Yes!" said a great voice behind their backs. "It is more magic."

They looked round. There, shining in the sunrise, larger than they had seen him before, shaking his mane (for it had apparently grown again), stood Aslan himself.

"Oh, Aslan!" cried both the children, staring up at him, almost as much frightened as they were glad.

"Aren't you dead then, dear Aslan?" said Lucy.

"Not now," said Aslan.

"You're not—not—a—?" asked Susan in a shaky voice. She couldn't bring herself to say the word "ghost."

17

Aslan stooped his golden head and licked her forehead. The warmth of his breath and a rich sort of smell that seemed to hang about his hair came all over her.

"Do I look it?" he said.

"Oh, you're real, you're real! Oh, Aslan!" cried Lucy and both girls flung themselves upon him and covered him with kisses.

"But what does it all mean?" asked Susan when they were somewhat calmer.

"It means," said Aslan, "that though the Witch knew the Deep Magic, there is a magic deeper still which she did not know. Her knowledge goes back only to the dawn of Time. But if she could have looked a little further back, into the stillness and darkness before Time dawned, she would have read there a different incantation. She would have known that when a willing victim who had committed no treachery was killed in a traitor's stead, the Table would crack and Death itself would start working backwards. And now—"

"Oh yes. Now?" said Lucy jumping up and clapping her hands.

"Oh, children," said the Lion. "I feel my strength coming back to me. Oh, children, catch me if you can." He stood for a second, his eyes very bright, his limbs quivering, lashing himself with his tail. Then he made a leap high over their heads and landed on the other side of the Table. Laughing, though she didn't know why, Lucy scrambled over it to reach him. Aslan leaped again. A mad chase began. Round and round the hilltop he led them, now hopelessly out of their reach, now letting them almost catch his tail, now diving between them, now tossing them in the air with his huge and beautifully velveted paws and catching them again, and now stopping unexpectedly so that all three of them rolled over together in a happy laughing heap of fur and arms and legs. It was such a romp as no one has ever had except in Narnia; whether it was more like playing with a thunderstorm or playing with a kitten Lucy could never make up her mind. The funny thing was that when all three finally lay together panting in the sun, the girls no longer felt in the least tired or hungry or thirsty.

"And now," said Aslan presently, "to business. I feel I am going to roar. You had better put your fingers in your ears."

They did. Aslan stood up, and when he opened his mouth to roar, his face became so terrible that they did not dare look at it. They saw all the trees in front of him bend before the blast of his roaring as grass bends in a meadow before the wind.

Then he said, "We have a long journey to go. You must ride on me."
He crouched down and the children climbed onto his warm, golden
back. Susan sat first holding on tightly to his mane, and Lucy sat behind
holding on tightly to Susan. With a great heave Aslan rose underneath
them and then shot off, faster than any horse could go, downhill and
into the thick of the forest.

THE LESSON
OF THE SWEETER DAY

Cliff Schimmels

Dr. Cliff Schimmels has been called a Renaissance man, yet he claims to think like a fourteen-year-old. In fact, at age forty-seven he went back to high school to find out what school is like for today's teens.

As a professor and author, Schimmels wrote a book in 1991 titled All I Really Need to Know I Learned in Sunday School. *The following selection describes Mrs. Henderson, one of Schimmel's favorite Sunday school teachers, and the song she affectionately bequeathed to him.*

The good thing about learning songs in Sunday school is that for the rest of your life, they take on the look of the person who first, to your hearing, sang them.

Of course, this isn't true with all songs or all singers, but some songs just seem to be tailor-made for specific people. How often, after all, have you heard someone sing a song, then said to yourself, "That fits"? From then on, anyone else who attempts to sing that song won't quite make it.

On the other hand, how often do you see someone who attempts to sing a song that doesn't quite fit?

During opening exercises at Sunday school, Mrs. Henderson didn't sing too much because Mrs. Smith always led while Mrs. Henderson sat out among the children herding, corraling, and coaxing. On special days, however, when we sang one special song, Mrs. Smith would step aside for Mrs. Henderson to lead. And that was so right. It was Mrs. Henderson's song, and everybody knew it. She's the one who taught it to us, led us in it, and corrected us if we didn't understand. And she's the one who knew what it meant.

> *Every day with Jesus*
> *is sweeter than the day before,*
> *Every day with Jesus*
> *I love Him more and more,*
> *Jesus saves and keeps me,*
> *and He's the one I'm waiting for,*
> *Every day with Jesus*
> *is sweeter than the day before.*

As she would lead by singing above us from her place in the front, even the restless and perpetually mischievous would cease their wiggling and gouging. They would stand still with calmness in body and soul, and the room would be filled with a certain quiet, a serene peacefulness rather than a forced or manipulated silence.

Although "hearty" was the descriptive word for most of our singing, "serene" would be appropriate to describe how we participated when Mrs. Henderson sang.

We never heard the age in her voice or saw the trembling in her hands. With our heads partially bowed in a reverence required by the moment, we watched and followed and said to ourselves, "This is so right."

This was Mrs. Henderson's song because it was her life.

Mrs. Henderson was everybody's grandmother; we children talked to her more than we talked to any other adult in church. Because of that we thought we knew her. In fact, everyone thought they knew her better than they really did—not because of deception, but a special kind of caring. In conversation with Mrs. Henderson, you talked and she listened.

She also frequently carried things in the pocket of her dress and surprised us with some little gift—a cookie, special piece of embroidery, or something she carved from a piece of twig. These gifts were conceived and designed for each specific child, and a gift from Mrs. Henderson became a prized possession, something each of us cherished for the reminder given that some adult really had thought about us.

She was the only Christian I've ever known who spent more time celebrating Easter than Christmas. She baked special goodies, mailed out announcement cards, and gave us gifts. Each year we had a children's Christmas play to satisfy the needs of the rest of the church, but we had an Easter play to satisfy Mrs. Henderson.

This is because Mrs. Henderson knew Jesus personally. She was on a first-name basis with Him. She prayed often and long, read her Bible thoroughly and deeply, and waited with great excitement for that day when Jesus would come again.

Each day with Mrs. Henderson was sweeter than the day before because each day she learned to love Jesus more. For her, this was life's true excitement. The Bible was a gold mine of rich nuggets contributing to plentiful living, and every day she dug and dug until she found that special nugget. On Sunday, she would describe those nuggets to us with such vividness that we learned to love Jesus more too.

One day in early June when the sky was luscious, the valley alive with plants, and it was early enough in the summer vacation that we hadn't grown bored yet, I went down to Mrs. Henderson's house to help her hoe her garden.

We worked together that afternoon and talked. Or rather I talked and Mrs. Henderson listened and asked things, and I talked more. Then, in what seemed to be a moment out of context, she said it would thrill her if I would sing to her. I winced and explained my sore rib syndrome, and that my nickname was Off-Key Cliff. She smiled with reassurance instead of ridicule and told me that she had a song with my name on it. She would teach it to me, and it would be my special song for the rest of my life. She was so convincing, and I was so excited about that possibility, that for a moment I actually believed I could do it. I listened and she sang—the only song I had ever heard her sing:

> *Every day with Jesus*
> *is sweeter than the day before,*
> *Every day with Jesus*
> *I love Him more and more,*
> *Jesus saves and keeps me,*
> *and He's the one I'm waiting for,*

Every day with Jesus
is sweeter than the day before.

When she finished, she pleaded with me to try—pleading with such gentleness and genuineness that I attempted this solo without any hint of fear that I might be off-key or any sense of disloyalty for taking her song.

I sang, but since my ears are on the side instead of the front, I couldn't hear myself, so I don't know whether it sounded good or not. But it felt good.

When I had finished, Mrs. Henderson had moisture in her eyes and told me I had done it beautifully. Then she told me I should sing that song because it fit me, and since I believe songs can fit the people who sing them, and because I had seen her sing this song, I believed her.

I have sung that song every day since. I don't sing out loud or in crowds. I probably don't even sing on key. And when it comes down to it, I don't know whether the song fits my voice or not, but I pray that it fits my life the way it fit Mrs. Henderson's.

THE LESSON
OF THE BROKEN CRAYONS

Cliff Schimmels

As a child, Cliff Schimmels's least favorite time in Sunday school was coloring time. He colored messy pictures and never stayed within the lines. Then a little girl named Edith joined the class and showed him that even the old, broken crayons can be used to draw beautiful pictures. Similarly, Schimmels shows how we can take negative situations and turn them into something worthwhile through Christ.

Coloring was not my favorite thing to do. It didn't even make the Top Ten. On a list of irregular duties and responsibilities, coloring was down around getting knots out of shoelaces when I was in a hurry to go swimming, or worse—pulling cockleburs out of cows' tails.

Just the thought of coloring in Sunday school was enough to haunt me awake at least twice every Saturday night with a jolt loud enough to wake up my brother and any other assorted animal life that happened to be sleeping in or around the bed.

The reason for my fear was justified, in part natural and in part theological. You see, in His infinite wisdom, God saw fit to make me an upside-down left-hander—at least by His design and my childish invention born out of necessity to write with some hand. Since I didn't know the difference between left and right, the pencil wound up in my left hand, which I turned upside down for better control.

That's how it happened. To some it might seem so very natural, but I still feel it was providential, and all those people who have laughed at my penmanship through the years will someday answer for their sins.

The result was that my coloring was not only awkward, but messy—and Sunday school coloring was the worst. Every Sunday morning I'd face that dramatic moment in the lesson when Mrs. Murphy, or sometimes Mrs. Smith, would roll her eyes around the room, grin rather falsely, and exclaim, "Have you ever wondered what those people in your lesson today must have looked like?"

Years later I've learned that educators call this moment and its subsequent activity "visualization." Teachers call it "time off."

Whatever you call it, the reaction was always the same. All the other children would wiggle with glee, and I would sit in utter dread as the teacher distributed sheets of paper with faint outlines of the heroes of the day.

Then, amidst the wriggling, would come the magic signal, "You may go get crayons now." A herd would rush full speed ahead to the cigar boxes in which were stored a giant assortment of crayons from present, past, and a long time ago. Have you ever wondered, by the way, what would have happened in those days of Sunday school and elementary education if there had been no cigar boxes?

The aggressive kids would get to the boxes first and rummage with the intensity of shoppers at a clearance sale until the most choice, new, and long crayons were in hand.

By the time the timid and coloring-haters got a turn to look, there remained only the stubby and broken bits of what used to be. Those broken pieces of color stuffed into my already awkward left hand squelched any Rembrandt fantasies I might have harbored.

Monochromatic assignments were at least manageable. Things like elephants, sheep, camels, and Mount Sinai allowed me to blob and smear without paying too much heed to that one artistic paradigm above all paradigms: "Stay within the lines." But multicolored assignments with small spaces brought definition to the label "Fine Arts" and terror to my soul.

One day near Christmas, Mrs. Murphy told us about the wise men who came to visit the Baby Jesus. They were kings, actually, dressed in the richest and brightest colors of the day, and we should color them so.

Now, I ask you, have you ever tried to paint royalty with only an ancient piece of purple crayon? I managed enough hand control to make the king's cloak purple, but I also managed to make his face purple too. When Mrs. Murphy and the aggressive colorers mocked, "Why is his face purple?" I explained that this wise man was happy. After all, he was the one who had brought the myrth.

That's when I learned that coloring poorly does have one serendipitous advantage: It causes one to develop a quick wit. This all changed, however, when Edith came to our Sunday school. I never really knew where she came from. She just showed up one day, and a year later disappeared.

Edith was not one of the aggressive ones. In fact, she was so unassuming that we would not even have known her name except that she had to wear a New Person name tag three weeks in a row.

On her first Sunday, when Mrs. Smith asked, "Is there anyone here for the first time?" Walter, who helped the teacher run things and always got the biggest crayon, pointed to Edith and shouted out loud, "I don't know that girl over there. I've never seen her before."

The second week she was there, we went through the very same ritual. But on the third Sunday, after cheeky Walter said his piece, Mrs. Smith suddenly remembered she had written the name "Edith" before; after that Edith didn't have to wear the New Person tag.

When it came time to color, Edith didn't rush over with the herd to the storage cabinet. She was so shy she was even behind me. Without a hint of frustration, she reached into the box and took one of the left-over bits.

What happened in the next few minutes revolutionized Sunday school art and my world in general: not only a thing of beauty but a joy forever for all upside-down left-handers everywhere.

With only a nub of a crayon in her hand, Edith proceeded to tear away its paper. She then placed the side of the crayon on the Walls of Jericho and began to move the flat edge around the design. The result was breathtaking. By pressing more firmly on the outside, she created a shading effect; with the continuous motion she eliminated the telltale blotches of children's art—all the while staying within the lines.

Besides that, she was the first one finished. When Mrs. Smith held up Edith's work for all to see and admire, the room was filled with another color, the envious green of aggressive kids shown up at their own game, and the world laughed joyously. After that even the aggressive kids picked the broken crayons, but they could never reach Edith's level because she was the master.

Through the years, this lesson of Edith and the broken crayon still haunts me with memories of delight and the joy of flexibility.

How often life deals us a broken crayon!

The dentist says, "I'm sorry. This is not your normal, run-of-the-mill cavity. This one requires a root canal."

You're in a hurry to a very important meeting with a very important person when you spot that cheery sign "ROAD CONSTRUCTION AHEAD."

The salesman says, "If you can't afford this one, I have another model *almost* as nice."

The boss says, "Could you have it by Monday?"

That teenager who is your very own flesh and blood, your posterity and hope, has a total vocabulary of three phrases: "Everybody else will be there," "That's not fair," and "You don't trust me."

At such moments I remember the Sunday school lesson from the day when Edith taught me to tear the paper off the crayon and make a beautiful picture anyway.

Somebody else really good at this wasn't particularly handsome. As a speaker, he put part of his audience to sleep one night—to the point that they fell out a window—and he was always getting beaten up or shipwrecked or run out of town.

Yet in the midst of all this adversity, this guy wrote a letter to a group of people in Rome who weren't exactly living in the Ritz themselves. He said, "For we know that all things work together for the good of those who love God and are called according to His purpose."

The Apostle Paul spent years and years taking the broken crayons he was dealt and drawing beautiful pictures in the lives of those he met. They were eternal pictures for God's palette, and they brought Him pleasure and honor.

THE BEST CHRISTMAS PAGEANT EVER

Barbara Robinson

Barbara Robinson has written a number of books, most of them hilarious. Robinson spends much of her time speaking in schools across the United States.

The Best Christmas Pageant Ever has been made into both a movie and a play. In the story, the irreverent, rough-and-ready Herdman kids volunteer to be in a church Christmas pageant and, in their earthy, confused transparency, bring a whole new freshness to the age-old nativity account.

The Herdmans were absolutely the worst kids in the history of the planet. They lied and stole and smoked cigars (even the girls smoked), and they talked dirty and smacked little kids and cussed their teachers and took the name of the Lord in vain and set fire to Fred Shoemaker's broken-down toolhouse.

They were just so all-around awful you could hardly believe they were real: Ralph, Imogene, Leroy, Claude, Ollie, and Gladys—six skinny, greasy-haired kids all alike except for coming in different sizes and having various black-and-blue places where they had clonked each other.

They lived over a garage at the bottom of Sproul Hill. Nobody used the garage anymore, but the Herdmans used to bang the door up and down just as fast as they could and try to squash one another. It was their idea of a good time.

I was always in the same grade with Imogene Herdman, and what I did was stay out of her way. It wasn't easy. You couldn't do it if you were very pretty or very ugly, or very smart or very dumb, or had anything unusual about you, like red hair or double-jointed thumbs.

But if you were sort of a basic, ordinary kid like me and kept your mouth shut when the teacher said, "Who can name all fifty states?" you had a pretty fair chance of staying clear of Imogene.

As far as anyone could tell, Imogene was just like the rest of the Herdmans. She never learned anything either, except dirty words and secrets about everybody.

My friend Alice Wendleken was so squeaky clean that she had detergent hands by the time she was four years old. Just the same Alice picked up a case of head lice when she was at summer camp, and somehow Imogene found out about it. She would sneak up on Alice at recess and holler "cooties!" and slap Alice's head. She nearly knocked Alice cross-eyed before one of the teachers saw her and took both of them to the principal.

My mother's friend Miss Phillips was a social service worker and she tried to get some welfare money for the Herdmans so Mrs. Herdman could just work one shift at the shoe factory. But Mrs. Herdman refused—said she liked working both shifts. Miss Phillips shook her head and told my mother that the woman insisted on two shifts because she didn't want to be cooped up all day with her own bratty kids.

So the Herdmans pretty much looked after themselves in a survival of the fittest pecking order. We figured they were all headed straight for hell, by way of the state penitentiary . . . until they got themselves mixed up with the church, and my mother, and our Christmas pageant.

Our Christmas pageant isn't what you'd call four-star entertainment. We don't add anything to jazz up the script like those people in Hollywood do. Primary kids are angels, intermediate kids are shepherds, big boys are Wise Men; Elmer Hopkins, the minister's son, has been Joseph for as long as I can remember, and Alice Wendleken is Mary because she's so pretty, clean, and holy-looking.

All the rest of us are the angel choir—lined up according to height because nobody can sing parts. In fact, nobody can sing, except for a girl named Alberta Bottles who whistles. Aside from that, it's always the same—kids shuffling aimlessly around in bathrobes, bedsheets, and sharp wings.

It was my brother Charlie's fault that the Herdmans showed up in church. For three days in a row, Leroy Herdman stole the cookies from Charlie's lunch box and Charlie finally just gave up trying to do anything about it. "Oh, go on and take it," he said. "I don't care. I get all the dessert I want in Sunday school."

Leroy's ears perked right up. "What kind of stuff?" he asked.

"Chocolate cake," Charlie told him, "and candy bars and cookies and Kool-Aid. We get refreshments all the time, all we want."

"You're a liar," said Leroy.

Leroy was right. We got jelly beans at Easter and punch and cookies on high attendance day and that was about it.

"We get ice cream too," Charlie fantasized.

"Who gives it to you?" Leroy wanted to know.

"The minister," Charlie said.

Of course, that was the exact wrong thing to tell Herdmans if you wanted them to stay away. And sure enough, the very next Sunday there they were, slouching into Sunday school, eyes peeled for the food.

"Where do you get the cake and ice cream?" Ralph asked the Sunday school superintendent. Mr. Grady said, "Well, son, I don't know about any cake but they're collecting food packages out in the kitchen." He meant the canned stuff we give to the Rescue Mission.

It was just our bad luck that the Herdmans picked that Sunday to come because they saw all the cans of spaghetti and grape drink and figured Charlie had been telling the truth. So they stayed. They didn't sing hymns and say any prayers, but they made out like bandits—I saw Imogene sneak at least one handful of coins out of the offering plate as it passed by.

After Sunday school, Mr. Grady announced that rehearsals would be starting for the Christmas pageant next Sunday after the service. All of a sudden Imogene Herdman punched me in the ribs so hard I squealed. "What's the pageant?" she said.

"It's a play," I said and for the first time that day Imogene looked interested.

"What's the play about?" Imogene asked.

"It's about Jesus," I said.

"Everything here is," she muttered, so I figured Imogene didn't care much about the Christmas pageant.

But I was wrong.

After church the next week we all filed into the back seven pews, along with two or three Sunday school teachers who were supposed to keep everybody quiet.

"Now you little children in the cradle room and the primary class will be our angels," Mother said. "You'll like that, won't you?"

They all said yes. What else could they say?

"The older boys and girls will be shepherds and guests at the inn and members of the choir. And we need Mary and Joseph, the three Wise Men, and the Angel of the Lord. They aren't hard parts, but they're very important parts, so those people must absolutely come to every rehearsal.

"Now, we all know what kind of person Mary was," Mother continued. "She was quiet and gentle and kind, and the little girl who plays Mary should try to be that kind of person. I know that many of you would like to be Mary in our pageant, but of course we can only have one. So I'll ask for volunteers, and then we'll all decide together which girl should get the part." That was pretty safe to say, since the only person who ever raised her hand was Alice Wendleken.

But Alice just sat there, chewing on a piece of her hair and looking down at the floor . . . and the only person who raised her hand this time was Imogene Herdman.

"Did you have a question, Imogene?" Mother asked. I guess that was the only reason she could think of for Imogene to have her hand up.

"No," Imogene said. "I want to be Mary." She looked back over her shoulder. "And Ralph wants to be Joseph."

"Yeh," Ralph said.

Mother couldn't believe this. "Well," she said with a frown, "we want to be sure that everyone has a chance. Does anyone else want to volunteer for Joseph?"

No one did.

"All right," Mother said, "Ralph will be our Joseph. Now does anyone else want to volunteer for Mary?" Mother looked all around, trying to catch somebody's eye—anybody's eye. "Janet? Roberta? Alice? Don't any of you want to volunteer this year?"

"No," Alice said, so low you could hardly hear her. "I don't want to."

Nobody volunteered to be Wise Men either, except Leroy, Claude, and Ollie Herdman. So there was my mother, stuck with a Christmas pageant full of Herdmans in the main roles.

There was one Herdman left over, and one main role left over, and you didn't have to be very smart to figure out that Gladys was going to be the Angel of the Lord.

"What do I have to do?" Gladys wanted to know.

"The Angel of the Lord was the one who brought the good news to the shepherds," Mother said.

Right away all the shepherds began to wiggle around in their seats, figuring that any good news Gladys brought them would come with a smack in the teeth.

Charlie's friend Hobie Carmichael raised his hand and said, "I can't be a shepherd. We're going to Philadelphia."

"Why didn't you say so before?" Mother asked.

"I forgot."

Another kid said, "My mother doesn't want me to be a shepherd."

"Why not?"

"I don't know. She just said don't be a shepherd."

One kid was honest. "Gladys Herdman hits too hard," he said.

"Why Gladys isn't going to hit anybody!" Mother said. "What an idea! The Angel just visits the shepherds in the fields and tells them Jesus is born."

"And socks 'em," said the kid.

Of course he was right. You could just picture Gladys whamming shepherds left and right, but Mother said that was perfectly ridiculous.

The next Wednesday we started rehearsals. The Herdmans got there ten minutes late, sliding into the room like a bunch of outlaws about to shoot up a saloon. When Leroy passed Charlie, he knuckled him behind the ear, and one little primary girl yelped as Gladys went by. But Mother said she was going to ignore everything except blood, and since the primary kid wasn't bleeding, and neither was Charlie, nothing happened.

"And here's the Herdman family," Mother announced. Then, "We're glad to see you all," which was probably the biggest lie ever said right out loud in church. Imogene smiled—the Herdman smile, we called it, sly and sneaky—and there they sat, the closest thing to criminals that we knew about, and they were going to represent the best and most beautiful. No wonder everybody was so worked up.

Mother started to separate everyone into angels and shepherds and guests at the inn, but right away she ran into trouble.

"Who were the shepherds?" Leroy Herdman wanted to know. "Where did they come from?"

Ollie Herdman didn't even know what a shepherd was or, anyway, that's what he said.

"What was the inn?" Claude asked. "What's an inn?"

"It's like a motel," somebody told him, "where people go to spend the night."

"What people? Jesus?"

"Oh honestly!" Alice Wendleken grumbled. "Jesus wasn't even born yet. Mary and Joseph went there."

"Why?" Ralph asked.

"What happened first?" Imogene hollered at my mother. "Begin at the beginning."

That really scared me because the beginning would be the Book of Genesis, where it says "In the beginning . . . ," and if we were going to have to start with the Book of Genesis we'd never get through.

The thing was the Herdmans didn't know anything about the Christmas story. They knew that Christmas was Jesus's birthday, but everything else was news to them: the shepherds, the Wise Men, the star, the stable, the crowded inn.

It was hard to believe. At least it was hard for me to believe—Alice Wendleken said she didn't have any trouble believing it. But the Herdmans just didn't know.

So Mother said she had better begin by reading the Christmas story from the Bible. This was a pain in the neck to most of us because we knew the whole thing backward and forward and never had to be told anything except who we were supposed to be, and where we were supposed to stand.

"Joseph and Mary," she read, "his espoused wife, being great with child . . ."

"Pregnant!" yelled Ralph Herdman.

Well, that stirred things up. All the big kids began to giggle and all the little kids wanted to know what was so funny, and Mother had to hammer on the floor with a blackboard pointer. "That's enough, Ralph," she said, and went on with the story.

I pinched Alice. She yelped and Mother separated us and made me sit beside Imogene Herdman and sent Alice to sit in the middle of the baby angels. I wasn't crazy to sit next to Imogene—after all, I'd spent my whole life staying away from Imogene—but she didn't even notice me. Not much, anyway.

"Shut up," was all she said. "I want to hear her."

I couldn't believe it. Among other things, the Herdmans were famous for never sitting still and never paying attention to anyone: teachers, parents (their own or anybody else's), the truant officer, the police. Yet here they were, eyes glued on my mother and taking in every word.

"What's that?" they would yell whenever they didn't understand the language, and when Mother read about there being no room at the inn, Imogene's jaw dropped and she sat up in her seat.

"Not even for Jesus?"

"Well, now, after all," Mother explained, "nobody knew the baby was going to turn out to be Jesus."

"You said Mary knew," Ralph said. "Why didn't she tell them?"

"I would have told them!" Imogene put in. "Boy, would I have told them! What was the matter with Joseph that he didn't tell them? Her pregnant and everything."

"What was that they laid the baby in?" Leroy said. "That manger . . . is that like a bed? Why would they have a bed in the barn?"

"That's just the point," Mother said. "They didn't have a bed in the barn, so Mary and Joseph had to use whatever there was. What would you do if you had a new baby and no bed to put it in?"

"We put Gladys in a bureau drawer," Imogene volunteered.

"Well, there you are," Mother said, blinking a little. "You didn't have a bed for Gladys so you had to use something else."

"Oh, we had a bed," Ralph said, "only Ollie was still in it and he wouldn't get out. He didn't like Gladys." He elbowed Ollie. "Remember how you didn't like Gladys?"

I thought that was pretty smart of Ollie, not to like Gladys right off the bat.

"Anyway," Mother said, "Mary and Joseph used the manger. A manger is a large wooden feeding trough for animals."

"What were the wadded-up clothes?"

"Swaddling clothes," Mother explained. "Long ago people used to wrap their babies very tightly in big pieces of material, so they couldn't move around. It made the babies feel cozy and comfortable."

I thought it probably just made the babies mad. Till then I didn't know what swaddling clothes were either, and they sounded terrible, so I wasn't too surprised when Imogene got all excited about that.

"You mean they tied him up and put him in a feed box?" she said.

"Where was the Child Welfare?"

The Child Welfare was always checking up on the Herdmans. I'll bet if the Child Welfare had ever found Gladys all tied up in a bureau drawer they would have done something about it.

"And, lo, the Angel of the Lord came upon them," Mother said, "and the glory of the Lord shone round about them, and—"

"Shazam!" Gladys yelled, flinging her arms out and smacking the kid next to her.

"What?" Mother said. Mother never read Amazing Comics.

"Out of the black night with horrible vengeance, the Mighty Marvo—"

"I don't know what you're talking about, Gladys," Mother said. "This is the Angel of the Lord who comes to the shepherds in the fields, and—"

"Out of nowhere, right?" Gladys said. "In the black of night, right?"

"Well, . . ." Mother looked confused. "In a way."

"Now when Jesus was born in Bethlehem of Judea," Mother went on reading, "behold there came Wise Men from the East to Jerusalem saying—"

"That's you, Leroy," Ralph said, "and Claude and Ollie. So pay attention."

"What does it mean, Wise Men?" Ollie wanted to know. "Were they like schoolteachers?"

"No, dumbbell," Claude said. "It means like the President of the United States."

Mother looked surprised, and a little pleased—like she did when Charlie finally learned the times tables up to five. "Why, that's very close, Claude," she said. "Actually they were kings."

"Well, it's about time," Imogene muttered. "Maybe they'll tell the innkeeper where to get off and get the baby out of the barn."

"They saw the young child with Mary, his mother, and fell down and worshiped him, and presented unto him gifts; gold, and frankincense, and myrrh."

"What's that stuff?" Leroy wanted to know.

"Precious oils and fragrant resins."

"Oil!" Imogene hollered. "What kind of a cheap king hands out oil for a present? You get better presents from the firemen!"

Sometimes the Herdmans got Christmas presents at the Firemen's Party, but the Santa Claus always had to feel around the packages to be sure they weren't getting bows and arrows or dart guns or anything like that. Imogene usually got sewing cards or jigsaw puzzles and she never liked them, but I guess she figured they were better than oil.

Then we came to King Herod, and the Herdmans never heard of him either, so Mother had to explain that it was Herod who sent the Wise Men to find the Baby Jesus.

"Was it him that sent the crummy presents?" Ollie wanted to know, and Mother said it was worse than that—he planned to have the baby Jesus put to death.

"He just got born and already they're out to kill him!" Imogene said.

The Herdmans wanted to know all about Herod—what he looked like and how rich he was and whether he really fought wars with people.

"He must have been the main king," Claude said, "if he could make the other three do what he wanted them to."

"If I was the king," Leroy said, "I wouldn't let some other king push me around."

"You couldn't help it if he was the main king."

"I'd go be king somewhere else."

They were really interested in Herod, and I figured they liked him. He was so mean he could have been their ancestor—Herod Herdman. But I was wrong.

"Who's going to be Herod in this play?" Leroy said.

"We don't show Herod in our pageant," Mother said. And they all got mad. They wanted somebody to be Herod so they could beat up on him.

I couldn't understand the Herdmans. You would have thought the Christmas story came right out of the F.B.I. files, they got so involved in it: wanting a bloody end to Herod, worrying about Mary having her baby in a barn, and calling the Wise Men a bunch of dirty spies.

And they left the first rehearsal arguing about whether Joseph should have set fire to the inn, or just chased the innkeeper into the next county.

Anyway, when the Reverend Hopkins heard that the Herdmans had grabbed all the main parts in the pageant, he was definitely worried. He told Mother that he was afraid it would be super low attendance Sunday for the pageant. He even toyed with the idea of calling the whole thing off. But he was wrong. Everybody came . . . to see what the Herdmans would do.

On the night of the pageant we didn't have any supper because Mother forgot to fix it. My father said he didn't expect supper anymore.

"When it's all over," he said, "we'll go someplace and have hamburgers."

But Mother said when it was all over she might want to go someplace and hide.

"We've never once gone through the whole thing," she said. "I don't know what's going to happen. It may be the first Christmas pageant in history where Joseph and the Wise Men get in a fight, and Mary runs away with the Baby."

But nothing seemed very different at first. There was the usual big mess all over the place—baby angels getting poked in the eye by other baby angels' wings and grumpy shepherds stumbling over their bathrobes. The spotlight swooped back and forth and up and down till it made you sick to your stomach to look at it and, as usual, whoever was playing the piano pitched "Away in a Manger" so high we could hardly hear it, let alone sing it. My father says, "Away in a Manger" always starts out sounding like a closetful of mice.

But everything settled down and at 7:30 the pageant began. While we sang "Away in a Manger," the ushers lit candles around the church, and the spotlight came on as the star; you really had to know the words to "Away in a Manger" because you couldn't see anything—not even Alice Wendleken's vaseline eyelids.

Then we sang two verses of "O, Little Town of Bethlehem," and were supposed to hum some more "O, Little Town of Bethlehem" while Mary and Joseph came in from a side door. Only they didn't come right away. So we hummed and hummed and hummed, which is boring and also very hard, and before long doesn't sound like any song at all—more like an old refrigerator.

"I knew something like this would happen," Alice Wendleken whispered to me. "They didn't come at all! Mary and Joseph have kidnapped the baby—and what's a Christmas pageant without Baby Jesus?"

I guess we would have gone on humming till we all turned blue, but we didn't have to. Ralph and Imogene were there all right, only for once they didn't come through the door pushing each other out of the way.

They just stood there for a minute as if they weren't sure they were in the right place—because of the candles, I guess, and the church being full of people. They looked like the people you see on the six o'clock news—refugees, sent to wait in some strange, ugly place, with all their boxes and sacks around them.

It suddenly occurred to me that this was just the way it must have been for the real Holy Family, stuck away in a barn by people who didn't care what happened to them. They couldn't have been very neat and tidy either, but more like this Mary and Joseph. (Imogene's veil was cockeyed as usual, and Ralph's hair stuck out all around his ears.)

Imogene had the baby doll but she wasn't carrying it the way she was supposed to, cradled in her arms. She had it slung up over her shoulder, and before she put it in the manger she thumped it twice on the back.

I heard Alice gasp and she poked me. "I don't think it's very nice to burp the Baby Jesus," she whispered, "as if He had a stomachache." Then she poked me again. "Do you suppose He could have really burped?"

I almost said, "I don't know why not," but I didn't. I wasn't sure, but He could have burped, or been fussy, or hungry like any other baby. After all, that was the whole point of Jesus—that He didn't come down on a cloud like something out of Amazing Comics, but that He was born and lived . . . a real Person.

Right away we had to sing "While Shepherds Watched Their Flocks by Night"—and we had to sing very loud because there were more shepherds than there were anything else, and they made so much noise, banging their crooks around like a lot of hockey sticks.

Next came Gladys, from behind the angel choir, pushing people out of the way and stepping on everyone's feet. Since Gladys was the only one in the pageant who had anything to say, she made the most of it: "Hey! Unto you a Child is born!" she hollered, as if it was, for sure, the best news in the world. And all the shepherds trembled, sore afraid—of Gladys mainly, but it looked good anyway.

Then came three carols about angels. It took that long to get the angels in because they were all primary kids and they got nervous and cried and forgot where they were supposed to go and bent their wings in the door and things like that.

We got a little rest then, while the boys sang "We Three Kings of Orient Are," and everybody in the audience shifted around to watch the Wise Men march up the aisle.

"What have they got?" Alice whispered.

I didn't know, but whatever it was, it was heavy—Leroy almost dropped it. He didn't have his frankincense jar either, and Claude and Ollie didn't have anything although they were supposed to bring the gold and the myrrh.

"I knew this would happen," Alice said for the second time. "I bet it's something awful."

"Like what?"

"Like . . . a burnt offering. You know the Herdmans."

Well they did burn things, but they hadn't burned this yet. It was a ham—and right away I knew where it came from. My father was on the church charitable works committee that gave away food baskets at Christmas, and this was the Herdmans's food basket ham. It still had the ribbon around it, saying Merry Christmas.

"I'll bet they stole that!" Alice said. But I knew better.

"They did not. It came from their food basket, and if they want to give away their own ham I guess they can do it." But even if the Herdmans didn't like ham (that was Alice's next idea) they had never before in their lives given anything away except lumps on the head. So you had to be impressed.

Leroy dropped the ham in front of the manger. It looked funny to see a ham there instead of the fancy bath salt jars we always used for the myrrh and the frankincense. And then they went and sat down in the only space left.

While we sang "What Child Is This?" the Wise Men were supposed to confer among themselves and then leave by a different door so everyone would understand that they were going home another way. But the Herdmans forgot, or didn't want to, or something, because they didn't confer and they didn't leave either. They just sat there, and there wasn't anything anyone could do about it.

"They're ruining the whole thing!" Alice whispered, but they weren't at all. As a matter of fact, it made perfect sense for the Wise Men to sit down and rest, and I said so.

"They're supposed to have come a long way. You wouldn't expect them just to show up, hand over the ham and leave!"

As for ruining the whole thing, it seemed to me that the Herdmans had improved the pageant a lot, just by doing what came naturally— like burping the baby, for instance, or thinking a ham would make a better present than a lot of perfumed oil.

Usually, by the time we got to "Silent Night," which was always the last carol, I was fed up with the whole thing and couldn't wait for it to be over. But I didn't feel that way this time. I almost wished for the pageant to go on, with the Herdmans in charge, to see what else they would do that was different.

Maybe the Wise Men would tell Mary about their problem with Herod, and she would tell them to go back and lie their heads off. Or Joseph might go with them and get rid of Herod once and for all. Or Joseph and Mary might ask the Wise Men to take the Christ Child with them, figuring that no one would think to look there.

I was so busy planning new ways to save the Baby Jesus that I missed the beginning of "Silent Night," but it was all right because everyone sang, including the audience. We sang all the verses too, and when we got to "Son of God, Love's pure light," I happened to look at Imogene and I almost dropped my hymnbook on a baby angel.

Everyone had been waiting all this time for the Herdmans to do something absolutely unexpected. And sure enough, that was what happened. Imogene Herdman was crying. In the candlelight her face was all shiny with tears and she didn't even bother to wipe them away. She just sat there—awful old Imogene—in her crookedy veil, crying and crying and crying.

Well, it was the best Christmas pageant we ever had. Everybody said so, but nobody seemed to know why. When it was over people stood around the lobby of the church talking. There was something special, everyone said—but they couldn't put their finger on what.

And this was the funny thing about it all. For years, I'd thought about the wonder of Christmas, and the mystery of Jesus's birth and never really understood it.

Now, because of the Herdmans, it didn't seem so mysterious after all.

When Imogene had asked me what the pageant was about, I told her it was about Jesus, but that was just part of it. It was about a new Baby, and His parents who were in a lot of trouble—no money, no place to go, no doctor, nobody they knew. Then, arriving from the East (like my uncle from New Jersey), some rich friends.

But Imogene, I guess, didn't see it that way. Christmas just came over her all at once, like a case of chills and fever. So she was crying and walking into the furniture.

Afterward there were candy canes and little tiny Testaments for everyone, and a poinsettia plant for my mother from the whole Sunday school. We put the costumes away and folded up the collapsible manger, and just before we left, my father snuffed out the candles.

"I guess that's everything," he said as we stood at the back of the church. "All over now. It was quite a pageant." Then he looked at my mother. "What's that you've got?"

"It's the ham," she said. "They wouldn't take it back. They wouldn't take any candy or anything. I guess tonight they just wanted to give."

Mother was right, and as far as I'm concerned, Mary is always going to look a lot like Imogene Herdman—sort of nervous and bewildered, but ready to clobber anyone who laid a hand on her baby. And the Wise Men are always going to be Leroy and his brothers, bearing ham.

When we came out of the church that night it was cold and clear, with crunchy snow underfoot and bright stars overhead. And I thought about the Angel of the Lord—Gladys, with her skinny legs and her dirty sneakers sticking out from under her robe, yelling at all of us, everywhere:

"Hey! Unto you a Child is born!"

THE LOST TOOTH

William Barton

Dr. William Barton was a well-known American minister who died in 1930. During his lifetime he wrote sixty books, including a dozen on Abraham Lincoln. His brief classic stories were written in the style of an ancient philosopher experiencing life in the twentieth century for the first time, and—as in this tale— introduce family members like his wife, whose pseudonym here is "Keturah."

The daughter of the daughter of Keturah came unto our habitation, and she sought the cookie box of Keturah. And thus did Keturah's own children in their day. And thus have I done often. Save that I never eat one cookie. I can eat none, or I can eat four or five, but I cannot eat one of the cookies of Keturah and stop. But this little maiden ate of the cookies of Keturah, and I think that there will always be cookies in her cookie box.

Now as the damsel ate, she cried out in terror. I wondered what had happened to her, for that is not the way the cookies of Keturah affect people. But the maiden cried not in pain, but in terror. And she said, "Oh, Grandpa, my tooth has come out!"

And she held up a tiny front tooth in her little hand.

Now the loss of a tooth is a matter of some importance to me; for I fear lest the time come when my grinders cease because they are few. But I knew that for her it was not a serious matter. So I comforted her, and said, "Fear not. It is of no consequence."

And she said, "Oh, Grandpa, canst thou put it back?" And I told her that I could not, and that I would not if I could. And she understood it not, but she was comforted when she saw that I did not share her fear.

And I said, "Have no fear, my little girl. The teeth that God gave thee when teeth first came unto thee were baby teeth, and they will leave thee one by one and fall out. Trouble not thyself, for there shall grow others in their place that will be stronger and better and last longer."

And she was comforted.

Then I considered the losses of life, and the pain and the fear of them, and how they are even as the fear that was in the heart of the little maiden when she lost the tooth. Yea, I went where people suffered by reason of losses, which I could not explain so easily, and my words of comfort had behind them no knowledge of what blessing God should provide instead of the thing that had been taken away. But I remembered that it is written in the Word of God how God hath provided some better thing.

And I took the little pearly tooth from the hand of the little maiden, and she sat upon my knee and ate the residue of her cookie, and I stroked her golden hair, and I prayed unto God for all those who have losses in life and who know not how God shall provide any better thing in place of them.

For their sorrow is like unto the sorrow of the daughter of the daughter of Keturah, and there are times when my wisdom stoppeth short of their need.

Concerning Rest

William Barton

This other tale by William Barton describes how an hour spent with his granddaughter was as refreshing to him as a long nap. Then he hypothesizes that this experience may capture something of what Jesus meant when he declared that his yoke upon us is easy, his burden is light, and he provides rest unto our souls.

There was a day when I was weary. For my days had been full of cares, and my nights had been broken. And I spake unto Keturah, saying, "I would fain lay me down upon my couch and rest. Trouble me not for the space of one hour." So I laid me down.

And I heard the patter of little feet, and there were little hands pushing at my door. And there came unto me the daughter of the daughter of Keturah. And she said, "Grandpa, I want to lie down with you." And I said, "Come and we will rest together. Close thine eyes tightly and be very still. So shall we rest both of us."

And the way she rested was this: She crept under the blanket that covered me so that her head and all the rest of her were covered and she said, "Grandpa, you have lost your little girl."

Then did I seek my little girl whom I had lost, and I said, "Where is my little girl? Where is my little girl?" And I felt all over the blanket, and I found her not.

Then did she cry, "Here I am." And she threw off the blanket and laughed. And she hid from me the second time, and the third time, and many times beside. And every time I found her again, hiding under the blanket.

And when this had wearied her finally, she sat astride me, so that one foot was on the right side and one was on the left, and she held me by my thumbs, and her little hands could not quite reach around my two thumbs. And she rocked back so that her head touched the couch between my knees, and she sat up with a bump upon my stomach. And she rode me to Banbury Cross and to many other places.

And she said, "You are having a good time with me, aren't you, Grandpa?"

And I told her that it was true.

Now at the end of one hour, I came forth leading the little damsel by the hand, and Keturah said, "Thou art rested. I behold that thy weariness is gone."

And it was even so. For the joy of playing with the little damsel had driven away my care and I was rested.

Now I thought of this, and I remembered that my Lord had said, "Come unto me, ye weary and heavy laden, and I will give you rest." And I remembered that He said that in resting I should bear a yoke and find it easy, and carry a burden and find it light. And, behold, I knew what He meant.

A Tale of Three Trees

A Folktale Retold by Stephen Fortosis

This is an anonymous folktale of three trees who wonder about their destiny and dream great dreams. They are eventually cut down and are heartbroken to find that their wood is used for humble and demeaning purposes—that is, until they realize Who it is that has need of their service.

Once upon a majestic mountain peak, three little trees stood side by side. They dreamed of what they wanted to become someday. The first little tree gazed up at the stars twinkling like gems above her. "I want to hold treasure," she said. "I want gold coins and diamonds to spill over my top. I will be the most beautiful treasure chest of all."

The second little tree looked out at the brook, bubbling its way to the ocean. "I want to be a great sailing ship," he said. "I want to travel the waters and carry famous kings. I will be the strongest ship in the world."

The third little tree looked down into the valley where bustling men and women hurried to and fro. "I don't want to leave this mountaintop at all," he said. "I want to grow so stately and tall that when humans stop to look at me they will raise their eyes to heaven and think of God. I will be the tallest tree in the world."

Years passed. The rains poured, the sun shone, and the little trees grew.

One morning three woodcutters climbed the mountain. The first woodcutter swung his glittering axe at the first tree. With three mighty swings, the tree toppled.

"Now I shall be made into a treasure chest," thought the tree. "I shall hold gold and diamonds."

The second woodcutter chopped the second tree down lickety-split.

"Now I shall sail into the bright sunset," thought the second tree. "I shall carry kings to distant shores."

The third tree tried to stretch straight and tall as the third woodcutter sharpened his axe. "Any sort of tree will do for me," muttered the woodcutter. He swung his axe again and again, and the third tree crashed to the earth.

The first tree smiled expectantly when the woodcutter brought her to a carpenter's shop, but the busy carpenter did not need a treasure chest. Instead his tough hands formed the tree into a feed box for animals.

The beautiful tree was not covered with gold or filled with treasure. She was coated with sawdust and filled with hay for hungry farm animals.

The second tree was taken to a shipyard, but no magnificent sailing ships were being made that day. Instead the mighty tree was hammered and sawed into a simple fishing boat. Too small to sail an ocean or even a river, he was taken to a small lake. Every day, he hauled in loads of dead, smelly fish.

The third tree was a bit confused when the woodcutter sliced him into big beams and left him in a lumberyard.

"What happened?" the tall tree wondered. "All I ever wanted to do was stay on the mountaintop and point toward God."

Many days passed. The three trees almost forgot their dreams. But one night as the first tree rested sadly with drowsy animals, a young woman entered the stable and laid her newborn baby in the feed box.

"I wish I could make a fine cradle for the child," her husband whispered.

The mother smiled at him as glimmering starlight shone on the humble, dusty feed box. And suddenly the first tree knew she was holding the greatest treasure in the world.

Years later, one evening a weary traveller and his friends crowded into an old fishing boat. The traveller fell fast asleep as the second tree quietly sailed out into the lake.

Soon lightning split the sky, thunder crashed, and the waves became big as mountains. The little tree creaked and shook. He knew he would soon fall apart in the storm.

The tired man woke up. He stood up, raised his hands and said, "Peace." The storm stopped and the lake became clear like glass. And suddenly the second tree knew he was carrying the greatest King who ever lived.

Early one morning, the third tree was yanked from the woodpile and made into a tall cross. He was carried by a bleeding man through an angry crowd calling out awful names. They climbed to the top of a mountain. There, soldiers nailed the man's hands to the wooden cross. The third tree tried to push the nails out of his wood but they were stuck fast. As the man died, the third tree cried and one last drop of sap rolled down his rough, gnarled side.

Finally they took the man down from the third tree and carried him away. For three lonely days the third tree stood sadly on the mountaintop. But early the third morning, out of the dawn mist walked the man they had killed. He was alive!

As he came closer, the third tree saw he had a kind face and he was smiling.

He reached out and touched the old cross with a faraway look in his eye. "For ages and ages to come," he said softly, "when humans see you, they will think of my love; and whoever comes to me, I will never turn away."

The third tree stretched out straight and tall for he knew: He was pointing the world to the King of heaven and earth.

Sacraments

Virginia Cary Hudson

In this humorous piece, glimpse how ten-year-old Virginia Cary Hudson viewed the sacraments of the church in 1904. While it is true that the sacraments are sacred, surely God looks with patience and, perhaps, even a bit of amusement at children's initial understanding of the spiritual significance of bread and wine, prayers and liturgies—and fishing.

Sacraments are what you do in church. What you do at home is something else. Cooking and sewing and running the Bissels sweeper and eating and sleeping and scrubbing yourself are not sacraments.

When you are little and ugly somebody carries you into church on a pillow, . . . and they pour water on your head, that's a sacrament.

When you are twelve you walk back in yourself with your best dress and shoes on, and your new prayer book your mother buys you, and you walk up to the bishop, and he stands up, and you kneel down, and he mashes on your head, and you are an Episcopal, then you are supposed to increase in spirit. Then everybody kisses you and that's a sacrament.

Only I left out the bread and the wine. That's a sacrament too. I tasted some of that bread in the choir room and it tasted just like my goldfish wafers.

When you are married, you go back to church dressed up like you never were before in all your days. Somebody sings "Oh Promise Me" and your sweetheart is waiting up by the preacher (if he doesn't forget to come) and you get a new, shiny, gold band on your finger and leave town. And that's a sacrament.

Miss Molly Anderson got all ready to get married and she let me see all of her lovely clothes all spread out on the bed in the spare room. Only she didn't get married. The bridegroom forgot to come back. He traveled. And I guess he took the wrong train or something. Mrs. Anderson shut the shutters, and nobody would come to the door, and when I went around to the kitchen door to take Miss Molly some cinnamon drops, the cook says to me, "Go away. Scat."

But Miss Molly didn't care if he did forget to come. She bought a new bath suit with a big sailor collar, and ruffles around her knees, and she married Dr. Thomwood, and I like him. He is handsome. That old absentminded bridegroom was always saying to me, "Little girl, isn't it time you were going home?" When I had only just got (I mean, gotten) there, and I barely had sat myself down in the parlor.

And then you get carried back in the church again, but you are dead and it takes six people to lift you, and everybody cries, and that's the last sacrament you are going to get.

Mrs. Park was so old and sick she didn't know her own children. Maybe she was tired of fooling with them all those years and just acted like she didn't know them. When Mrs. Park died I sure didn't cry because I bet when she waked up and found she was dead she was just tickled to death.

One day we got tired of playing hopscotch and skin-the-cat, so Edna Briggs said, "Let's play Baptizing."

I said to Mrs. Williams, "Can we, I mean may we, play Baptizing in your rain barrel?"

She said to me, "Yes, indeed," and just went on tatting.

So I put on my father's hunting breeches and got Judge Williams's hat off the moose horn rack, and I dressed up like the Baptist preacher. That was when Edna ran to get all the kids. And I said to them—I said, "The Lord is in his Holy Temple, keep silent and shut up. All you sinners come forward and hence."

Nobody came but Melvin Dawson, who is just two years old. Poor little Melvin—he is so unlucky. I got him by the back of his diaper and dipped him in the rain barrel once for the Father, and once for the Son, and when it came time for the Holy Ghost, poor little Melvin's safety pin broke and he dropped in the bottom of the rain barrel, and everybody ran, and nobody would help me, and I had to turn the rain barrel over to get him out, and then I put him stomach-first on my knee and galloped him like a pony to get the water out of him, and then I sat him inside his house, and I went to Mrs. Harris's house and got under her bed, and when she looked under there and saw me all soaking wet, Mrs. Harris said, "Rain and hail in Beulah land, what has happened now?"

And when I told her what had happened she just patted her foot and sat and sat. Then she said, "You know what?"

And I said, "What?"

She said, "The bishop sure needs such a barrel in the churchyard to give some members I know just what little Melvin got."

And then Mrs. Harris said, "Let's talk about fishing." And we did.

Thank God for fishing. Thank God for Mrs. Harris and God bless poor little Melvin. Amen.

GROWING PAINS

IN SEARCH
OF A PROPER MATE

Mark Littleton

Mark Littleton is the author of more than a dozen books, many of them award-winning. His Sports Heroes series has expanded to eight titles, and its popularity grows.

This story is drawn from a collection called Tales of the Neverending. *It would be difficult to picture more vividly than Littleton does the compassionate condescension Christ has shown in considering the wayward and blemished church as his eternal bride.*

Christ also loved the church and gave Himself for it, that He might sanctify and cleanse it with the washing of water by the word, that He might present it to Himself a glorious church, not having spot or wrinkle or any such thing, but that it should be holy and without blemish.

Ephesians 5:25–27 (NKJV)

At first I wasn't sure what he wanted. Princes don't often reveal their heart desires at the start of this kind of business.

Actually, I didn't even think he knew what he wanted. Of course, my opinion changed. I know now he had her pictured from the start, even before I got involved. He knew her before she was born. That's the kind of person the prince was. He could see her—every line, every curve, every movement of her soul. He knew her before her parents' parents were even a gleam of spirit light.

That's what mystified me about it all. Why he chose her became the raging question of my mind. I almost was afraid to ask him, though. She was so much less than he could have had.

But I'm getting ahead of things.

I'm a simple man. I do a job, and I try to do it well. But from the start I knew he didn't come for my advice, or even for me to make the match. He already had the match. He simply wanted it all down on paper, clearly drawn out. He likes things that way.

It wasn't really an investigation, not like I usually make. He just wanted me to get all the details in front of him. "Lay it all out," he said. "So I can see it straight."

Understand, this was the most distressing, astonishing case of my career. If he weren't the prince, I would have told him "no, I wouldn't be party to this," and been done with it. Actually, if it had been up to me, I'd have never brought her up in the first place. He wouldn't have ever known she existed.

But, of course, that was impossible.

So he wanted the facts? All right, that's what I'd give him. That would end it for sure. He certainly couldn't go through with it once he knew everything. She'd be a girl of the past.

How little I understood then.

Her name was Clesia. Not your typical name, I know. But, of course, he knew that beforehand too.

He came in on a Friday. I knew he wanted every important detail, so I figured it would take the whole weekend. I realized I'd have to be careful about it—how much I revealed and when. He was a hard case. Set on his course. If I were to retain any semblance of integrity and reputation, my work was cut out for me.

He arrived in the morning. Sure. Smiling. Ready for the miracle of his life. I couldn't believe it. Did he really think she was some kind of gem? Could he have thought so, knowing what she had done? Or was he just looking through a dozen fresh roses at a distance on a windy day?

He smiled.

Then I showed him the photo. With you, I'll be frank. If the picture was bad, the photo was wretched. She was, as they say, a no-hoper. Pocked cheeks. Stringy hair. Makeup a mess. I'm not misogynist, and I try to be fair with every woman, but I'm telling you this honey was no bunny. She was, as my son says, "hurtin' for certain."

I don't mean to be colloquial, serious as this was. The photo could easily have sent men with strong stomachs to the latrine—immediately. And to think that he planned to marry her!

We got through the photo. He was pleased. He nodded his head and simply said, "This is Clesia."

I nodded, as though to confirm it, but he didn't sound disappointed. He said it with pride and a kind of leaping joy, the kind you feel deep in your heart so you want to jump.

I was nearly sick. But I pulled out the notebook and eyed him. "Are you sure you're ready for this?"

He nodded. "Of course. How could I not be? I have waited for this for many years."

He should have waited a lot longer, if you ask me. But I began the rundown on her—measurements, that stuff.

He just waved his hand and shook his head. "I already know that."

She had the figure of an eighty-year-old woman who'd never had a figure to begin with, but he didn't even seem interested.

So I gave him the results of my personal interview. "Highly unintelligent. 'Dense,' as they say. Untrusting. Ceaseless complaints. Worried about everything. No interest in history. Reads little." I asked him if I should go on. It made me tired just to read the litany.

He nodded. "Read it all."

"Bad teeth. Poor eyesight. Poor housekeeper." I told him that every time I visited her, her house was in a state of such confusion and disgust that I had to interview her outside. Flies everywhere. The stink! Ugh! I wanted to retch on the spot. Did the woman know what soap was? Had she ever cleaned anything?

And her parents. The worst sort. Divorced. Her father a pimply man living with another woman. Her mother a nag and a witch. I mean a black magic, lotion potion, dead frogs, and bat's wings witch, if you understand.

Still, you couldn't feel sorry for Clesia. She could have done something for herself. She wasn't totally helpless. I told him, "Manifestly lazy. Picks her teeth. Discourteous. Raucous. Abrasive voice. Likes to prance around in outlandish costumes and admire herself . . ."

He asked me if I saw anything positive. It was then I began to think he really was looking for the worst possible case he could find. But he didn't seem like the type. He wasn't punishing himself, I was sure of it. You can tell in such cases by the way they talk. He just wasn't that type.

I was frank. "No. Not a shred of anything."

He just cleared his throat and looked away. "OK, go on."

I didn't want to break the really bad things to him if I could help it. I mean, he'd planned this, they said, for something like eternity. I didn't know precisely what that meant, but it had to be a long time. Still, he was forcing me to show him the worst. So I had to watch my step. Too much, and it might incite him.

I began: "She's a gossip of the worst sort. Keeps no secrets. No confidences. Lives for learning the dirt on everyone."

He didn't even blink. I knew the prince was a private man, so I thought that would throw him, but he didn't even clear his throat. He simply sat there.

So I went on. "It's my judgment that she's a very angry woman. Bitter. Resentful. Unforgiving. She's suspicious, extremely sensitive about every little thing. And jealous."

He laughed. I tell you, he laughed! I almost thought I had him. So I said, "I'm telling you, this woman is a major wretch."

He immediately fixed his eyes on me and gazed for what seemed a whole minute. I knew then that I'd overstepped my bounds, but he smiled and said, "Go on."

I felt apologetic. "Sorry, I'll try to keep my own opinion out of it." But I had nothing good to say about her. So I told him the first major thing I thought might give him pause.

"She's a slut."

I said it matter-of-factly. I didn't try to indicate whether I thought this was immoral or anything, though I knew very well what he thought on that score.

"I know she's not a virgin," he said.

"Not a virgin!" I cried. I couldn't hold it in. "Do you know what this woman does every chance she gets? She's been with every second guy in town," I said, hoping to see him blanch or something. "The doctor said she's a disease-carrying piece of vermin. He wouldn't touch her."

The prince didn't give a hint of pain or rejection. "She's committed adultery," I said, "though I don't know why any woman's husband would want her."

He waited, saying nothing.

"And she's accepted money for it. You know, prostitution."

Not a shadow of a doubt crossed his features. Was the man catatonic? Now I knew I had to start bringing out the really bad stuff. Ha! Bad stuff? As though I hadn't given him enough.

"She's an habitual liar. Can't trust a word she says. Uses drugs. Alcoholic. Several abortions." He didn't flinch.

All right, he asked for it. "She is wanted for hundreds of crimes. Even now she awaits sentencing."

"What crimes?" he asked.

So there was life in him! Gladly I would tell him. "Perjury. Theft. Extortion. Blackmail. Sodomy. Perversion." I let it all come out in slow but staccatoed shots. I wanted it to sink in.

"Larceny. Embezzling. Cheating. Fraud."

Did I detect the slightest droop of his head?

"Picking pockets. Arson. Child molestation."

How any one person could do all this was beyond me. But of course, she was much more than your normal person.

"Loan-sharking. Idolatry. Witchcraft."

I let that last one out after a long pause. But I think the droop I'd spotted earlier was just a change of his position. He hadn't even sighed once. So I let him have it.

"Infanticide and murder."

"Is that all?" he asked.

Was the man insane? "Is that all?" Didn't he know who he was? Or his father? I felt like strangling him. Wasn't this enough to push him away? I knew I'd have to really knock him. I said, "You realize that she's a slave."

"Yes."

"You'll have to buy her from her owner."

"I understand that." He didn't even blink.

All right, the big one. The really big one. "You realize you'll have to pay for all her crimes?"

A long pause. I almost found myself praying. At last there was a hint of integrity in him.

"Execution, you mean?"

I wanted to hit him hard. "Absolutely! No escape."

He waited. He seemed to be thinking. I could hardly hold myself back. At last he was going to turn it over, leave this obsession.

"I'll have to die first?" he said. The same even voice.

"Absolutely. This woman is wanted in every country of our planet."

He cleared his throat again. "All right. I understand."

I slumped down in my seat. What was left? If that didn't put an end to it, what would?

There was one last thing: "She wants nothing to do with you. You do realize that, don't you?"

He laughed. *He laughed.* What did he think this was—*Challenging Situations,* the new TV game? Good grief! I was boiling. It made me sick to think he was not only considering this now, but had been for years. He'd planned it. He would do it, regardless of what I said.

Then he said, "I guess that's to be expected, considering . . ."

"Yes," I said, as contemptuously as I could. "That is to be expected. And if I were you . . ."

He held up his hand. "Don't say it. I didn't come for your advice about what to do."

I threw the brief onto the table. I wanted to belt him in the face. Bring him to his senses. "So you're going to go through with it?"

He looked at me, amazed. Amazed! "Of course I am. It is written."

All right, I'd seen a lot of kooks, lamebrains, weirdos, and idiots in my life but he made them all look like Marcus Aurelius, Aristotle, Socrates, and Virgil thrown together. Where was his reasoning? What on earth was he doing?

I had to ask him. "Why do you want her, Immanuel?" I addressed him by his name. I felt fatherly all of a sudden. Maybe I shouldn't have, but he didn't act as though I was out of line or anything.

He glanced around the room and finally fixed his gray eyes on me. He was such a handsome man. Godly. Earnest. Sincere. Every attribute—he had it. "I want her because it is my father's will that I take her."

So Dad was the problem.

"But what does he see in her, for heaven's sake?" I cried, throwing up my hands.

He laughed. "Nothing." He said it so matter-of-factly that I almost fell over.

"Nothing?" I roared. "Nothing?"

He gazed at me as though he felt sorry for me. "Did you think my father or I saw something in her?"

I stammered and hemmed and hawed for a moment. It had never occurred to me, actually. "You see nothing in her? Nothing?" I said again, a bit more meekly.

"There is nothing in her that has made my father choose her," he said. "That's what I meant to say."

I had to agree. "But why, then, have you chosen her to be the bride? Your father, that is. Why has he chosen her for you? You could have someone so much greater and more beautiful. Someone who could give you a reason for choosing her, at least."

He ran his fingers through his hair. "So you think there might be someone out there who merits the choice?"

I laughed. "Of course. There are many. I could give you five, ten, a hundred, a million better than Clesia. Right now. This very minute."

He shook his head. "You are looking at the surface of things, Levi. Every last one of them is as bad off as Clesia. Do you understand that?"

No, I didn't understand. What could he mean?

"Please understand," he said. "My father didn't choose Clesia because she is better than others. Or worse. Or ugly. Or beautiful. There is nothing in her or about her that caused my father to choose her."

I was curious. I really wanted to understand this. "So why did he choose her then? If there was nothing in her or about her, as you say, what caused the choice?"

"My father's sovereign right to choose," said the prince. So coolly. So plainly. "Because he is king."

I sat back in my seat and breathed deeply. I had to get this straight. "You mean to tell me that the only reason your father chose Clesia is because he has a right to do that, and he has exercised that right?"

The prince smiled and nodded like he was glad I understood. "Yes, I guess you could say it that way."

"All right," I said. I wanted to get a little deeper. "Then why didn't he choose any of the others? Why didn't he choose all of them? You could marry all of them if you wanted."

As I asked that question, I was frightened. Genuinely frightened. I don't even know why. But I thought I realized something about the king and the prince that I'd never seen before. I wasn't sure then what it was.

"You ask the key to a great mystery, Levi ben Jacob," the prince said. "If I answered your question, you would have to have a mind able to comprehend the mind of my father himself."

"But is it fair?" I shouted. "Choosing Clesia but all these others just left aside?" Now I felt angry and upset.

He looked down and grimaced. "You ask a hard question. But let me answer it this way. Is there anything in Clesia or any of the others that requires that I choose them—I, the prince, or my father, the king?"

I looked bewildered. "You are a wise man, Levi," he responded. "But you have much to learn. We must make preparations for the wedding. But first, the hard part."

"The hard part?" I didn't know what he was referring to.

"Yes," he said. "You did say she had committed crimes worthy of death?"

"Yes."

For the first time, he blanched. He closed his eyes. I could see pain jolt through him. I reached out to grab him. "I'm all right," he said. "It's just that even now I'm not sure how great the cost will be. But if I am to marry Clesia, I must pay it, mustn't I?"

It was almost as though he were hoping I would tell him there was some way around all that. But I knew there wasn't. And so did he. He got up and turned to go. Then he turned around and held out his hand. "You have done a good job, Levi. I am grateful. Perhaps what you have done will help her understand. Do you think so?"

I looked at her picture lying on the table. It was a stifling feeling. What he had to do. What he was going to do.

And her. The kind of woman she was. Would she ever understand what he would do for her, what price he had to pay to make her his bride? Could she? Ever?

THE GOOD BISHOP

Victor Hugo

Victor Hugo is famous as a French novelist, poet, and dramatist of the nineteenth century. His best known novels are The Hunchback of Notre Dame *and* Les Miserables.

In this exerpt from Les Miserables, *Hugo paints a picture of a bishop who is both good and wise. When an ex-convict the bishop has hired betrays him, the churchman astounds the man by showing only generosity in return.*

Whoever wants to become great among you must be your servant, and whoever wants to be first must be your slave.

Matthew 20:26–27

Jean Valjean was a woodchopper's son who, while very young, was left an orphan. His older sister brought him up, but when he was seventeen years of age, his sister's husband died, and upon Jean came the labor of supporting her seven little children. Although a man of great strength, he found it very difficult to provide food for them at the poor trade he followed.

One wintry day he was without work, and the children were crying for bread. They were nearly starved. And, when he could withstand their entreaties no longer, he went out in the night; and, breaking a baker's window with his fist, carried home a loaf of bread for the famished children. The next morning he was arrested for stealing, his bleeding hand convicting him.

For this crime he was sent to the galleys with an iron collar riveted around his neck, with a chain attached, which bound him to his galley seat. Here he remained four years. He tried to escape, and three years were added to his sentence. Then he made a second attempt and also failed, the result of which was that he remained nineteen years as a galley slave for stealing a single loaf of bread.

When Jean left the prison, his heart was hardened. He felt like a wolf. His wrongs had embittered him, and he was more like an animal than a man. He came with every man's hand raised against him to the town where the good bishop lived.

At the inn they would not receive him because they knew him to be an ex-convict and a dangerous man. Wherever he went, the knowledge of him went before, and everyone drove him away. They would not even allow him to sleep in a dog kennel or give him the food they had saved for the dog. Everywhere he went they cried, "Be off! Go away, or you will get a charge of shot." Finally he wandered to the house of the good bishop (and a good man he was).

For his duties as bishop he received from the state 3,000 francs a year; but he gave away to the poor 2,800 francs of it. He was a simple, loving man with a great heart, who thought nothing of himself, but loved everybody. And everyone loved him.

Jean, when he entered the bishop's house, was a most forbidding and dangerous character. He shouted in a harsh loud voice, "Look here, I am a galley slave. Here is my yellow passport. It says, 'Five years for robbery and fourteen years for trying to escape. The man is very dangerous.' Now that you know who I am, will you give me a little food, and let me sleep in the stable?"

The good bishop said, "Sit down and warm yourself. You will take supper with me and, after that, sleep here."

Jean could hardly believe his senses. He was dumb with joy. He told the bishop that he had money and would pay for his supper and lodging.

But the priest said, "You are welcome. This is not my home, but the house of Christ. Your name was known to me before you showed me your passport. You are my brother."

After supper the bishop took one of the silver candlesticks that he had received as a Christmas present, and, giving Jean the other, led him to his room, where a good bed was provided. In the middle of the night Jean awoke with a hardened heart. He felt that the time had come to get revenge for all his wrongs. He remembered the silver knives and forks that had been used for supper, and made up his mind to steal them and go away in the night. So he took what he could find, sprang into the garden, and disappeared.

When the bishop awoke and saw his silver gone, he said, "I have been thinking for a long time that I ought not to keep the silver. I should have given it to the poor and certainly this man was poor."

At breakfast time five soldiers brought Jean back to the bishop's house. When they entered, the bishop, looking at him said, "Oh, you are back again! I am glad to see you. I gave you the candlesticks too. They are silver also and will bring forty francs. Why did you not take them?"

Jean was stunned indeed by these words. So were the soldiers. "This man told us the truth, did he?" they cried. "We thought he had stolen the silver and was running away. So we quickly arrested him."

But the good bishop only said, "It was a mistake to have him brought back. Let him go. The silver is his. I gave it to him."

So the officers went away.

"Is it true," Jean whispered to the bishop, "that I am free? I may go?"

"Yes," he replied, "but before you go, take your candlesticks."

Jean trembled in every limb and took the candlesticks like one in a dream.

"Now," said the bishop, "depart in peace, but do not go through the garden, for the front door is always open to you day and night."

Jean looked as though he would faint.

Then the bishop took his hand and said, "Never forget you have promised me you would use the money to become an honest man."

He did not remember having promised anything but stood silent while the bishop continued solemnly: "Jean Valjean, my brother, you no longer belong to evil but to good. I have bought your soul for you. I withdrew it from black thoughts and the spirit of hate and gave it to God."

I Saw Gooley Fly

Joseph Bayly

Joseph Bayly served for many years as a publishing executive for David C. Cook Publications. He is also a skilled writer—known for best-selling books such as The Gospel Blimp, View from a Hearse, *and* Psalms of My Life.

The following parable that he wrote is about a campus klutz named Herb Gooley who learns a secret that no one else seems to know. And soon both students and administration become extremely curious about what makes the supernatural Gooley tick.

Herb Gooley was just an ordinary sort of guy until the night he stepped out of his third-floor dorm window and flew away into the wild blue yonder.

But I'm getting ahead of my story.

I first met Gooley in that little hamburger and malt joint just off campus—Pete's Place. I'd never have noticed the guy except that he dropped a mustard bottle, and the stuff squirted down the front of his storm jacket. Now I'm a sophomore at the time and this guy's a frosh. (No mistaking them during those early weeks of the quarter.) But he's making such a mess out of wiping the stuff off that I help him. Brother,

66

what a mess. But Herb was the sort of fellow who could hardly wipe his nose himself, let alone the mustard.

When we had the stuff pretty well wiped off his coat and shirt (you could still see these bright yellow streaks), I ask him where he sacks out.

"Pollard," he says.

"That hole. Must be a frosh, huh? You'll learn. Course you can transfer after a quarter. Me, I'm at Sigma Phi House. Know the place that looks like a country club over on Lincoln?"

He doesn't know it. So we pay Pete and walk out. That is, I walk out. Herb trips over a cigarette machine that stands near the door.

Next time I notice the guy is at Homecoming.

It's during the Frosh-Soph Tug-of-War. (They really had pressure on those fire hoses that year.) We're ready for the final pull and the gun goes off. Suddenly the whole frosh team's yelling to stop pulling. So, after they turn the hoses on us, we stop; and here's Gooley, looking sort of dazed, with the rope twisted clear around his arm. I'll never know how he did it. They get it off and take him to the infirmary. Nothing broken, but he sure must have had a painful arm for a few days.

I remember sometime the following fall seeing a crowd gathered around the front of Hinton's department store. So I pull over to the curb, and here is the college station wagon half-in, half-out of Hinton's show window. What a scene. Bodies all over the place, one of them broken in two across the hood. Gooley's standing there holding a head.

Maybe losing his driving privileges for a while got him interested in flying. At any rate, he comes back from Christmas vacation his junior year able to fly. Able to fly, mind you, not just able to fly a plane.

His roommate (Jerry Watson, it was) told us about it the next day. Seems Gooley had been studying late, and finally he turns the book over, switches off his desk light and says, "Think I'll go down to Pete's for a malted."

"Too late," Jerry says. "It's three minutes to twelve and he closes at midnight."

"I'll fly down." Gooley says it matter-of-factly, just like he's saying he'll run or something.

So over to the window he goes (Jerry all the while thinking Gooley is suddenly developing a sense of humor), lifts it up, and steps off the ledge.

Their room is on the third floor.

Jerry waits a second for the thud, then dashes into the hall and down the stairs yelling, "Gooley fell out the window! Somebody call a doctor."

No Gooley on the ground or anywhere around. So they think Jerry's pulling their leg.

"Honestly, fellows, Gooley stepped out of our window. Said he'd fly down to Pete's. Honest, he did."

So they wait around for Gooley to come back, and when he does, they start firing questions.

"Sure I can fly. Jerry was telling you the straight stuff. Here, I'll show you." And with that he takes off into the wild blue yonder.

None of us believed the story when we heard it. Would you? In the first place, people can ride bicycles, people can row boats, people can fly planes even, but nobody can fly.

In the second place, if anybody could fly, Herb Gooley wasn't the man. That guy couldn't even walk.

It began to snow about suppertime the next day and it snowed all through the night. Next morning the ground is covered, but some of the walks are shoveled off. I'm walking down the cleared path at the quad when I notice something. Fresh footprints go out on the snow a few yards, then there's nothing. Nothing. No trampled snow, no feet turning around. Just footprints going out and stopping.

Within a few days nobody needs any more circumstantial evidence. We've all seen it—Gooley flying.

He'd be walking along with you, and suddenly he's airborne. Nothing spectacular. I mean it was all very quiet. His rise was almost vertical, and he flew along at about fifteen or twenty miles per hour. Just above the treetops. He'd sort of bank to turn.

That winter and spring you should have seen Gooley come into class on the third or fourth floor of Old Main. Brother, that was a sight to behold. It got to be a regular custom to open the window just before the bell. I'll never forget the day we had a visiting lecturer. Nobody had told him.

Let me tell you there was a run on the library for books on aerodynamics, aircraft design and any other subject that even faintly bears on flying. Guys and girls were spending their free time soaking up all they could learn.

I don't want you to get the idea that we talked a lot about it. Nobody would admit wanting to fly, but most everyone did. Nothing in the world I wanted more. Seems sort of funny now.

The college flying course tripled in size—flying planes, that is, but it was as close as we could come to personal flight. In bull sessions we talked into the small hours about how Gooley probably did it.

You see, Gooley wasn't saying.

Of course, later there was some reaction—a lot of people began to call Gooley a freak. It sort of made us laugh, though, when one of the most outspoken anti-Gooleyites was found with a brain concussion at the foot of the Old Zach monument. (He got over it all right.)

I think the college administration was sort of ashamed to have Gooley as a student. So they bring in this guy Sevorsky for a special lecture series called Flight Emphasis Week. Brother, were those lectures packed out. Standing room only.

Halfway through the week we realize that Sevorsky can't fly. We're standing outside Old Main, waiting for him to leave the president's office, which is on the second floor. So how does he come down? He walks down the stairs and out the front door. This guy can design airplanes, we say. He has the latest scoop on jets and helicoptors. But he can't fly.

About a dozen students show up for his final lecture.

Most of us had heard a myth about some ancient Greek who could fly until he got too near the sun. So we think maybe there's a clue. Interest switches to books on ancient Greek mythology, and the library puts them on the reserve shelf.

You know, I've always been surprised that Gooley didn't tell us how to do it, or at least how he did it. He couldn't help knowing how interested we all were. But he kept his mouth shut. So none of us learned to fly.

It's a funny thing, but I still sense a loss at not learning Gooley's secret, and other grads have confessed the same thing to me.

What happened to Gooley? I've often wondered about that. He transferred that fall to another college where, they say, all the students know how to fly.

PILGRIM'S PROGRESS

John Bunyan
Retold by Stephen Fortosis

Bunyan's classic transforms Christian conversion and growth into a helpful allegory. This contemporary version presents the first segment of the book, from the time the pilgrim first realizes his need for forgiveness and peace, to the point of his conversion.

"Honey, it's 7:30," said Alyson. "You'd better get up. You'll be late for work."

Craig groaned and covered his head with a pillow. "I had the worst nightmare ever," he mumbled. "Think I'll just stay home today."

"Just because of a dumb dream?"

"I had this massive load stuck on my back. It smelled like a rotting corpse. I tried everything to get rid of it, but nothing worked. Then a voice said, 'Your load will sink you down to hell. Seek God while there's time.'"

Alyson laughed. "Come on. I've had scarier dreams than that. I wake up sweating. Then ten minutes later I forget all about it."

Craig sat up in bed, looking already exhausted and listless. "I'm gonna take a sick day. I don't feel so hot."

The following week grew worse. Craig barely slept at night and his days were spent in almost constant troubled thought. He began driving off alone to spend hours wandering aimlessly in the forest near his sub-division. His family, friends, and relatives began to grow anxious, and even discussed among themselves how to get Craig some professional therapy.

Then one evening as he wandered, Craig met a man named Evangelist, who carried a Holy Book.

"Sir," said Craig, "you look like a religious person. I've heard people like you speak of being saved. Can you tell me what it means? I happen to feel very lost."

Evangelist showed him some truths out of the Book. Then he pointed to a white gate in the distance surrounded by an ethereal glow.

"You must begin your spiritual pilgrimage. Go toward the light. When you reach the gate, you'll be told what to do next."

When Craig didn't show up for dinner that evening, Alyson asked the neighbors if they'd seen him. No one had, but two neighbors, Obstinate and Pliable, agreed to search the area. After about an hour they spotted Craig crossing a meadow far in the distance. When yelling didn't help, they lit out after him. When they overtook him, Craig said, "Don't try to convince me to return home. The town where we live is actually the City of Destruction. Come with me to the City of the Great King."

"Give me a break," said Obstinate. "You think we're gonna leave our friends and families to follow you on a stupid wild goose chase?"

"Anything you forsake isn't worth being compared with the freedom I'm searching for. The Book says the Great King has a rich inheritance for humans that will never fade away."

"Wait a minute," said Pliable. "Let's at least hear him out. It sounds as if he's on a different spiritual plane."

"What? The guy's brain dead. He's got his head stuck in a cloud bank."

"Pliable, I know there are spiritual realities," said Craig, "and many more glories than we know. The Book tells of many such things."

"Believe it or not," said Pliable, "I think I'll give Craig some company. Craig, do you know the way to this paradise?"

"Yes, we must go toward the light. There we'll receive further instructions."

Obstinate turned in silent rage and stalked back toward town while the two companions set off.

"Tell me more about this new world," said Pliable.

"It's an endless kingdom with everlasting life. There are crowns of glory and clothes that will make us shine like the sun. In this place there'll be no more crying, or sickness or sorrow, and the Owner will wipe all tears from our eyes."

"Wow! That sounds great. Let's get a move on."

"I can't go very fast because of this huge burden on my back."

Suddenly the two plunged into a patch of quicksand called the Marsh of Despond. As they wallowed helplessly, Pliable laid into Craig.

"Is this the utopia you've been raving about? If this is an omen of what's to come, you can just count me out. If I get out of this, you've seen the last of me."

Finally Pliable struggled to the bank and crawled out of the bog. He disappeared into the forest and Craig never saw him again. As Craig sank up to his chin in the slime, he cried out for help.

"What are you doing here?" said a voice. "Didn't you see the steps?"

"Who are you?" called Craig.

A man appeared on the bank. "My name is Help. This marsh is the hopeless despair people feel when they're under great conviction of sin and they wonder if there is really any deliverance from it."

With that, Help held out a branch to Craig and, with a great sucking sound, Craig was hauled out of the bog. After Help left, Craig continued on. As he walked across a flower-strewn meadow, he saw a man approaching who identified himself as Worldly Wiseman from the town of Carnal Policy.

"Where are you headed looking so down?" he asked.

"I'm going toward the light. I've got to get rid of this heavy burden."

"I see. Mind if I give you a suggestion? You're in for a pack of trouble trying to unload your burden this way. There's a city nearby named Morality and, in the town, there's this guy named Legality. He and his son, Civility, are known for their goodness and sense of fair play. They can release you of your burden. Then you can send for your wife and children. The homes in Morality are very reasonable, the neighbors are all honest and reliable. You'll love living there."

"That sounds interesting. How do I find this town?"

"See that high mountain? Go around it and the first house you'll see is Legality's."

When Craig reached the mountain, he noticed boulders hanging off a precipice. They looked so precarious that Craig was afraid to make the pass. Lightning flashed out of the mountain, and he began trembling uncontrollably.

Evangelist appeared suddenly. "What are you doing here, Craig?"

Craig stood speechless.

"Aren't you the man I found crying outside of the City of Destruction?"

"Yes," said Craig sheepishly. "I met a gentleman who persuaded me a guy named Legality could help."

"The Book says, 'The just shall live by faith alone. If anyone draws away, the Great King will have no pleasure in him.' This doctrine you almost fell for seeks to avoid the Cross. To get to the Cross you must enter in at a narrow gateway. Few there are who find it."

"I'm really sorry for getting so sidetracked. Is it possible to get back on the right road from here?"

"Yes, only see that no one turns you out of the way." With a smile and a wave, Evangelist turned and disappeared in the mist.

Craig hurried back toward the light, refusing even to speak to anyone on the way. When he reached the gate, a sign read: KNOCK AND IT SHALL BE OPENED TO YOU.

A man named Goodwill peered over the gate at Craig.

"Sir, I'm a poor burdened sinner. I come from the City of Destruction but I want to reach Mount Zion so I can be delivered from the wrath to come. May I come in?"

"Yes, all who search honestly may enter."

As Craig passed through the gate, Goodwill quickly made him duck down.

"There's an evil castle nearby," he explained. "It's ruled by Beelzebub. His knights shoot arrows toward those who arrive at the gate on the chance they may be killed just before they enter."

"Whew! Getting rid of this burden's no picnic. You can help me with it, right?"

"Yes, but first you need to learn a few things. Head down the trail a ways and you'll come to the house of a man named Interpreter. He'll show you some wonderful truth."

When Craig reached Interpreter's home, he was welcomed warmly.

"Come with me," he said. "We'll start our lessons right away."

As they walked down a hallway, on a wall Craig spotted a portrait of a Spirit whose eyes were lifted to heaven. A crown hung over His head, the Book was in His hands, the Law of Truth was upon His lips and the world was behind His back.

"Who's the serious-looking guy?"

"This Person is the one appointed by the Great King to be your guide in all difficult places. Make sure not to follow anyone but Him."

Interpreter led Craig to a large room filled with dust. A man was instructed to sweep, but he only stirred up the dust until it was so thick Craig began choking and gagging. A girl appeared and began sprinkling the room with water. As the dust settled, she swept the room clean.

"This room represents the heart of a person who is without Christ. The dust is the sinfulness we possess from birth. The man symbolized the Law. The girl symbolized the Gospel. Instead of cleansing the heart, the Law only makes us more aware of our sinfulness. The Gospel cleanses the life of sin, the soul is made clean, and the King of Glory can then inhabit it."

Next, Interpreter took Craig to a room where two children sat. One was named Passion, the other, Patience. Passion was obviously very discontented, while Patience sat quietly.

A man entered the room and handed Passion a bag of gold coins. Passion began celebrating excitedly, jeering all the while at Patience. But before long, Passion had wasted all the money and she wore only rags.

"Passion represents selfish folks of this world," said Interpreter. "They lavish money on expensive toys and they have all their enjoyment now. Patience, however, is willing to bide her time and wait for the timing of the Great King. Her rewards will come eventually. The things that are seen are temporary, but things unseen are eternal."

Craig followed Interpreter to a wall where a fire burned brightly. Though someone kept pouring water on it, the flames only leaped higher.

"The fire represents the work of grace the Great King does in a heart. He who throws water on it is the Devil. How do you think the fire only burns brighter?"

"You got me there," answered Craig.

Leading him behind the wall, Interpreter showed Craig another man who secretly fed kerosene to the fire, keeping it hot and vibrant.

"This symbolizes the Spirit of Christ who, with the oil of His grace, continues the work begun in the heart."

With a gesture, Interpreter led Craig up a hill. From the hill, Craig saw a stately palace. Outside the palace stood a great crowd of people but most made no move toward the gate. On the edge of the moat a man sat at a table, ready to record the name of anyone who wished to enter.

Many evil-looking knights stood menacingly in front of the castle gate, prepared to attack any who approached.

Finally a lone man stepped up and signed his name at the table. Then he bravely put on his helmet, drew his sword and rushed the gate. The knights fell upon him with deadly force. Not willing to retreat, the man began cutting and hacking fiercely. Finally, after receiving and giving many wounds, he cut his way through them all and pressed forward into the castle. Those lining the top of the castle wall sang, "Come in, come in. Eternal glory you shall win."

Craig smiled grimly. "I realize it will be through many trials that I'll finally enter the City of the Great King."

"My young friend, watch and be sober that you enter not into temptation. May the Comforter always be with you to guide you in the way that leads to the city."

"Thanks a lot, Interpreter. You've shown me things that'll help a lot in the days to come. I need stability. I don't want to blow it along the way."

Craig waved good-bye and headed up a highway which was lined on both sides with a wall called Salvation. He tried to run but only staggered under the load on his back. Suddenly he saw a rugged hill. On the top he saw a Cross, and on the bottom a Sepulchre. Craig couldn't tear his eyes away from the Cross. The sudden tears that came surprised him. As he approached the Cross, his burden loosened and dropped from his shoulders. It tumbled down the hill and disappeared forever in the mouth of the Sepulchre.

Shining beings then appeared, smiling gently at Craig's tears. One said, "Your sins are forgiven. Your name is now to be Christian." One stripped him of his rags and clothed him in a new outfit. Another placed a mark on his forehead and gave him a small scroll with a seal on it. "Show them this scroll when you reach the Celestial Gate," said that shining one.

With a shout of joy, Christian sprinted down the hill, excited to begin in earnest his journey to the City of the Great King.

My Salvation and Yours

David M. Griebner

The Bible teaches us that, with reverence and awe, we are to work to the finishing point of our salvation. Throughout this deepening process God allows hardships, obstacles, even tragedies. Sometimes when we slam up hard against these troubles, it feels as if we're starting all over again in our Christian experience. But God simply breaks us down, forming us into an increasingly beautiful representation of his character. This is God's incomparable goal for us.

Once there was a woman who made stained glass windows for a living. Now I know what you are thinking, but she didn't make the kind of windows that had people in them or scenes from the Bible. Instead her delight was in the color of the glass. She had a special gift for putting colors together, so she worked mostly with large pieces of wonderfully colored glass, which she arranged beautifully. She was satisfied and so were her customers.

Then one night she had a dream that would change everything. In her dream if felt as if someone spoke to her and seemingly placed an order: "Make me a window of my salvation and yours." When she woke she remembered the dream for a few minutes, as we often do, and then she forgot it. However, the dream returned the next night, "Make me a window of my salvation and yours."

Soon she was having this dream every night; even though she didn't understand the request exactly, she decided to make a window for the sake of a good night's sleep. At first wondering where to begin, she decided to do what she did best. She gathered some beautiful pieces of stained glass, arranged them in a way that seemed right to her, and leaded the whole thing together. She went to sleep that night expecting to be left alone. She was not. "Make me a window of my salvation and yours."

She walked toward her studio the next morning uncertain of what to do now. *Should she make another window? Move to another town? See a psychiatrist?* Then her thoughts were interrupted by what she saw when she opened the door. Her beautiful window had somehow tipped over and shattered on the concrete floor. *How? Now what? Is this why the dream came back?* She sat there for a few moments looking at the fragments of her window. Then, despite her own resistance and uncertainty, she picked up a piece of the broken glass and another and another. Somehow she could see how these pieces went together even more beautifully now than they had when they were larger.

She worked through the day and by evening she had a new window. While it was the same glass as before, now there were many more pieces and much more detail. In fact the window contained more pieces than she had ever worked with before. She was happy with her work, and she went to sleep exhausted. But that night the same voice as before unsettled her sleep: "Make me a window of my salvation and yours."

Weary and angry she stayed away from her studio all the next morning. When she finally opened the door after lunch, a sight greeted her that she almost expected. Her latest window was in pieces on the floor— far more pieces than the last time! Fighting despair and the urge to run away, she cradled her head in her hands and peered out at the broken glass through the space between her fingers. After several painful and uncertain moments, she tenderly reached out with one hand and put two pieces of glass together . . . and then another.

It took her longer than a day to make a window this time. There were so many pieces and so many ways to arrange them. Oddly enough, while she was working on this window her dreams were silent. This silence left her hopeful. Finally her latest window was done as well. The pieces of glass were so small it was almost like a mosaic. And it was exquisite. She hadn't imagined that she was capable of creating such symmetry. Surely now her dreams would be silent. Yet that very night after finishing, she heard again, "Make me a window of my salvation and yours."

So it went. She made window after window; every one broken in turn, each time into smaller and smaller pieces. Thus each subsequent window became more and more detailed, etched with subtler shades of color, more grandeur, greater wonder.

In time, the woman became accustomed to the dream, the breaking down, and the building up.

Then one day she died. Her friends found her in her studio. Next to her was a pile of tiny slivers of glass. They left the pile undisturbed, closed the studio, and locked the door. But on the day of her funeral, a great wind broke through the window of the place, swept up that pile of fine glass and cast it into the sky where it ignited in the sun like a million rainbows.

At her funeral some said they heard a voice say "Well done" just as the preacher finished the prayer.

We Understand So Little

A Folktale Retold by Stephen Fortosis

This is an anonymous Jewish folktale that repeats for us the lesson that, behind even the mundane scenes in life, God is always accomplishing far more than we know.

I tell you the truth, unless a kernel of wheat falls to the ground and dies, it remains only a single seed. But if it dies, it produces many seeds. The man who loves his life will lose it, while the man who hates his life in this world will keep it for eternal life.

John 12:24–25

Once there were two brothers who had spent all their lives in the city, and had never even seen a field or pasture. So one day they decided to take a trip into the countryside. As they were walking along, they spied a farmer plowing and were puzzled about what he was doing.

"What kind of behavior is this?" they asked themselves. "This fellow marches back and forth all day, scarring the earth with long ditches. Why should anyone destroy such a pretty meadow like that?"

Later in the afternoon they passed the same place again, and this time they saw the farmer sowing grains of wheat in the furrows.

"Now what's he doing?" they asked themselves. "He must be a madman. He's taking perfectly good wheat and tossing it into these ditches!"

"The country is no place for me," said one of the brothers. "The people here act as if they had no sense. I'm going home." And he went back to the city.

But the second brother stayed in the country, and a few weeks later saw a wonderful change. Fresh green shoots began to cover the field with a lushness he had never imagined. He quickly wrote to his brother and told him to hurry back to see the miraculous growth.

The brother returned from the city, also amazed at the change. As the days passed the brothers watched the green earth turn into a golden field of tall wheat. And now they understood the reason for the farmer's work.

When the wheat grew ripe, the farmer came with his scythe and began to cut it down. The brother who had returned from the city couldn't believe it. "What is this imbecile doing now?" he exclaimed. "All summer long he worked so hard to grow this beautiful wheat, and now he's destroying it with his own hands. He is a madman after all! I've had enough. I'm going back to the city."

The other brother had more patience. He stayed in the country and watched the farmer collect the wheat and take it to his granary. He saw how cleverly the farmer separated the chaff, and how carefully he stored the rest. And he was filled with awe when he realized that from a bag of seed sown, a whole field of grain could be harvested. Only then did he truly understand that the farmer had a reason for everything he did.

"And this is how it is with God's works, too," he told his brother. "We see only the beginnings of God's plan. Can we ever understand the full purpose and end of His creation without faith in His wisdom?"

ADULT MATURINGS

One Changed Life

Keith Miller

*Since the 1960s, Keith Miller has been gracing the Christian
world with books that are both stimulating and refreshing in their
candor and insight. Beginning with* A Taste of New Wine *and*
A Second Touch, *Miller moved on to produce other popular titles.*

The story "One Changed Life" is taken from his book
Habitation of Dragons. *This is a true account of how one hour of
gospel witness to a wayward businessman resulted in a spiritual
harvest Miller never imagined.*

For years I was hesitant about the idea of new Christians trying to
influence other people before they really understood the implications
of the Gospel.

Then I went on a speaking trip to another state, where I was restless
and tired. Feeling phony and miserable, I did not want to speak to this
particular group. How could I possibly project hope and purpose about
the Christian life?

Waiting my turn to speak, I looked over those hundreds of strange
faces. I wondered if anyone else had come to this meeting unwillingly.
I could not shake loose from the slough of self-pity and frustration of

not being able to control my circumstances. But after I had finished speaking, I found myself still standing before the lectern, hesitating. Finally, I heard myself saying something I'd never said before—something a little embarrassing because it sounded like a gimmick: "You know, I have the strangest feeling that I came all this way to talk to one of you who may be going through some of the same feelings of frustration and self-pity that I am. If you think you are the person, I would like to meet you after this session."

As I sat down, I mentally kicked myself in the backside: "Why did you say a stupid thing like that? These people will think you're some kind of a kook." But it was too late.

After the program a large number of men came to extend the courtesy of greeting the speakers. As the line came by, I forgot all about my closing remarks until a short, heavy-set man with glasses and black wavy hair walked up to me. When he shook my hand, he gripped it with great intensity. I looked into his eyes and saw a couple of tears start down his cheeks. Leaning forward, I said quietly, "Say, if you have a minute, I'd like to talk to you." He nodded. I pointed to a corner and said I would be there in a few minutes.

As soon as I could break loose, I went to him.

"I am an attorney and travel a lot," he told me. "Although we belong to this denomination," and he nodded toward the group still clustered around the speaker's platform, "it hasn't really meant anything to me in years. I certainly never planned to come to this meeting. As a matter of fact . . ." He stopped and looked at me a little uneasily.

"As a matter of fact," he continued, "I have a mistress in this town and was coming to see her—though I was supposedly on a business trip. For weeks I've been feeling very guilty. I wanted out of this relationship, but couldn't seem to break it off. Anyway, when I got out of my car a block from this church, in front of her apartment, who should come charging up to clap me on the back but three guys from my home church. I almost fainted when one of them asked, 'What are you doing here, Joe?'

"I lied. 'I'm just passing through,' I told them, scared to death they were going to see the guilt written all over me.

"'Hey, great,' they told me. 'We're just going down to hear some Christian businessmen speak. You've gotta come with us.' I was afraid to say no, for fear I'd somehow give myself away.

"Then as I sat here in this meeting and heard you speak about a new start in life—a life with purpose and meaning—I was amazed. I had

84

given up on having any purpose and meaning. I've been filled with self-pity, but with no idea what to do. When you stood up there and looked squarely at me and said what you did, I knew I was the one you were talking about." He stopped talking and looked at me.

"Listen," I said, suddenly realizing I had to catch a plane. "We haven't much time. Would you like to commit your whole future to God, including your relationship with this woman?"

He stood there biting his lips. Finally he said, "I would."

"All right," I said. "There are a couple things involved in beginning. One is to confess that you really want your own way more than God's. If you can do that, then ask God, as He is revealed in Christ, to come into your life and show you how to live for Him. Then give Him permission to make you want to."

In a prayer, standing in the corner of that huge church, Joe made a new beginning. I pointed out that Christianity was not a "ticket to heaven" but a way of life that starts now and transcends death, and that all he had done with me was to make a simple beginning. Now he had to begin to learn to live again.

I heard my name called and noticed that the people who were to drive me to the airport were looking at their watches. Hating to leave this man, I said, "Listen, Joe. I'll make a deal with you. I'll pray for you every morning for a month if you will pray for me. If you want to go on after that, write me a card and say, 'You're on for another month,' and I'll stay with you a month at a time from now on."

Joe was in tears as he took my business card and shook my hand. I hated to leave him but I knew I must. Glancing at my watch, I realized the whole interview had lasted about twelve minutes.

When I got home from that trip at the end of the month, there was a letter from Joe. He had begun to live for God. He started by breaking off the relationship with his mistress. Already it was hard, but he was going to try for another month if I would stick with him.

Yet I knew Joe was in for some real adjustments. As the months went by, I was amazed at the way God was getting hold of this man. He began reading the Scriptures and all the books he could get his hands on about living the Christian life. He began going to his church and having long talks with his minister. Joe began to see his self-centeredness, and changed his behavior toward his family and friends in the little southwestern town of a few thousand in which he lived. During all this time

I had not seen Joe or talked to him. All he knew was that someone he had met one day was praying for him at 6:00 every morning.

About a year later Joe wrote and said he had told a few people about what was happening to him, but he did not feel they understood him. If I would come to his church, he said he would get these people together for a discussion about living for Christ as a businessman.

This was a very busy time in my life. But I had gotten Joe into this, and the circumstances were so unusual that I thought that the least I could do would be to go and visit with the little group to which he was trying to witness. So I went.

I arrived just in time for the meeting. Joe met my plane and was very excited as we drove to his church. He said he was sure glad I was there, because several people in town had come right out and asked him what had happened in his life. Since I had never written any books or articles, his friends would only know me as "a friend of Joe's." As we arrived at the church, the minister said how glad he was that I'd come, and how Joe had helped him personally.

By this time we were a few minutes late. We went through a door at one end of the church to meet with the friends who were curious about Joe's life. I stopped for several seconds . . . looking into the faces of more than eight hundred people crowded into every corner and aisle of that church and adjoining rooms.

I realized in that moment that all of the promoted programs and Christian education plans in the world are virtually worthless to motivate people to become Christians until they see some ordinary Joe who is finding hope and a new way to live in Christ.

A Man
Called Norman

Mike Adkins

Mike Adkins had no idea what he was getting into when he offered
to help Norman, his eccentric, elderly neighbor, crank up a stubborn
lawn mower. But, out of those moments, a friendship germinated,
and Adkins was to benefit from the close relationship at least as
much as Norman. You will be changed internally as you see
illustrated in this story the true meaning of Christian friendship.

I had to get rid of an old tree stump in my front yard, so I figured if I
dug around the roots long enough with my oversized trowel, I'd expose
it enough to get a chain around it and haul it out. It was a steaming day,
and I wore out fast, so I began distracting myself by checking out my
new neighbors.

A couple of houses down from ours was an old place that seemed
abandoned. The front porch sagged. The windows were filthy. Choco-
late-colored paint was peeling off everywhere. The house seemed to be
hiding behind the limbs of a lonely oak out front—like a person who's
afraid, shielding himself with his arms.

Suddenly I saw someone emerge. *Oh, no!* I thought, *that's weird Norman over there. God, how could You have me buy a house across the street from Norman?*

Norman Corbin was the odd, creepy guy every town seems to have. I'd known of Norman since grade school. The big man spent his days tromping up and down Main Street twice as fast (or slow) as most folks—rubber galoshes, instead of shoes, flopping on his feet. He wore dirty overalls and a hat that was so grease- and oil-stained that you could barely tell it had once been a fedora. Sometimes on his way through town he'd stop, run his fingers through his bushy, graying hair, stare up at the sky, and shout something like, "Whoa? What'uv bestin franguss? Dreetmack cripno!" It made you wonder where the men in the white coats were; I assumed Norman was at least several cards short of a full deck.

Anyway, while I dug my trowel around the tree roots, Norman began tinkering with the gas-powered lawn mower over in his yard. He kept pulling on the cord to no avail. Suddenly he saw me. Raising his arms like the Incredible Hulk he screamed, "Yeeeaaaooow!" Then he charged toward me with his arms raised as if he was going to attack. I felt a surge of pure adrenaline. I was scared silly. He glowered at me, arms raised, then turned back to the lawn mower.

I thought: *God, I know we're supposed to love everybody, but if he comes over here I'm going to defend myself.* I gripped my tool more tightly.

He came rushing at me again: "Aaargggh! Aaargggh!" He did that three times in all, stopping on his side of the street, then loping back to his lawn mower.

Suddenly a feeling settled down on me that lifted me up as it fell. It was like a misty rain, fresh like that, and at the same time peaceful and quiet like a fog. I'm trying somehow to describe the presence of God, and a boldness that came to me that I don't normally have. I knew I was supposed to talk to Norman.

I stood up and walked right over to him. His eyes looked huge behind thick lenses. He needed to look in a mirror when he shaved—I saw whole patches of heavy stubble he'd missed. His downcast eyes searched the grass and he shifted from one foot to the other like a nervous animal. I had the feeling he wanted to swing the mower over his head and smash it to bits.

"Having trouble with your lawn mower, Norman?" I asked.

He stared at me, then said, "Having trouble with your lawn mower, Norman?"

I thought: *Didn't I just say that? Why is he repeating me?*

The voice was gruff and low, with a reedy rumble, like the sound you make by blowing on a thick blade of grass between your thumbs.

"Well, Norman," I continued, "I'm not much of a lawn mower mechanic, but let me see what I can do here."

I tightened the screws on the housing and cleaned the spark plug. As I worked, I heard him softly repeat what I'd just said. I yanked the cord and the motor started purring like brand-new.

Norman's eyes kept shifting here and there. Finally a slow grin spread across his face. I glimpsed a green-and-yellow tooth here, one there, and two more down below. As I went back across the street, I thought maybe the grin was the start of some kind of a friendship.

Every Sunday evening after church, just about everybody ended up at the local Dairy Queen. Norman always seemed to show up too. We always just pretended he wasn't there. None of us wanted to be thought strange, and talking to Norman posed the risk of being grouped with someone so clearly an outcast.

Then one Sunday night that fall, my wife Carmel and I were sitting at the Dairy Queen when Norman came in. I sensed God telling me to go over and talk to him. I didn't want to go, but finally, after asking Carmel to pray for me, I went anyway.

Norman sat at a booth close to the counter. I bought another ice cream cone at the counter and quickly slipped into the booth opposite him. His ice cream had smeared into the whiskers around his mouth.

I kept my voice low, "Do you remember who I am, Norman?" I said.

"Do you remember who I am?" he repeated.

"I'm your neighbor."

"I'm your neighbor."

If he was going to repeat everything I said, this was going to take all night. I cut to the point. "Do you know who Jesus is? Did you ever think about asking Jesus to come into your heart and be your Savior and Lord?"

I was expecting him to repeat that too. He studied me for a long moment, his eyes intent. Finally he lowered his ice cream and said, "I've given it some serious consideration."

I was so stunned I didn't know what to say. I went back to my wife. I had to ponder who Norman really was, and what friendship with him might mean.

A few weeks later I saw Norman in his yard again. I wanted to invite him over, but Carmel had been fixing up our place so the interior looked like something out of a magazine, and it was difficult for me to see Norman in that picture. I didn't really know how I would make conversation with him anyway. Then I remembered there was going to be a Christian musical special on TV.

I shouted across the street to Norman, "We'd like you to come over to our house to watch television tonight. Six-thirty."

He stared at me and said, "Uh-huh," but I didn't know if he'd come or not.

It began to get dark at 6:30, and I went to my window. I spotted Norman, all dressed up for the occasion—including a garish tie that hung at a crazy angle across one side of his chest.

I also noticed upon opening the door that he hadn't bathed. I thought of the best seat in the house—my chair. Although I love my chair and was sure Norman was going to soil it, I sat him down in it. I showed him the foot elevator, and he got a kick out of that.

Throughout the musical special Norman sat still, hardly breathing. It definitely kept his attention. When it was over, he just got up and said, "Thank you very much."

I walked him over to the door, saw him down my narrow steps, and told him to come back again. I'll admit, though, when I went back into my living room, I checked my chair for damage. There wasn't a single mark on it. Carmel had sprayed with an air freshener by then, leaving no trace that Norman had been in our home.

Some time after this I decided I'd go over and visit Norman on his own turf. As I approached his door one spring evening, I wondered whether he'd want anyone to see how he lived. But he opened the door and let me in. I couldn't believe how filthy his living quarters were. A heavy coat of smut covered everything. The windows were so dirty that the outside appeared pitch dark. The floor was so caked with grime you couldn't detect the linoleum pattern. Open cans of spaghetti, ravioli, and tuna fish covered the aluminum table and the counter space next to the sink. Forks and spoons sprouted out of their tops. Suddenly I realized Norman must eat all his meals out of those cans, cold.

His furnishings came from the 1920s. There was an old Victrola in the living room that you had to hand wind. His ancient bed was lumpy and unmade, with mildewed covers.

After that visit, I dropped by once in a while just to see how Norman was doing. At first he wouldn't look me in the eye and only muttered replies to my questions. Gradually he became less shy. Once in a great while, he would even throw back his great tousled head and let me see that four-tooth, jack-o'-lantern grin. He told me he'd lived with his mother until her death some ten years before. Besides cutting lawns in the summer, he made his money from cleaning furnaces in the winter.

However, his coal-burning furnace didn't work worth a hoot, and he must have been hard-pressed to keep from freezing in his own home.

As my relationship with Norman progressed, I tried to understand him—though I was still somewhat afraid of him. A butcher knife, its blade bigger than your wrist, lay on his kitchen table, and I kept wondering whether he might do something crazy. I could almost hear the thunk of that knife being plunged into my back.

These fears persisted because of a confrontation I had on the street with a confused man who thought of himself as a prophet. He walked up to me and warned me wildly not to have anything to do with Norman. He said Norman was demon-possessed and might harm me, and that God had finally abandoned my friend to the devil for good.

I heard other opinions at work. One guy said Norman had probably been struck by a Greyhound bus. Another thought he was really a genius who got so much knowledge stuck in his head that one day his mind imploded. Yet another theory was that Norman was an idiot savant—someone mentally defective but with a special genius.

I wasn't sure what to believe, but I did recall that children used to poke Norman hard and scream out a series of numbers. He would yell back a great-big number as if he'd added their sums together.

As I continued visiting Norman, I realized how bad off his little house really was: The walls were tea-colored from water stains. Long strips of the wallpaper hung down. The grime made so much of it indistinguishable. I decided to buy gallons of white paint and blue, and set to work painting the interior. Then I painted the exterior. Carmel helped me clean the kitchen floor so the brick design of the linoleum appeared again, and I redid some wiring.

As we worked on Norman's house, my kids began to pitch in; they liked Norman so much that gradually he became a family favorite.

Soon, when some Methodists nearby experienced a spiritual renewal, about twenty of them showed up one weekend with mops, brooms, and vacuum cleaners, announcing that they wanted to help clean up Norman's old shack.

For two weeks that group worked like all get-out. The women even tried to help Norman—a real pack rat—organize collections he insisted on keeping, like the paper bags piled in his bathtub. Meanwhile the men replaced some of the plumbing and rotting floorboards; we cleaned the windows.

Norman looked shocked. He must have thought he lived in a house with permanently stained glass. But he didn't know how to express his gratitude in the way most of us have come to expect, and I began to feel as if I was doing a rather thankless job. Maybe that's why one night when I was at a high school basketball game with my brother and several friends, I blurted out in the middle of a discussion, "Hey, you know what? I've been helping out Norman."

Everyone stared at me for a moment. Then my brother said nonchalantly, "That's nice, Mike," and turned the conversation back to basketball.

I suddenly realized I wanted recognition for what I was doing. I wanted my neighbors to see how dedicated I was. I also wanted applause from God. One way or another, I was playing to an audience.

Though I began to wrestle with my true motives for befriending Norman, I didn't abandon him. In fact, I realized we'd never done anything fun before. So one summer day I asked, "Hey, Norman, are you a baseball fan? Do you root for the Redbirds?"

He just sort of grinned to himself.

"No, I mean it, Norman. You ever been to see the St. Louis Cardinals play?"

"No. Like to. Seen 'em on television."

"Why don't we go to a game then?" I said. "I'll get tickets."

When I went to pick him up, Norman came out wearing a heavy tweed overcoat. It was mid-July so I told him to go back in the house and put it away. He loped back inside, but came back to the car still wearing the coat. We repeated this until finally I gave up.

In the car, Norman's eyes were glued to my CB radio. He'd never talked on one, so I got on the thing and told whoever was listening that I had a CB greenhorn in the car and suggested we give him a handle. I added how Norman did yard work, so someone suggested he be called the Old Grasscutter.

Then I gave the mike to Norman, who said gruffly, "Hello? This is Old Grasscutter."

Several listeners responded and he began talking to them the entire trip.

Once in St. Louis most people treated Norman like he was demented. But the radio must have given him a connection, a non-threatening way to relate and enjoy other people.

I asked him how he felt when kids poked him and screamed out numbers. His reply was ironic. "Oh, I don't know, Mike," he said. "I guess I always thought they were kind of crazy."

When we reached Busch Stadium, it was sweltering outside. Again I pleaded for Norman to remove his coat. Finally he did, but as he turned to walk toward the ballpark, I saw he was wearing two pairs of slacks, both with wide rips all the way up the back. I decided to let him wear the coat.

The game began, but Norman didn't watch the play at all. He gazed, slack-jawed, at all the shouting fans.

"Never seen so many people in one place before," he said. "Only been out of town once. Went thirty miles one time."

I tried to focus his attention on the game, but he just stared hungrily at the hot dog vendor. He wanted a hot dog with a dab of mustard. Then he wanted another. A few minutes later he decided to scarf down two more. Before the end of the third inning, I'd also bought him a soft drink, peanuts, popcorn, nacho cheese chips, and ice cream. The trash around our feet looked as if we'd fed all the inhabitants at a zoo, but I knew Norman had had a rare afternoon of sheer enjoyment.

Sometime during the next year Marie, Norman's next-door neighbor, stopped me to report Norman seemed to be growing crippled. She made an appointment with a foot doctor and asked me if I'd take Norman.

The podiatrist checked Norman's feet, then took me aside. Obviously having trouble keeping his lunch down, the doctor first asked me whether Norman ever washed his feet. Next he reported that Norman's feet were severely deformed from wearing shoes too small for too many years. The doctor had pulled the dead nails from each toe and carved a cone of callous from the ball of each foot, then packed the surgical wounds with sulfur and salve and bandaged them. I bought Norman a bucket and made sure he soaked his feet every evening for a while.

By this time I'd gained Norman's confidence, but still hadn't convinced him to wash up. I then conceived an idea that I thought might persuade him. I carried a brown suit over to his house that I wouldn't wear anymore. I felt pretty proud of myself until I went to hang it up in his closet and discovered a closetful of other people's cast-offs.

A voice echoed inside my head: *How about loving your neighbor as yourself?*

I prayed, "God, if you give me some money, I'll buy Norman a suit more expensive than I've ever bought for myself."

Not long thereafter I was asked to provide the music for some special meetings at the Methodist church. Surprisingly an offering was collected for me and I knew instantly that the money was for Norman.

We hustled down to the best men's store in town. When the impeccably dressed salesman led Norman to the suit rack, he selected a navy suit with intricate stitching. We also bought him a shirt, socks, and shoes.

On the drive home, I asked Norman if he'd like to go to a gospel concert at a church that evening. "You'd be my guest," I said. "You could wear your new suit."

"I like music," he rumbled. "Let's go."

"But Norman," I continued. "Have you ever been clean?"

There was a pause.

"We're pretty good buddies, Norman, right?"

"Yep, Mike, we're pretty good buddies."

"Then today's the day. Today's the day you take a bath."

As I helped him get ready I asked, "Why don't you take regular baths?"

"Well," he muttered, "I figured, who'd care?"

He explained slowly that his dad had died in the coal mines, and just hadn't come home one day after work. Norman remembered seeing his uncle at the funeral, but that was the last time he saw him too. Then he told me that following his mother's passing, he just sort of gave up on taking care of himself.

I thought of this as I bought Norman some Lava soap, a giant sponge, and SOS pads. I cleared out the paper sacks he had collected in his bathtub, then filled the tub with water, told him to climb inside, and call me when he'd finished washing.

The first time he called, all he'd succeeded in doing was smearing the grime onto different parts of his body. I got him in a gentle headlock and began to wash his hair. I scrubbed and scrubbed. Suddenly I glimpsed a dignified patch of pure white hair in place of the dull muddy-gray he'd always displayed.

I had to show him spots he'd missed at least half a dozen times before he was actually clean. Then I got him brushing his four teeth and I shaved off his whiskers. He combed his hair and finally climbed into his new suit. I couldn't believe it! That evening it looked like Carmel and I were escorting a state senator to the concert.

Norman just grinned a little and said, "Do ya think they'll notice my new suit?"

After that busy, busy year I was ready for a family vacation; every time I thought about it, a little voice in my head said, "Norman's never had one of those. Why not take him along?" I kept arguing with the voice, but it won out in the end.

We decided to go to the amusement park at Opryland in Nashville, and bought Norman a new designer T-shirt for the occasion. At this point he was—we estimated—sixty-two years old and I feared he might have a heart condition so we steered clear of the Wabash Cannonball. However, I figured he could handle the bumper cars. He'd never been in one, so I told him to get in, push the pedal, and have a good time.

The ride started and, before anyone knew it, somehow Norman had backed the entire crowd of bumper cars into one side of the rink. Everyone was getting incensed, but he honestly didn't know how to break loose. Finally someone broke out, circled the entire rink and—boom—slammed headfirst into Norman. That freed the logjam and then everyone tried to get even, laughing like hyenas all the while. Norman went into panic mode and tried to climb out of the car. Afraid he might get an electric shock, I shouted for the operator to stop the ride. Thank the Lord, the time ran out before Norman could unhinge his bulky frame from the car.

I ran over to Norman, who instead of yelling at me like I expected, trembled like a child. He looked at me through those thick glasses of his, seeming to say, "I trusted you. How could you do that to me?"

Suddenly I realized that one person or another had been intimidating Norman all his life. Even when children showed him attention, they weren't doing it affectionately and he knew it.

Maybe it was time to talk to Norman about taking a spiritual bath. I'd noticed a Bible on his lamp stand and figured maybe he'd been reading it, but I wasn't sure what to say to him. I asked a local pastor along who was good with people.

Actually Norman had revealed himself as one of the finest people we knew: He was rarely angry at anyone. He definitely wasn't conceited. He made almost no demands. Still, the pastor explained from the Book of Romans, even a good man needed to turn to Christ for repentance. Norman needed to be clean inside.

For a while he just shook his head and looked confused. Then his clouded expression grew clear. He said: "Oh, I—I know what you're sayin'. Luh—like my windows there, bein' so blamed dirty. Wouldn't do much good to just clean the outside of 'em. I'd have to clean the inside, too."

He was finally getting the idea. "That's right, Norman," I said.

We bowed our heads and it was quiet. I didn't want simply to give Norman words to parrot back at me, but I didn't know if he understood how to form a prayer. Then I heard that rumbling voice: "Well, God, I want to ask You to come into Norman's heart and be my Savior, because that's what the preachers used to say on the radio on Sunday mornin'. Mama used to listen to them. And, God, that's what that Bible over there says, that I've been readin' for myself. And so, come on into my heart. Come into Norman's heart and be my Savior. Amen."

He raised his head, "Did I do OK?" he asked.

Both the pastor and I had tears in our eyes, and just nodded. Finally I choked, "You did fine, Norman. Just fine."

That winter I went for some special job training in West Virginia. Near the end of one week Carmel called: Norman was hurt bad. I hurried home and found him in a hospital bed with a dislocated knee—most of the ligaments torn, and the bone chipped.

Norman had fallen three times—the first time downtown, then twice trying to get home. He couldn't get help so he'd done extra damage sliding on icy sidewalks for so many blocks.

The doctors kept him in the hospital for a few weeks, but even back home, he still was largely immobilized. Meals on Wheels helped him out, but it was up to me to tend to the chamber pot, bathe him, exercise his leg, and tend his temperamental coal furnace on those freezing winter evenings. Some of the lowest moments in my friendship with Norman came on those lonely nights. I wanted to be out serving God in big churches with my music and speaking ability. I couldn't figure out why he had me helping this old man in a God-forsaken shack in West Frankfurt, Illinois.

Slowly Norman got so that he could pull himself out of bed. Then he graduated from crutches to only a cane. One night I was getting ready to leave him and thought I should start praying with him. It quickly became a habit.

Another night I got Norman out of the tub and gave him his pajamas— just the tops. (They were so long they reached down to his knees.) I turned out the lights and said good-night, then locked the door behind me. As I walked away, I remembered I'd forgotten to pray so I went back to his bedside.

"Norman," I said, "I forgot something. You know what, don't you?"

He said, "Yep, you forgot my shorts."

We both started laughing. I gave him his underclothes and turned my back while he put them on.

Then I said, "What I meant, Norman, was I forgot to pray."

At first, I did all the praying. But one night I said, "Norman, you pray."

The old clock was tick-tocking on the mantel, wind wheezed through cracks in the walls, and the boards creaked and moaned.

Finally Norman said, "Well, God, I just want to thank You for Mike, because I don't know what I would've done without him. Amen."

After we said good-night and I crossed over to my yard, I began to realize that if you're going to love somebody, it's got to be for his or her own sake and not in expectation of some reward or pats on the back.

Sometime later the grocery store manager in the area gave me a call.

"We love Norman, Mike. Don't misunderstand. But the truth is, he stinks. My customers are complaining openly. Much as I hate to do it, I've got to ask you to tell him not to come into the store."

I was shocked. I thought I'd gotten Norman into the habit of bathing, and he appeared pretty clean last time I saw him. I figured maybe it was just some cantankerous people—until I received another call from the Dairy Queen, whose manager said the same thing.

Now I was angry with Norman. Was he making a mockery of his Christian experience by continuing to act as if no one cared about him? After all I'd tried to do to help, had Norman really not changed at all?

I stomped over to his house, charged through his back door, and sat him down at his kitchen table. "Don't say a word to me," I told him. "I'm going to do the talking. I'm getting calls from businesses saying you can't come in anymore because you stink. You can't go back. You've embarrassed me and shamed yourself. You're supposed to be a Christian."

He tried to interrupt.

"Don't say a word," I said, raising my voice. "This time I'm not going to listen. I've scrubbed your floors, I've carried your coal, emptied your slop jar, but I'm not messing with you anymore."

I was really steamed now. "Before I leave you're going to take a bath," I shouted. "I'm leaving this house for the last time with you in the tub getting clean."

Norman stood up like a little child and went in the bedroom. I sat in the kitchen to make sure he didn't con me. As he stepped out of his bedroom into the hallway, my eyes were drawn to his calf and an abscess there the size of a grapefruit. His leg looked as if a bunch of rats had eaten it away; the wound was green and running, and the stench unbearable. Then I noticed that his entire leg was almost double its normal size. Gangrene had begun.

Norman had never said a word about his leg. Maybe he was so used to quietly accepting adversity that he thought he should just grit his teeth and bear it. In any case I was so ashamed of my outburst, I didn't know what to say. Norman smoothed things over. On the way to the hospital, he chuckled to himself quietly. Finally I had to ask, "Why are you laughing?"

"Boy, were you mad," he rumbled. "You were beatin' on my kitchen table and everything."

It turned out Norman had cut himself on the bucket I'd bought for him to soak his feet in. The superficial wound had quickly turned infectious because the circulation in his leg was so bad. He didn't lose the leg, but it still swells some and must constantly be bandaged.

Maybe my commitment to Norman was like God's training camp for me, because at about this time my father, a Christian just these last two years, was diagnosed with pancreatic cancer. The doctors gave him six months to live. One day near the end, I went to see him. He was so near death. His breathing worsened. I combed his hair, parted it, and styled it just right. He had never gone anywhere without his hair combed.

I was struck once again by the closeness in age between Norman and my dad. Through Norman I started living the life of faith in earnest, and my father had seen what faith can do.

My father's breathing became slower and slower until finally it just stopped, and I knew he'd found new company and was washed, combed, and ready.

Not long after my father's death, a Christian television company heard a song I wrote about Norman and invited the two of us to appear on a program. I sang that song, and a local businessman presented Norman with a brand-spankin'-new lawn mower. Then the host's wife kissed Norman on the cheek, which pleased him no end.

That evening, back in our hotel room, the two of us saw a rebroadcast of the program. When Norman saw the host's wife kiss him again, he threw back his head and chuckled.

"I think she likes me," he said.

"I'm sure she does, Norman," I said, "but she already has a husband."

He looked at me as if I were the afflicted one. "I didn't mean anything like that."

It struck me that probably no one had kissed or hugged Norman since his mother died ten years back. What a lonely life he'd lived. But in Christ Norman needed no pity. He had more love than he could ever understand or absorb, and he was washed, combed, and ready.

THE PINEAPPLE STORY

Otto Koning

This is a true story about a missionary who learned the lesson of unconditional love the hard way. It may not be especially overwhelming to spread the gospel message when the recipients are reasonably polite and unobtrusive. But when they actually do a missionary wrong and won't even admit it, God's love is truly put to the acid test. Otto Koning tells us all about it first-hand.

My family and I work with these people way back in the bush, and one day I decided to order in some pineapple plants. The people had heard of pineapples and even tasted them, but they didn't have any source by which to get them. In fact, back in the jungle you long for fresh fruit because you don't get much of it or fresh vegetables either.

So I brought in one hundred plants from another mission station. Then I got one of the local men to plant all these pineapple shoots for me. I paid him, of course—salt or whatever he wanted for the days worked.

It seemed to take awfully long—about three years—for those little shoots of pineapple to become big bushes and yield fruit. Finally that third year we could see fresh pineapples coming on, and we were just waiting for Christmas when the fruit ripens. My wife and I would go for walks to watch for pineapples ready to eat. But we never got a single one of them! The natives stole every one—and before they were ripe. That is their art, you see: Steal before the fruit is ripe or the owner gets it.

Now here I was, a missionary, getting mad at these people. Missionaries aren't supposed to get mad. You know that. But I got angry.

I said: "Look, you guys! I've been waiting for these pineapples for three years. I didn't get any of the first fruits. Now there are others getting ripe. If any more of these pineapples are stolen, no more clinic for you."

See, my wife was running a clinic. She would give the people all their pills free because they didn't have anything to pay anyway. We were knocking ourselves out trying to help, taking care of their sick, saving the lives of their babies.

So when one by one the pineapples got ripe, and one by one they were stolen, I felt I had to stand my ground. I couldn't just let these people run all over me. Yet my real reason was selfish: I wanted to eat those pineapples myself. So no more clinic.

The people let their sick babies die. They couldn't care less. Life was cheap over there. People with bad pneumonia would be coughing and begging us for medicine.

We would say, "No! Remember you stole our pineapples."

"I didn't steal them," they would say. "It was the other guys that did it."

They would go on coughing and begging. We couldn't take it any longer.

I broke down and said, "OK, tomorrow morning we will open the clinic again."

When we opened the clinic they started stealing the pineapples, and I felt bad again.

Man! These rascals!

Then we found out the real thief—the guy who had planted the pineapple shoots. I called him on the carpet. I said, "Look, buddy! What are you doing stealing my pineapples? You're my gardener."

He said, "My hands plant them. My mouth eats them." That is the rule of the jungle. If you plant something, it's yours. Who heard of paying for services? So he said, "They are all mine."

"Oh no!" I said. "They are mine. I paid you to plant them." But he just couldn't understand how that made them my plants.

I thought, *Well, what do I do now? This is the rule of the tribe—I'd better learn to live by their rule.*

So I said, "All right, I'll give you half of these plants. Everything from here to over there is yours; if they get ripe, they are yours. But these are mine."

He sounded like he was in agreement. Still my pineapples got stolen.

Finally I said, "Look, I'll give you all these pineapples, and then I'll start all over again. Now you make a garden and you take all these pineapples out of my garden so I'll have room to plant new ones. I don't want your pineapples in my garden if you feel they are yours."

So my gardener said, "Too-wan"—which means outsider—"you will have to pay us."

I said, "Now, look!"

They said, "No, no! You are asking us to move your pineapple bushes and that is work."

They made a big ruckus about the plants being mine. I said, "I'll pay you one day's work. Take them all away."

Then they said, "We don't have a garden ready. Will you pay us to get it ready?"

I said, "Forget it!" I was so fed up with them. I told my wife, "This is impossible! I'm just going to pay some guy to root out everything and throw the plants on the trash heap. Then the people can just take what they want!"

So we did. We rooted out all the pineapple plants and threw them on a heap. It was hard to do. These had been nice pineapple bushes. But I bought new plants and told the people, "Now look, I'm going to pay you to plant them, but I eat them—me and my family. You don't eat any."

They said, "You can't do that. If we plant them, we eat them."

I said, "Look, I don't have time to mess with a garden. I have too much to do. There are so many of you, and there is only one me. You've got to help me. I want you to plant them, and I will eat them. I'll pay you too. I'll give you this nice knife if you will agree to do it."

They started to think. *He'll pay us that knife so he can eat our pineapples.*

Finally they agreed.

During the next three years I reminded the guy who planted them, "Look! Who is going to eat these pineapples?"

"You are," he said.

"Fine!" I said. "Have you still got the knife?"

"Yes."

"Well, take good care of it." If he lost the knife I'd be in trouble again. The pay would be gone.

Finally, after three more years the pineapples began to ripen. My wife walked through the garden again. I said, "Man! Pretty soon we're going to have a crop of our own pineapples."

We started to thank God for providing them. But do you know what happened? Every one was stolen. I would see the natives go through the garden by day to spot where the pineapples were; then at night they would go right to them.

I thought, *What am I going to do? We can't cut out the clinic. But we could cut out the trade store.* That's where the people bought their matches, salt, fish hooks, and other things like this that they used to do without.

So I said, "OK, no more store. You stole my pineapples."

When we closed the store, though, the people began to say, "We had better leave because we don't have any salt. If he isn't going to have a store, there is no advantage for us being here with him. We might as well go back to our jungle houses."

So they took off to live in the jungle; there I was, sitting by myself eating pineapples. No people, no ministry.

"Look," I said to my wife, "we can eat pineapples back in the States, I mean, if that's all we're here to do."

A runner returned and I said, "Get them all back. We'll open the store next Monday." I thought and thought: *How am I going to get to eat those pineapples? There must be a way.*

Then I got an idea. A German shepherd! I got the biggest German shepherd I could find on the island. I brought him into the garden and let him loose. The people were afraid of him. They had never seen a dog this big. They had little, mangy dogs that they never fed—diseased dogs. And here was this well-fed German shepherd. The people looked at the food the dog got. It was better than anything they got. So I began to feed the shepherd when the people weren't around because they resented the dog's food.

But that dog did the trick. Most of the people didn't dare come around anymore. So now we had the same result as closing the store. People didn't come. I didn't have anybody to talk to. I couldn't get anybody to teach me the language.

I thought, *What do we do?*

The dog wasn't working. In the meantime, the dog was starting to breed with the village dogs and would raise up a wicked half-shepherd, wild and hungry. The doctor said, "Hey, if your kids or anybody gets bitten by that dog, I'm not going to treat them."

He was using the same tactics I was using on the natives. I said to my wife, "We've got to get rid of the dog."

103

We did. I hated to do it. But now the dog was gone. The people came back and then the pineapples were gone too. I thought, *Boy! There must be a way. What can I do?*

When I went home that year for a basic youth seminar, I learned that we must give everything we own to God. The Bible says: If you give, you will have; if you keep for yourself, you will lose. Give your things to God, and God will see that you have enough. This is a basic principle. I thought, *Man! I don't have anything to lose. I'll give that pineapple garden to God because I'm not eating the pineapples anyway.*

Now I know that's not a very great sacrifice. We're supposed to sacrifice something valuable to us. But I would give it to God and see if He could control it.

"Man!" I said, "I'm going to see how He's going to do it."

So I stood out in the garden one night to pray. The people had gone home; I didn't want them to see me out there. I prayed, "Lord, see these pineapple bushes? I've fought to have fruit from them. I've claimed them. I've stood up for my rights. It is all wrong, and I realize it now. I've seen that it's wrong and I give them to You. From now on, if You want me to eat any of Your pineapples, fine. You just go right ahead and give them to us. If not, fine. It doesn't really matter."

So I gave them to God, and the natives stole the pineapples as usual. I thought to myself, *See, God, You can't control them either.* Then one day they came to me and said, "Too-wan, you have become a Christian, haven't you?"

I was ready to react and say, "Look here, I've been a Christian for twenty years."

But instead I said, "Why do you say that?"

They said, "Because you don't get angry anymore when we steal your pineapples."

This was a real revelation. Now I was living what I'd been preaching to them.

I had been telling them to love one another, be kind to one another, and I had always been standing up for my rights, and they knew it.

Finally one bright lad started thinking and said, "Now, why don't you get angry anymore?"

I said, "I've given that garden away. It isn't my garden anymore. So you aren't stealing my pineapples. I don't have to get angry anymore."

Another guy started to think even more and he said, "Who did you give the garden to?"

They looked around. "Did he give it to you?" "Did he give it to you?" "Whose is it anyway?" "Whose pineapples are we stealing?"

Then I said, "I have given the garden to God."

They said, "To God? Hasn't He got any pineapples where He's at?"

I said, "I don't know whether He has or not, but I have given it to God."

They all started thinking about that one. They came back in a group and said, "Too-wan, you should not have done it. Why don't you get them back from God?"

"No wonder we aren't getting the pigs when we go out hunting."

"No wonder our babies are getting sick."

"No wonder our wives are not giving birth."

"No wonder the fish aren't biting."

Then they said, "We shouldn't steal them anymore if they are God's, should we?"

They were afraid of God. So then the pineapples began to ripen. The natives came and said, "Too-wan, your pineapples are ripe."

I said, "They aren't mine. They belong to God."

They said, "But they are going to get rotten. You had better pick them."

And so I got some and I let the natives take some. When my family sat down to eat them, I said, "Lord, we're eating Your pineapples. Thank You for giving them to us."

All those years those natives were watching me and listening to my words. They saw that the two didn't match. But when I began to change, they did too. Soon many natives decided to become Christians. The principle of giving to God really was working. I could hardly believe it myself. I started giving other things to God.

One day my son was near death and there was no way to get him to a doctor. I suddenly realized that I'd never given my son to God! So I prayed, "God, I give my son to You. Whatever You want to do is fine."

That was harder than giving God the pineapple garden. I was prepared for God to take my son. But that night the fever broke, and my son got well.

The natives began bringing things for me to fix. I said, "God, my time is Yours. If You want me to fix harmonicas and pots and shovels out here on the mission field, fine!"

I wasn't getting as much Bible translation done, but more people were being won to Christ. They kept saying, "Too-wan has become a Christian. He tells us to love one another and now he is starting to love us."

One day I was fixing a broken chair. A native saw me and said, "Here, let me help you hold it."

After we fixed it I said, "Well, aren't you going to ask me for any salt?"

He said, "No, Too-wan. Don't you remember? You helped me fix my shovel. Now I help you fix your chair."

I thought, *Man! That's the first time he did anything for me without getting paid for it.* Then one day I saw something in the Bible (Lev. 19:23–25) I had never noticed before:

> And when ye shall come into the land, and shall have planted all manner of trees for food. . . , three years shall it be uncircumcised unto you; it shall not be eaten of. But in the fourth year all the fruit thereof shall be holy with which to praise the Lord. And in the fifth year shall ye eat of the fruit thereof, that it may yield unto you the increase thereof: I am the Lord your God.

Finally I understood. God never intended me to eat those pineapples the first year they were ripe. He wanted me to dedicate them to Him. Then He wanted me to give them to the natives so that they could see my good works and glorify our Father in heaven. If I had only done this, the natives would have urged me to eat the pineapples the fifth year.

Man! All the trouble I could have avoided.

A Small Happening at Andover

Joseph Bayly

*In this story, Joseph Bayly reveals how a Christian can think she is
right about everything, yet ignore the most important truths of all.
A prim and proper retired schoolteacher learns that people are
more important than "righteous" agendas.*

It really seemed to make no difference one way or the other. Surprisingly, either way looked right.

This was perplexing, she thought, tilting her head first to one side, then to the other. Why, almost never was there more than one way that anything looked right. Cups and saucers, for instance. You didn't say saucers and cups, and you didn't place the saucer on top of the cup. She smiled at the absurd thought. Not even the lovely bone china ones, with the saucer design so much prettier than the plain, everyday ones. No, that was the right way. Then again . . . she was wrong. Her face clouded. The afternoon Edna had called, she was just pouring water over the metal tea holder in a cup. It was the Royal Albert Laurentian Snowdrop pattern. The water had boiled exactly seven minutes, the right length of time for tea water. But she knew Edna would be long and the tea would become over-cool. So she made a hasty decision, of the sort one later regrets: She placed the saucer on top of the cup—to keep the tea warm. It worked. But to have done it right—reboiling the seven-minute water after Edna had said good-bye—would have been the right course of action.

She should never have told Edna about that. How Edna had laughed at her insistence on the rightness of things. Somehow it made her uncomfortable, even now, to know that Edna knew. For Edna had not permitted her to forget that she knew.

Well, Edna would not learn of the present puzzling predicament. The letter "P" was such a delightful letter. Perfect P, she called it. Perhaps (that lovely, door-opening word), perhaps the letter P owed its delight to the fact that it was only one letter removed from R. Of all the letters, only R could vie with P. Only Rightness achieves Perfection.

Strange that Q should come between. Queer, quack, quandary. Why, it sounded somewhat like a Latin declension. Queer, quack, quandary. For a moment she imagined that tomorrow morning she would pack her lunch and set out precisely at 7:55 to walk the mile to Andover High School. Tomorrow was Thursday. That meant dry toast with grape jelly and a Jonathan apple, and vocabulary tests.

It would be grape jelly on toast tomorrow, with an apple, but no longer in a paper sack. Nor would there be vocabulary tests. Tests had ended, along with grading and lunch-carrying. Therefore, it was not right even to imagine them back. Resolutely, she turned her thoughts from the past. Retirement, not teaching, was right now.

Since there seemed to be no possibility of resolving the present problem, she would read the Bible and go to bed. Besides, the right time had come—9:45—she noted as the clock chimed.

Tomorrow she would find which was right. Obviously one was wrong, even though both appeared to be equally correct.

She turned to Leviticus 5, the reading for tonight. Yes, that was the right chapter, for this was the night of April fifth, the ninety-fifth day of the year, and that was the ninety-fifth chapter of the Old Testament. She had just begun to read when the telephone rang.

That would be Edna, of course. Edna knew perfectly well that nothing, absolutely nothing, should interfere with her nighttime reading at the right time. Well, she would not answer. It would not be right to interrupt the reading to answer the telephone. Edna knew that. But it was like Edna to try to get her to do something that was not right.

Edna had two faults. First, she was not a Christian. Second, of course related to the first, she did not do things rightly. She went up Main Street without wearing gloves. She had no regular time, no right time, for arising in the morning and going to bed at night. In fact, occasionally she did not go to bed the same day she got up!

That's how Edna would say it, too—she did not observe the right rules of English grammar. Edna seemed to find perverse delight in annoying her by improperly ending a sentence with a preposition, in splitting infinitives, and in using adjectives where adverbs would be right.

The ringing stopped.

Well, now, that was more like it. Noise, of whatever sort, was not right at this hour.

She closed her Bible after a few minutes and carefully placed the folded afghan on the floor. Today's date was odd-numbered, and so the brown side should be uppermost. As she knelt on the faded blanket at the platform rocker, she examined the rug briefly—where the man had stepped when he came to repair the radio. She was pleased to find no trace of the mud flecks he had left. The thin wire brush might be sixty years old, but it was still the right instrument for such a job, she observed with satisfaction.

Then she prayed. She asked that Edna might become a Christian— a prayer of 43 years' standing. And, as always, she prayed also that if there was anything in her that might be keeping Edna from faith, let the Lord remove it, whatever it might be.

But her mind was on the evening's problem. So she told the Lord that He knew—He knew—there was only one right way for a thing to be, even though to her eyes either of two ways might be, or might seem to be, equally right. He knew that both could not possibly be right.

Accordingly, she asked Him to show her which was right—whether the African violet she had purchased at Dustin's Greenhouse should be placed on the right or left end of the bookcase. She told Him she was willing to do that which was right, even though it might mean reversing the position of her mother's and father's photographs above the bookcase. But she did want it to be right. For she knew that it had to be right in order to please Him.

Having prayed, she arose, neatly folded the afghan and placed it on the blanket chest, checked the doors and went to bed. The time was precisely right—10:20.

Now it came to pass that the Lord heard her prayer, and He had pity on His child, who had been bound these many years.

The fullness of time having come for her deliverance, that same night, He caused a spark from the furnace to lodge in a broken place in the chimney. There it smoldered until 3:00 A.M., when the house burst into flames.

The fire department responded to the urgent call too late, and the dwelling was destroyed with all that was therein—all except the Lord's child, who was saved, in her nightgown and wrapper.

Now the Lord moved Edna to invite His child to come live with her. Other doors being closed, she accepted the kind invitation, albeit with great reluctance and misgivings.

As day followed day, and week followed week, and month followed month, a change took place in the Lord's child. The Lord completed her deliverance.

The signs of this were found in freedom to go to Main Street—at least in summer—without wearing gloves; freedom to stay up until midnight, and to have breakfast at nine in the morning. She even had freedom to keep her cup of tea hot with the saucer on top. (But seldom did she split an infinitive.)

And Edna, who had received the Lord's child into her home, also received the Lord into her heart.

CHARLEY

Ethel Barrett

Because of Ethel Barrett's remarkable ability as a storyteller, she gained enthusiastic audiences on the radio, on television, on platform, and in print. She wrote many books, including such titles as Sometimes I Feel like a Blob, There I Stood in All My Splendor, *and* Storytelling: It's Easy.

The following story is about Charley, told in the words of his mother. You will sense Barrett's ability as you step inside this mother's mind and travel with her in the rearing of a very special son.

Aunt Agatha and I walk down the center aisle of the large church, get our programs, and are ushered down front into one of the finest pews. The church is already well-filled. I resist the temptation to look back up and see if the balcony is filled too, and settle down next to Aunt Agatha to wait for Charley. As I wait I think on Charley, which is a pretty big order, for Charley is something. I muse and the years flip back, back, back . . .

Of course it had been apparent from the beginning that Charley was a very unusual child. At least it had been apparent to me. Things had started out well enough, except for the fact that I named him Charles after his father, which was the last thing I should have done for it led to the "big Charley, little Charley" business to avoid "Junior."

Other than that he was off to a good start, an absolute cherub. When a nurse first brought him to me, I'd looked him over carefully. I decided he was quite above average, and my mind buzzed with plans for the new chapter in my life.

I am a very methodical person and have always believed that if you add two and two, you have to get four. It's simply a matter of cause and effect, knowledge and application. So I fortified myself with books and more books on the care and feeding of children, and also a shelf of psychology books. I was prepared for anything.

Any resemblance between Charley and the baby in the books, however, was purely coincidental. For he had a most decided mind of his own. I insisted that it was a matter of figuring which category he fell into, and the rest would be easy. There was only one catch to that. Charley didn't seem to fall into any category at all. By the time I'd decided he was something no psychologist had ever written anything about, the preschool years were over. My hopes went up again when I deposited him in school; perhaps the teachers would discover how he was above-average. But I waited in vain for the good news. In school, and in Sunday school, Charley was utterly, completely average.

Sunday school. It was Charley who went there first, and I can never think of it without a tightening of my throat in gratitude all over again.

Charley came home from Sunday school with a little wordless book. "Now. It's a story without words, see," he told me.

"Uh huh."

"So, um, here's first—the golden page. Do you know what that stands for? That's heaven. 'In my Father's house are many mansions. If it were not so I would have told you. I go to prepare a place for you . . .'"

"Where'd you learn that?"

"That's in the Bible."

"Hmmm. Well, go on."

"That—that's heaven. Would you like to go there when you die?"

"Well, I expect I will."

"No, Mother. That's just it. You won't."

"Why?" I was half-amused, half-taken aback.

"Now that's just what I wanted you to ask, on account of here—there, that's the next page, all black."

"So it is."

"That's you."

"Hey now, wait a darn minute . . ." This was getting a bit thick.

"I'm not telling you that you're dirty," Charley said, wide-eyed. "God tells you you are. You're not going to argue with Him, are you?"

"No—I guess not." I settled back, wary now.

"'For all have sinned and fallen short of the glory of God.' Now it says that—right in the Bible. For all have sinned and come short of what God asks. That means you too, Mom."

"That means me too. Go on."

"Now there's a red page. The blood of Jesus Christ, His Son, cleanses us from all sin."

"Jesus Christ, God's Son?" I was listening now, in spite of myself.

"And here's a white page. 'Wash me and I shall be whiter than snow.' That's the only way, Mom, you can get to heaven. D'you see?"

Yes. Wonderfully, miraculously, I had seen. It always amazes me that I'd seen. I had found this Jesus, and had claimed His righteousness for my salvation. In the simplest possible way I had walked into God's arms like a child. I'd gone to church first. Then to Sunday school. It was a new chapter. No, it was a new life.

And then big Charley had seen it. We'd had two terrific years.

But I lost big Charley.

That was when Aunt Agatha moved in, came to tide me over for a month and just stayed. Now I pressed against her gratefully in church as I thought of it. Agatha had stayed and little Charley had been leading us on a merry chase ever since.

"But, Charley, you stood up there on the platform and didn't open your mouth. What was the matter?"

"I don't know."

"Your whole class recited the Scripture. You know that Scripture."

"Sure. 'Put on the whole armor of God, that you may be able to stand against the wiles of the devil. For we struggle . . .'"

"Why didn't you say it?"

"Hmmm?"

"Why didn't you say it—when you were up there with the class?"

"I dunno."

"And you knew the song?"

"Sure." He began to sing it, all stops pulled out. "A call for loyal soldiers comes to one and all, soldiers for the conflict, soldiers for the—"

"Why didn't you sing it when the rest of them did?"

"I dunno."

"Oh brother."

Of course with Charley, it could never be said that two and two actually equaled four. But then it could never be said that there were many dull moments.

"Don't know why I have to practice this dumb thing. Guys don't play pianos. Guys don't—"

"Charley—"

"Guys just don't. The name of the dumb thing is 'A Happy Farmer Coming Home from Work.'"

"Charley—"

"So if the farmer doesn't have to take piano lessons he oughta be happy."

"Dear, stop muttering."

"Hmmm?"

"You have that wrong, darling."

"I can't hear you. I'm practicing."

"You sound as if you're playing with your elbows . . . in the cracks. With all those keys on the board, why do you have to play in the cracks?"

"I don't see why I have to practice this thing—"

"You're going to sit there and practice until you get that straight."

"Mom, the phone's ringing."

"I hear it. Keep on practicing. I'll be back."

"Hap-py Far-mer . . ."

"Charley, will you stop that for a minute so I can hear?"

"Oooh-Kaaay. First I have to practice this nice piece and now I have to stop this stupid thing. Is it a nice piece or . . . ?"

"Charley, it wasn't the telephone. It was the doorbell."

"My piano teacher?"

"No, it's the new pastor. Will you please run upstairs and wash your face?"

"I already washed it on the side my teacher sees. She sits . . ."

"You-get-up-the-stairs-and-wash-it-on-both-sides. And your hands too—and your hands have BACKS!"

"OK, OK."

Smile now. Let pastor in. Keep smiling. Kids will be kids, and Charley is the only one you have.

"Well, Dr. Bailey! Of all people! How good of you to call. Come in."

"Hello, Mrs. Martin. Just thought I'd drop by and—oooooof!"

"Oh no!"

Must keep head. Don't blow top. Send Charley upstairs with firm and objective dignity. Help Dr. Bailey up. There, that's it. You're doing fine. That's it, hold your temper until he leaves. Will he ever—no, please God, let him stay. If he leaves now, I will kill Charley. Let him stay till I cool off. I must not even think of murdering Charley. If I stop thinking of the whole business, maybe it will go away. Must keep head. Must—oh, pastor's going. At long last, he's gone. Now.

"Charley? He's gone. Come downstairs now." Ah. You are deadly calm. He stayed long enough.

"Mom, I'm really sorry."

"Why did you have to slide down the bannister?"

"I guess you didn't hear me coming."

"Why did you have to slide down that bannister?"

"You always tell me I make too much noise when I walk down. I thought I'd come down quietly."

"But why did you have to—"

"How'd I know he was standing right there at the foot of the stairs? I thought you'd invite him into the living room!"

For the most part, the rest of Charley's boyhood was one big blur to me. But bits and fragments come back, plucked from nowhere:

"How do I look, Mom?"

"Mmm. Wonderful."

"Pretty cool, huh?"

"Mmm. Pretty cool."

"D'you think she'll like me?"

"I'm sure she will. Do you have your money?"

"Uh huh."

"Corsage?"

"Yup."

"And don't forget—hey, wait a minute. Your neck is dirty. . . ."

Some memories seemed of no significance . . .

"So, Mom, there it is."

"Charley! I never thought I'd live to see this day."

115

"Yeah, I'm pretty smart after all."

"Oh I never doubted that for a moment. But an A in English! Were there many others who got A's?"

"Yup. Teacher was a pushover. Almost everybody got an A."

"Oh good grief."

Then again some of the memories were milestones.

"I learned some stuff in manual training today. I'm going to be real helpful around the house, Mom. I learned how to change a—fix a—put on a new, um . . . oh yeah, a washer. Fits the water tap."

"Hmmm? Well."

"Well, I'm going to fix these—we've got two drips in the house."

"Three. Aunt Agatha's with us."

"No, you know what I mean. I mean faucets. I've learned to fix 'em. And that's just what I'm going to do."

"Uh-oh."

"What?"

"Nothing darling. I think that's wonderful. Where're you going?"

"Down the cellar. I have to turn off the main water."

"You do?" Keep calm. Display confidence.

"Sure, you have to do that. Gimme a light, will you?"

"Please may I have a light?"

"That's what I said. Gimme a light."

Don't follow him down there. Turn on the light and leave him alone. That's the only way he'll learn.

"Do you know how to do it, Charley?"

"Sure, I know how to do it. I know where the valve is. I'll just have it off for a few minutes. I've got this down pat. I know how."

He knows how to do it. Leave him alone. That's the only way he'll . . .

"You just twist this . . . uh . . . kinda rusty. Just . . . uh, Mom—I busted something! There's water . . ."

"Oh no!"

"Flood! Oh boy. Can't stop it. Mom, call a plumber, quick."

Quick. Call a plumber. Easy now. Yellow Pages. Can't Charley do anything right? Plumber, plumber, plumber. Oh brother. Don't get angry. You can't think when you're angry. Plumber, plumber. Send Charley off to camp or away to school. Plumber. Here we are. No, leave Charley home and I'll go off somewhere. Anywhere. Why doesn't the plumber answer? That cellar will be half full before . . .

"Yes? Plumber?"

After the leak was fixed and cellar bailed out I came to a conclusion that I told my aunt: "That settles it, Agatha. He isn't my child. He can't be. They switched babies on me in the nursery, that's what they did."

"Well, don't act as if the world has come to an end, Jane."

"But Agatha, he turned something and broke something down in the cellar. The water had to be turned off for the whole street."

"Well, what of it? It isn't a matter of life or death."

"Matter of life or death? It practically is. It's Monday morning. Everybody's washing. I'll—I'll have to go down the street with a bag over my head for a month. I won't be able to face anybody. And all because he wanted to change a—fix a—put on a washer. What is the matter with that boy? Agatha, where have I failed? What can I do with him?"

"If you'd just talk to him more—try to reach his mind."

"He doesn't have a mind!"

"Oh, Jane!"

"He doesn't have a mind, Agatha. If I could look inside his head, it would be filled with little pebbles. I know it would."

"Jane, calm yourself!"

"Calm myself! Agatha, other people's children don't act like that. They grow up normally. They go through Sunday to Monday, normally. He starts the week on Wednesday and lives it toward both ends. There simply never was another boy as crazy as he is."

"Nonsense. There are at least ten million mothers in this country alone who would throw up their hands in protest if they could hear you say that."

"Well, I'll bet you one thing. I'll bet—Oh, hello Charley. I didn't hear you come in."

"I'm really sorry, Mom. They'll have this fixed in a little while. The faucet for turning off the water was old, rusty. It just snapped. I'm sorry. You know I'm sorry, Aunt Agatha."

"Of course you are. You certainly didn't do it on purpose. It isn't anything that can't be fixed anyhow. No great harm done . . ."

Aunt Agatha interjected, "The mail is here, Charles. You've got some pamphlets from some colleges. Christian colleges."

"Yeah, I gotta start thinking about the rest of my education. What's the matter, Mom?"

"You mean you've been thinking?"

"Sure. Thinking about what I want to be . . . What's the matter?"

"Oh nothing. It just never occurred to me that you—that you wanted to be anything."

"Aw, sure, I-I want to be a minister."

I saw him then, suddenly, at just that moment. Charley—Charley the person. He was looking at me, his eyes vulnerable, pleading for recognition. I stood in the doorway and stared when a revelation came—sharp, sudden, stinging my eyes. In that moment I lost my child. This Charley was a stranger. But ineffably dear. I longed to know him. I would know him. He was so worth knowing.

"Aw, Mom, you're crying. Mom, don't cry. Where're you going?"

I stanched my tears and laughed sheepishly instead. It was better. "I'm going to burn up and throw out a collection of old books I've had hanging around. Psychology books. Stop laughing. Both of you!"

I chuckle again, sitting here in church, thinking of it. Agatha's whisper brings me back with a jolt.

"Jane, Jane."

"Hmmm?"

"Isn't that Dr. Thornton over there? He's nodding to you, dear."

"Where? I can't see him without my glasses."

"Well nod anyway. Over there."

"How do you do, Dr. Thornton?" I mouth it and nod.

"They're about to begin, dear." Agatha settles back and draws a big breath and it comes out trembling. "This is going to be a big evening for all of us. Charley's ordination at last!"

An impressive-looking procession files out on the platform and there—there is Charley. I catch my breath. Charley—tall, incredibly impressive, and his neck is clean.

"Nod back to him," Agatha says. "He's smiling at you."

My throat is getting alarmingly tight.

"Is he?" This will never do.

"Yes. Nod."

"I can't—see him."

My eyes are blurred. He was my little boy, and now this! I didn't pray enough, I didn't understand enough, and, most of all, I didn't laugh enough. Yet God was faithful. Oh, God has been so good. I reach over and squeeze Agatha's hand. Yes, all in all, I got far better than I deserved.

TRAGIC SON,
TRAGIC FATHER

J. Ellsworth Kalas

J. Ellsworth Kalas is pastor in residence at Asbury Theological
Seminary and is the author of several books. He enjoys retelling
biblical stories through a unique starting point, often creatively
through the lens of a minor or unsympathetic character.

In this selection, Kalas presents Jephthah, a judge in Israel, in
the light of his tragic upbringing. He demonstrates how Jephthah's
past was allowed to taint his future. However, he also explains how
a painful past does not need to be duplicated. We are not doomed
to repeat family dysfunctions; we can break the sin cycle.

Some of the most fascinating and instructive persons in the Bible are hidden away in places where we might easily miss them. Give that person a
name virtually unknown in our time, and he or she still is more likely to
be missed. Then let that person's story be of a kind far removed from our
time and culture, and we'll almost surely miss the acquaintance.

I don't want that to happen to Jephthah. For more than thirty years he has been one of my favorite biblical characters. If you know his story, you may think it perverse of me to be drawn to such a person. You may even do some amateur psychologizing to see if you can understand why I feel as I do.

His story seems to be classic tragedy. He began life as a tragic son and ended it as a tragic father. For me, he symbolizes one of those persons whose life seems stalked by tragedy, as if a chosen victim. From birth to adult life and finally to death, the victim's path is a series of confusions and pains. Perhaps that isn't too surprising because in the reproductive strategy of our world like begets like; why shouldn't tragedy produce more tragedy, until the victim concludes that life is just one pain after another?

See how the writer of Judges introduces Jephthah to us: "Jephthah the Gileadite was a mighty warrior. His father was Gilead; his mother was a prostitute." The biblical writers rarely waste words. They give us the data in quite stark terms and leave it to us to interpret the implications.

But the next six words give our imagination room to work: "Gilead's wife also bore him sons." Gilead was apparently a person of some economic substance, so he took the baby Jephthah into his home. Give him credit for that. And give credit, too, to his wife, that she accepted responsibility because it surely must have been an unwelcome one. How could she help resenting the boy? After all, he was a daily reminder of her husband's infidelity. Now she was left to bear much of the brunt of it.

We don't know Gilead's feelings, and he may well have adored the boy. Still, Jephthah was a living embodiment of Gilead's transgressions, and while a conscience is exceedingly valuable, you may hate to see it put its feet under your table three times a day.

As for the half-brothers, I think they must have sensed the strangeness in Jephthah long before they knew the story behind his birth. Our human instincts are peculiar in such regards. We so often intuit what no one has verbalized. I think therefore the brothers must have formed a childhood league against the one who was different, and of course that increased Jephthah's differentness. When people treat you as if you are odd, after all, it's difficult not to fulfill their opinion.

So what went through Jephthah's mind in those growing-up years? Once he knew his heritage, did he curse his mother's profession and his father's passion? Did he compensate by proving in boyish ways that he was stronger, more careless of danger than his half-brothers? Did

121

he sometimes tell them that he would someday outshine them all? But then, in the darkness of falling asleep, did he lose heart and curse the God who permitted his conception?

Inevitably the day came when Jephthah's brothers drove him from the house. You knew they would. "You shall not inherit anything in our father's house," they said, "for you are the son of another woman." It's sad, isn't it, how humans can be so unkind in rejecting certain people for matters not of their doing.

So Jephthah fled, probably rejoicing that he was getting free of this hostile atmosphere, and he settled in the land of Tob.

There he became a leader. It may have been in his blood or it may have been the drive that sometimes inhabits an immigrant or a slum-dweller, but he quickly gathered a group of men around him—one translation calls them "outlaws," and another "worthless fellows." It was the kind of crowd only a powerful, instinctive leader could have melded into a unity, and Jephthah did it. They became raiders, fearsome soldiers of fortune.

In time the Israelites faced war with a neighboring nation, but lacked the kind of military leader who could give them a shot at victory. So they sent a delegation to Jephthah, pleading with him to lead their forces. Jephthah was quick to remind them that they had once cast him out. Can you blame him? If he were to return, he'd said, and was successful in battle, they must make him head over the people. The delegation was desperate enough to accept his conditions. After all, the alternative was subjection to the despised Ammonites, so Jephthah didn't look so bad.

He must have been a brilliantly able man. Perhaps the mottled circumstances of his life had built strengths others might not easily have cultivated. With remarkable statesmanship, he tried first to avoid war by a series of conferences with the Ammonites.

Eventually, however, it was clear that no reconciliation could be had. As his people organized for battle, Jephthah made a vow to God: "If you will give the Ammonites into my hand," he pledged, "then whoever comes out of the doors of my house to meet me when I return victorious from the Ammonites shall be the Lord's to be offered up by me as a burnt offering."

It was a strange, violent contract. Some theologians feel that Jephthah thought the first thing to come from his house would be an animal, but the language of the vow seems to indicate he expected to sacrifice a fellow human being. Probably he thought the person coming first would be one of his servants or some other associate, which meant he was prepared to take the life of some person whose devotion to him was so great that he or she would lead the way in loving celebration.

However one views it, the vow is incomprehensible in our day and culture. Many people still bargain with God, promising that they will go to church faithfully if they recover from surgery, or that they will give a certain sum to the church if they succeed in a business deal. But even those who engage in such divine speculation couldn't imagine vowing a human sacrifice.

Let me make clear that the Hebrew Scriptures never approved of human sacrifices. Such procedures were fairly common among some of Israel's neighbors, but they were strictly forbidden to the Jews. However it isn't unusual for people to pick up the sins of their neighbors. As a matter of fact, it's astonishing to see how quickly reprehensible conduct observed can become conduct copied. Jephthah was a rugged man. He had struggled for every success he achieved. He believed in winning so much that he might well have said that "winning is the only thing." A person with such a passion for winning often feels the price is almost incidental—and that is as true in politics, sports, and business as it is in the world of the military.

Well, Jephthah won. He gained a magnificent victory and returned home exultant. But as he approached his home, the first to come out of his house to meet him was his daughter. The sacred writer makes a point in stark pathos: "She was his only child; he had no son or daughter except her." She came playing the timbrels and dancing, rejoicing in her father's victory, proud of his achievement. She was all of his life, just on the edge of womanhood, a beautiful thing. And she adored her father, so that his victory was now her greatest pride.

As the girl ran to Jephthah, it was as if the heavens fell. The warrior tore off his clothes and wept. "Alas, my daughter!" he cried. "You have brought me very low; you have become the cause of great trouble to me. For I have opened my mouth to the Lord, and I cannot take back my vow."

You and I can have several reactions to his statement. We want to tell him that it is not his daughter who has brought him low, but his own foolish vow. We want to grasp him by his armor and tell him that God would honor him more in the breaking of the vow than in his keeping it. But Jephthah is a man of severe commitments. Life has been to him a pattern of high stakes, and now it's simply risen to the ultimate measure.

This is a strange story, but perhaps its strangest aspect is its commonness. We know this story well, you and I, for we have seen it played out any number of times. We know Jephthah—not in his warrior garb, but in a Brooks Brothers suit. He may belong to your neighborhood bridge group. Perhaps you've lent him your power mower. I'm not speaking, of course, of Jephthah the son of a harlot, but of Jephthah who sacrifices his daughter in winning a battle.

Tragic man, he sacrificed what was dearest to him in order to win something that had little meaning without that dearest thing. You know him well.

Let me dare to spell it out. Sometimes it's the businessman whose life is a continual flurry of activity: meetings, plane trips, conferences, executive meetings. "You have to make it while you can," he explains. "I have three kids to get through college. I want them to have the advantages I never got." But when Jephthah brings home his greatest triumph, he sometimes discovers that he has sacrificed his son or his daughter to get it.

This kind of sacrifice is not limited to fathers. I remember a young woman whose life was already severely complicated by bad choices. When I asked her to trace her troubles back to some starting point, she spoke sadly—but with no real malice—of a mother never around, especially in this daughter's teen years. "I wanted so much to talk, just talk," the girl said. But the mother was busy about good things, perhaps winning battles for other people or for good causes.

A familiar story, isn't it? So why are we so shocked when we read it in Scripture? True, Jephthah is more primitive, but he's no more at fault than a million modern parents. Jephthah didn't know when he left for battle that with that vow he would lose his daughter, the only thing that really mattered to him.

Jephthah was the leader of Israel for six years after that. He won other triumphs, but the thing he loved most was gone.

Men and women cheered, of course, when Jephthah passed by in parade, and common folks envied him. "He's a big man," they told their children. "Probably the greatest general since Joshua." And people who knew him only from a distance said, "He's got it made. Lucky fellow."

But Jephthah himself, on quiet nights when there was no state activity, would watch while embers slowly died in a fire and ask the meaning of it all. Why had he been born in such tragedy, son of a prostitute? Why had he lost his daughter in still more tragedy? Tragic son, tragic father! Why had tragedy dogged his private life, even while he won success in his public life?

We shouldn't really be surprised that tragedy begets tragedy. That's the law of genetics, is it not, that like begets like? Not only do dogs beget dogs, and people beget people; poverty begets poverty, and wealth—wealth. Of course, we often experience the reproduction of tragedy on a smaller scale: When we suffer some indignity or reversal, we're thrown off balance, and when the next issue comes along we become still more susceptible to defeat. When a person's life begins in tragedy, then, it isn't surprising that worse tragedy follows.

Except for grace.

I wish I could have told Jephthah about grace. I wish, especially, I could have intercepted him in the days before his daughter's death, to say that a tragic son can become a blessed father.

I wish I could have told him of a friend of mine—a minister, who not long before his retirement, dared to tell his congregation in a Father's Day sermon of the grace of God in his life. He recalled that his own father had been consumed by addiction. So his father never gave him a hug, a kiss, or even a word of affirmation. His father never participated in any important event of his life or offered one gift in all of his childhood and adolescence. When his father died, my friend officiated at his funeral; only one person was there besides the six children.

With such a tragic, paternally loveless upbringing, my friend was set up to repeat the process. Instead, however, he and his wife have brought up a beautiful family of strong, loving adults. The two sons are even ministers. By the grace of God, the genetic process of tragedy begetting tragedy was broken.

I pondered it again not long ago as I officiated at a baptism. I have seen hundreds of proud and dedicated parents through the years, but—perhaps because I knew their story—these parents stood out.

As an infant, this father had been left by his own father, who then saw his son only once—in his teens. But the grace of God, communicated through his mother, some friends, and church, made all the difference. The cycle of tragedy was being broken.

That's partly why I'm so fascinated by the Jephthah story: I believe tragedy is avoidable. It doesn't have to repeat itself because God has a lively commitment to our human struggle. Graciously, He brings new factors into the chemistry of our lives which can make the bitter waters sweet, cause the distresses and reversals of life to become productive, build where life is a shambles, and redeem when all seems lost. God, who is gracious and omnipotent, can bring good from the womb of sorrow—that is, if we will work with Him toward that end.

And so it shall be that the Jephthahs who are born in tragedy shall come to live in peace, and die in the love of God. That, in some small but crucial and intimate measure, is what we mean by His grace. That's how, at last, the son of tragedy can become the father of blessing.

Concerning Lemons

William Barton

A third tale by William Barton in this collection again is crafted in the style of an ancient philosopher experiencing life in the twentieth century. Here, the philosopher learns that the Good News that is good to give away is also good to enjoy at home.

Now it came to pass that I journeyed to a far country called California and found a friend, a citizen of that country, who had an automobile. He took me on swift journeys to show me orange groves and grapefruit orchards and vineyards, and many trees that grew prunes.

Often I heard of a town called Corona, and always this was said of it: Corona, Home of the Lemon.

Now on a day we passed through Corona, and the day was warm and dusty and I spake to my friends: Behold, this is Corona, Home of the Lemon. Let us tarry, I pray thee, for of lemons is concocted a cunning drink that maketh glad the heart and doth not intoxicate.

So we rode through the street, and we came to a place where it was written: "Ice cream, soda water, sundaes, and all kinds of soft drinks."

We alighted from the chariot and went in, where, behold, was a man in a white apron. And I was about to speak to him, but my friend spake: "Be thou silent and keep thy money in thine own pocket; I am paying for this."

And I kept silent willingly, for those are pleasant words to hear.

Then spake my friend to the man in the white apron. "Hasten thee, lad, and prepare for us four good, ice-cold lemonades, and make them good and make them speedily."

And the man in the white apron heard him as one who understood not what he said.

Then spake my friend again, "This friend of mine is from Chicago, and these other friends are from Boston and they think they know what good lemonade is, but I want them to have a drink of lemonade that is real lemonade. Hasten thee and prepare it for them."

Then spake the man in the white apron, "We have no lemonade."

And the man of California grew red in the face and he said, "What? No lemonade in Corona, Home of the Lemon?"

And the man in the white apron answered, "We have soda water, root beer, ginger ale, ice cream, but no lemonade."

Then spake my friend, "Hasten now to the grocery store and buy a half-dozen good lemons and quickly make us lemonade."

And the man in the white apron hastened, then returned and said, "There isn't a lemon in town. They ship them all to Chicago and Boston."

When I heard this, I meditated and I said, "I have suffered for lack of good fish at the seashore, and fresh eggs in the country, when both were abundant in town, and now I behold that the place to buy good lemonade is where they do not raise lemons."

As I meditated, I remembered that in many other things "the shoe-maker's family goeth unshod." Yea, this shall be to me as a parable, lest having preached to others I should be a castaway. So I resolved that with all my exportation of the Gospel, I would keep some for home consumption.

THE MILLIONAIRE AND THE SCRUB LADY

William Barton

It is notoriously easy for us as humans to get carried away with our own perceived respectability and importance, William Barton shows us. Consider the millionaire who, in one fatal instant, was put in his place and had to abandon his arrogance at the bottom of a very long staircase.

There is a certain millionaire who hath offices on the second floor of the First National Bank building. And when he goeth up to his offices he rideth in the elevator. But when he goeth down, then he walketh.

He is a haughty man, who once was poor, and hath risen in the world. He is a self-made man who worshipeth his maker.

He payeth his rent regularly on the first day of the month, and he considereth not that there are human beings who run the elevators, and who clean the windows, hanging at a great height above the sidewalk, and who shovel coal into the furnaces under the boilers. Neither doth he at Christmas remember any of them with a tip or a turkey.

There is in this building a poor woman who scrubbeth the stairs and the halls, and he hath walked past her often but never seen her until recently. For his head was high in the air, and he was thinking of more millions.

Now it came to pass on a day that he left his office and started to walk down the stairs, that the scrub lady was halfway down; for she had begun at the top and was giving the stairs their first onceover. Upon the topmost stair, in a wet and soapy spot, there was a large cake of yellow soap, and the millionaire stepped on it.

Now the foot which he set upon the soap flew eastward toward the sunrise, and the other foot started on an expedition of its own toward the going down of the sun. And the millionaire sat down upon the topmost step, but he did not remain there. As it had been his intention to descend, so he descended, but not in the manner of his original design. As he descended, he struck each step with a sound as if it had been a drum.

And the scrub lady stood aside courteously, and let him go. At the bottom he arose and considered whether he should rush into the office of the building and demand that the scrub lady be fired. But he considered that if he should tell the reason there would be great mirth among the occupants of the building, so he held his peace.

But since that day he taketh notice of the scrub lady and passeth her with circumspection. For there is no one so high and mighty that he can afford to ignore any of his fellow human beings. For a very humble scrub lady and a very common bar of yellow soap can take the mind of a great man off his business troubles with surprising rapidity.

Wherefore, consider these things, and count not thyself too high above even the humblest of the children of God. Lest happily thou come down from thy place of pride and walk off with thy bruises aching a little more by reason of the fun thou hast afforded her.

For these are solemn days, and he that bringeth a smile to the face of a scrub lady hath not lived in vain.

LIFELONG
LESSONS

Love in a New York Apartment Building

Joseph Bayly

We hear much today about the importance of random acts of kindness. In this story by Joseph Bayly, meet one source of such acts—a woman whose very lifestyle consisted of kindness, and who left behind a legacy as great as any evangelist or missionary.

Mrs. Mary Conover is a tenant, together with 150 other people, in a New York City apartment building. A widow of five years, she lives with her employed daughter.

New York apartment houses aren't especially friendly places. People have been known to die in them and not be discovered for days. In this particular building, the entrance doors have little mirrored peepholes. You can look out of them into the hall without being observed, and if you don't want to talk to whoever has rung the bell, you just don't open the door.

But when Mrs. Conover rings the bell, doors open promptly for she may be bringing a freshly baked apple pie or homemade laundry soap.

Or she may be returning Mr. Coletti's shirt, which the retired barber asked her to turn the collar on because his wife doesn't sew.

Pie-baking, soap-making, and sewing are carryovers from Mrs. Conover's growing-up days in a small town. But that background doesn't explain her kindness to other people. A lot of New Yorkers come from small towns, but one or two years in the big city is long enough to dry up any milk of human kindness. (Mrs. Conover has lived in New York for close to thirty years.)

In addition to her small-town background, Mrs. Conover is a Christian, and this is known by many people in the apartment building. So they've come to accept small kindnesses, and even call on her in times of crisis. For instance when Mr. Kraemer had his heart attack, which turned out to be fatal, they asked Mrs. Conover to come down and stay with Mrs. Kraemer until the doctor came, and help make the funeral arrangements.

During the long months when elderly Mrs. Scott was so sick, she gratefully accepted Mrs. Conover's help, even though it was constantly accompanied by a simple Christian witness. Mrs. Scott, you see, believed in Christian Science.

If you asked a number of people in that apartment house what a Christian is like, they'd probably reply, "Mrs. Conover. She's been a Christian friend to me."

Not that she's always on the giving end. Last Mother's Day, for instance, Mrs. Conover was swamped with cards and gifts from people in the house: Barricini chocolates, stockings, hard candy from Italy, cosmetics.

There's a little Jewish lady—eighty-seven years old—from another house, about a block away, who stops at Mrs. Conover's door almost every Saturday night with a bag of baked goods. Pastry, rye bread, bagels: the contents of the bag change from week to week. Mrs. Conover has difficulty understanding the old lady's German-accented speech. But she knows that her son-in-law has a bakery, and these baked goods come from there.

A few months ago the little Jewish lady came to her door with a box.

"This is my birthday," she explained, opening the box to show Mrs. Conover a beautiful cake. "My son-in-law made this for me. But I don't eat cake any longer. My cake is for you."

After she left (her visits are always brief), Mrs. Conover decided to take a piece out of the cake, and to give most of it to two small boys in another apartment. Their father had just undergone surgery for a malignancy, and their mother was away from home in another hospital having a baby.

Taking the cake, she went up to the apartment, where a young black girl was staying with the children.

"How wonderful," the girl exclaimed, when she opened the door and saw the cake. "I felt so bad that I didn't have time all day today to make a cake for Bobby's birthday. It was so nice of you to remember . . ."

Mrs. Conover said she hadn't remembered. She hadn't known. But she wanted Bobby and his brother to have part of this cake that had been given to her. She was so glad it was Bobby's birthday.

Christian love is possible, even in a New York apartment house, and love begets love . . . and hope . . . and sometimes faith.

(Since this was first published, Mrs. Conover has died. So now I can tell you her real name: Mrs. Mary Bayly, my mother.)

THE SKYLARK'S BARGAIN

G. H. Charnley

What would you trade to get what you want? Would you trade time, a possession, a relationship, your moral standards—or maybe even your life? This allegory by G. H. Charnley begs the question through a bird who didn't realize he'd traded in his soul until it was too late.

What is a man profited if he gains the whole world, and loses his own soul? Or what will a man give in exchange for his soul?

Matthew 16:26 (NKJV)

There was once a young skylark who was very fond of worms. He used to say that he would give anything if he could make sure of getting all the worms he could eat.

One day, as he was flying up into the sky, he looked down and saw something rather unusual traveling along the cart track which ran through the forest. Feeling curious the young skylark dropped lower and lower until at last he could see. It was a queer sight indeed. He saw a tiny coach, painted black with red blinds and yellow wheels, drawn by two magpies. Walking in front of the coach was an old man, very little and ugly, wearing a black coat with red trousers and yellow stockings. He carried a bell, and as he walked he kept swinging the bell and shouting:

> Who will buy? Who will buy?
> I am selling in all weathers,
> Fine and fat and juicy worms,
> In exchange for skylark's feathers.

The skylark was attracted and flew down. "Good morning, my young friend," said the old man. "What can I do for you?"

"How much are they?" asked the skylark.

"Two for a feather, my friend, and the coach is full of them."

"Are they fresh?"

"Yes, indeed, all gathered fresh this morning, my pretty bird."

The skylark gave a painful little tug at his wing, and, dropping the feather into the old man's hand, said, "Two, please."

As the coach passed on, the skylark felt a little guilty, but he enjoyed the feast and was pleased to find afterwards that no one noticed the missing feather.

The next day he flew with his father. "My son," said the old skylark, as they rose higher and higher, far above the tops of the tallest trees, "I think we skylarks should be the most content of birds. We have such brave wings. See how they lift us up into the sky, nearer and nearer to God."

"Yes," said the young bird, "ye—es . . ." But all the time he was watching a tiny speck, which crept like a black beetle far below on the forest track, thinking: *There, I've missed the coach.*

The following day he waited close to the cart-worn track. When he heard the bell ringing, he plucked another feather. It came out so easily, he pulled two more after it. Then he heard the hoarse voice shouting:

> Who will buy? Who will buy?
> Surely we can come to terms,
> In exchange for skylark's feathers
> I am selling luscious worms.

"Three here," said the skylark.

"Very good, very good indeed. That will be six worms, and here's an extra one for luck," added the old man with a chuckle.

My word, thought the young skylark, *that's a bargain.* So the skylark became a regular customer.

He found after a bit that he could not fly so high, but he did not mind greatly. There was less fear of the coach passing without being seen. Then one day, when his wings seemed thin, worn, and ragged, he suddenly felt that he'd been making a terrible mistake. He tried to fly up into the warm sunshine but fell back to the earth like a stone.

Dear me, of course! he thought. *Why didn't I think of this before! I know what I'll do. I will dig worms and trade for feathers.* Day and night he diligently searched and gathered and stored. Then he hid himself in the tall grass, waiting for the coach to pass without being seen. Soon he heard it, and he stepped boldly in front of the coach, saying, "Please, sir, I want to know how many feathers you will trade me for all of these worms?"

The ugly coachman laughed and set off at once, saying over his shoulder, "Worms for feathers is my business, not feathers for worms."

So the young skylark died and was buried under the green grass. Now they say that every summer the older birds take the young birds and fly mournfully about the grave, calling one to another as they fly:

> Here lies a foolish skylark,
> Hush your note each bird that sings,
> Here lies a poor lost skylark
> Who for earthworms sold his wings.

THE KING
FROM THE TOWER

Peter Leithart

Peter Leithart, a Presbyterian minister, became frustrated about the shortage of quality, biblically based bedtime stories for his children. So he decided to write his own, and out of this dream came his book Wise Words, *which illustrates biblical proverbs.*

The following tale from that collection tells of a proud king stuck in his ivory tower who decides to meet his subjects. To his great displeasure, he finds that no one recognizes him—that is, until he does a feat worthy of a king.

A man's pride will bring him low, but the humble in spirit will retain honor.

Proverbs 29:23 (NKJV)

There was once a king who lived in a tall tower in the midst of a city. The top of the tower poked through the clouds, so that from his porch, the king could nearly touch the sun, and, though he had never tried it, he was sure that with a little effort he could step onto the moon. He knew he was the highest king in the world.

This king spent his days strolling around the porch of his tower, watching the sun rise over the clouds and looking at the curious tiny specks that swarmed through the streets of the city below. Though he was king, he had never visited the city. From what he could see, the only people who lived there were small as ants.

One morning, as he was watching the sunrise, the king decided to visit his subjects. He carefully dressed himself in his most impressive purple robe, buckled the clasp of his golden belt, and put on his shiniest black shoes. He looked at himself in the mirror to make sure he looked like a king. He looked and looked for quite some time. When he was satisfied, he descended the long staircase that led from the tower to the city.

When he reached the bottom, he took a deep breath. The tiny people of the city, he thought, would be awestruck at so gigantic a king. Everyone would bow to the ground before him, kiss his feet, and fight for a chance to touch the hem of his robe. He must make every effort to put them at ease. Spreading his hands in a sign of blessing, he stepped out onto the walkway beside the street.

The king noticed immediately that the tiny people of the city were not so tiny as he had thought. Most of them, in fact, were quite a bit larger than the king himself.

He also noticed that no one bowed to him or kissed his feet. Instead, everyone ignored him. The men and women on the walkway hurried past without even looking. One man, reading a book as he walked, slammed into the king, nearly knocking him to the ground, then walked off without so much as an "excuse me." Just when the king had regained his balance, a cart rolled by and scattered dust onto his gorgeous purple robe.

It was then that the king noticed everything in the city looked dry as a desert. There were no fountains in the town square, no puddles on the street, and everyone seemed hot and thirsty.

"I say," he said to the next man who passed by, "I am the king from the high tower. Shouldn't you be bowing or something? Do you want to touch my beautiful purple robe or kiss my shiny black shoes?" But the man only looked suspiciously at the dusty king and crossed to the other side of the street.

For a moment, the king thought he would return to his tower and never come back. It was already clear that no one in the city appreciated or honored him as he deserved. Just then, he spied a wine shop down the street. Being thirsty from his long walk down the staircase, he swaggered up the street and into the wine shop.

"I say," the king said, "give me a bottle of your best wine."

The shopkeeper looked at him and began to laugh. "Give you a bottle of my best wine? We do not give anything away in this shop, Buster. Besides, it has been so dry here that water and wine are as valuable as gold."

The king stuck his nose in the air and sniffed. "But I am different," he said in a very kingly voice. "I am not 'Buster.' I am the king!"

"I don't care if you are Julius Caesar," the shopkeeper said. "You do not get free wine. And if you are not going to buy anything, get out." The shopkeeper picked up a barrel and threatened to throw it at the king.

Afraid for his life, the king fled from the wine shop. He presently passed a bakery. In the window was the most beautiful wedding cake he had ever seen, and he realized suddenly how hungry one becomes when threatened with a wine barrel. So he strutted into the bakery and up to the counter.

"I say," he said in a most impressive manner. "I would like that wedding cake in the window."

The baker looked up and wiped his forehead with his hand, leaving a streak of white flour that made him look like a head-hunter from a South Pacific island.

"Give you that cake?" said the baker with a snort. "It is already sold. I can't give it to you, fella. I could make you another just like it, if you pay me."

"I want that cake and no other," said the king. "Perhaps you do not know who I am. I am not 'Fella.' I am the king and I demand that particular cake."

"I don't care if you are Charles the Great," said the baker. "I do not give away cakes. Buy something if you will. Otherwise, get out." He hurled a huge lump of dough that missed the king's head by a hair's breadth. "Get out!"

The king was so angry he wanted to destroy the city and everyone in it. Then he remembered he had no army and would have a hard time getting soldiers so long as no one knew he was king—a thought that filled him with sorrow. *Some king I am*, he thought. *None of my subjects even recognize me, and none obey me.*

He slowed as he turned down another street, and presently he came to a jeweler's shop. In the window was a sparkling golden crown covered with diamonds, rubies, emeralds, and sapphires. It was more beautiful by far than the king's own crown, which the king suddenly remembered he had left at home in his tower. *Perhaps that is why no one recognizes me,* he thought. So he walked into the jeweler's shop and up to the counter.

"I say," he said in a most impressive manner. "I would like to have that crown in the window."

The jeweler looked up from his work and fixed a sharp eye on the king. "Listen, guy. Do you know how much it costs?" he asked.

"No," the king answered with a nervous smile. He still was shaking after the threat at the winery. "But the cost is not important. You see, I am not 'Guy.' I am the king from the tower. That is the most beautiful crown I have ever seen. I need it so everyone will recognize me. I want you to give it to me."

The jeweler looked surprised at first, then his eyes flashed with anger. "Give it to you! I don't care if you are Napoleon Bonaparte, I would not give you that crown. It is worth a fortune. If you are not going to buy something, get out." The jeweler brandished a pair of scissors. "Get out!"

Frightened nearly out of his wits, the king raced out the door and down the walkway. Suddenly the king heard a sound that made him stop dead still. It was very faint at first. As he listened, he realized it was the voice of a child who seemed to be crying for help.

The king looked at the people around him. None of the others seemed to hear the voice. They just kept walking busily up and down the dry street.

"Don't you hear anything?" the king cried out. But the people walked on.

For a moment, the king thought he had imagined the voice. Then it came again. "Help!" This time he was certain he heard it.

The king called again to the hot, red-faced people swirling around him. No one even looked. "Why should I do anything?" he asked himself. "I have more important things to do than to help little children. I am the king, after all."

He started back to his tower. Up in the clouds, he would be at peace. Up in the tower, he would be too high to hear voices crying for help. When he was up there, these nasty, sweaty people would turn back into the tiny ants they were supposed to be. He could hardly wait to get back up to his tower.

As he walked toward the tower, however, the voice seemed to get louder. Every time he turned a corner, the voice seemed closer. Then he heard the voice coming from directly behind a high hedge of thorn bushes.

"There is a child who needs your help!" he called out frantically. "Someone!" But no one came.

There was nothing for the king to do but find out why the child was calling. As he fought through the hedge, thorns pierced him, and he felt trickles of blood roll down his face. Finally he broke through the hedge into a small courtyard. From a well in the center of the yard he heard a child's voice echoing, "Help me!"

The king hurried to the well and peered down. He could see nothing. The king looked for a rope to lower, but there was no rope. The only way to rescue the child was to descend into the pit himself. He knew the danger and hesitated. Then he said, "Don't worry. I am coming."

Climbing over the side of the well and digging his fingers and toes into the cracks in the wall, he groped down into the darkness. As he lowered himself into the well, a sharp edge on the wall sliced his right thumb. His foot slipped and his left shoe went plunging to the bottom. When he tried to find a toehold, his foot slipped again and the big toe on his foot scraped against the rough wall. He could feel the blood soaking his silk stocking.

Still he struggled on, inch by inch, down into the well. It was dark as midnight around him. After what seemed like many hours, his feet finally rested on the dusty floor of the well. A child's arms grasped his leg with such force that he would have fallen if the well had not been so narrow. It was a little boy. The king knelt before the boy and hugged him, while the grateful child wept on his shoulder.

"I was playing on the well," the boy whimpered, "and I slipped and fell."

"It's a true miracle you are not dead," the king said.

"I thought I was," the boy answered, "at first."

The king rested at the bottom of the well. Suddenly the dry floor of the well became damp. Before long, a puddle had formed. A minute later, the water was up to the ankles.

"The well," the king said in amazement. "The water is flowing again. We must get out before we drown."

The boy climbed onto the king's back, and together they began the long ascent from the pit. As the water churned and gurgled under them, the king inched his way up the wall. More than once, the water reached his chest, but each time he found a new toehold and inched higher. After what seemed like forever, the king heaved himself and the boy out of the well. He and the boy fell to the ground, exhausted.

A light, warm rain was falling on the brown grass, pricking their faces. The king finally said, "We must find your home. Let me carry you."

Shielding the boy with what was left of his robe, the king pushed his way back through the thorns to the street. He stood for a moment, his wet and tattered robe flapping in the breeze. In the street, people dashed this way and that, like ants when their anthill has been kicked. Raindrops had gathered into puddles, and children danced and splashed, shrieking with joy. Across the street someone saw the king, cried out, and pointed. A great noisy crowd flooded toward him. Someone shouted, "Look, it is the widow's son. He is alive. The king has saved him."

A woman pushed through the crowd and the boy reached to grasp her neck.

"Mama," he cried, as the weeping woman caught him.

"How can I ever thank you, O king?" cried the widow.

"What did you call me?"

"Are you not the king from the tower?" the widow asked doubtfully.

"Yes, but how did you know?"

"Because you saved my son," she replied. Then, looking at his tattered clothes, bloody face, and body, she added, "and because you look like a king."

Behind him the king heard a shout. He turned and looked through the opening he'd made through the hedge. "The well's filled with water!" a man shouted. "The springs are flowing again."

Dozens of people, cups and buckets in hand, pressed through the hedge for water.

While the king watched, he felt a hand on his shoulder. He turned to see the wine seller balancing a barrel on his neck. The king ducked.

"I'm not going to throw it at you," said the wine seller. "This is yours. Wine fit for a king greater than Caesar." There too was the baker, lugging the wedding cake. "Take it," he said. "I can make another for the wedding. Food fit for a king greater than Charles." Finally came the jeweler, holding the sparkling crown. "I believe this crown fits you, your majesty. A crown for an emperor greater than Napoleon."

The king knelt and accepted the gifts. Then he called out, "This is a great occasion. The widow's son who was thought dead is alive.

The drought is over. Let us celebrate. I will share my food and drink with you."

The people of the city crowded into the town hall, where they ate wedding cake and drank their fill of wine. It was almost morning when the last of the banqueters sloshed happily home.

The next day the king took his crown and returned to the tower that stretched above the clouds. But before he departed, he announced that everyone in the city was welcome to come and go freely to his tower. Anyone who wished an audience with the king needed only to ask. And so the king ascended, content to know that, at least once in his life, he had truly acted like a king.

THE GIFT OF THE MAGI

O. Henry

O. Henry is the pen name of newspaperman William Sidney Porter. Though he was born in North Carolina and also died there, O. Henry's stories of New York City are his most popular.

It was actually while he was in prison for embezzlement that O. Henry began writing in earnest. This marked the beginning of a long career which eventually made him one of America's most widely read story writers.

In "The Gift of the Magi," a young couple learns how to give the wisest sort of gifts because they are from the heart.

One dollar and eighty-seven cents. That was all. And 60 cents of it was in pennies—pennies saved one and two at a time by bulldozing the grocer and the vegetable man and the butcher until one's cheeks burned with the silent imputation of parsimony that such close dealing implied. Three times Della counted it: $1.87. And the next day would be Christmas.

There was clearly nothing to do but flop down on the shabby little couch and howl. So Della did it. Which instigates the moral reflection that life is made up of sobs, sniffles, and smiles, with sniffles predominating.

While the mistress of the home is gradually subsiding from the first stage to the second, take a look at the home. A furnished flat at $8 per week. It did not exactly beg description, but it certainly had that word on the lookout for the mendicancy squad.

In the vestibule below was a letter-box into which no letter would go, and an electric button from which no mortal finger could coax a ring. Also appertaining thereunto was a card bearing the name "Mr. James Dillingham Young."

The "Dillingham" had been flung to the breeze during a former period of prosperity when its possessor was being paid $30 per week. Now, when the income was shrunk to $20, though, they were thinking seriously of contracting to a modest and unassuming D. But whenever Mr. James Dillingham Young came home and reached his flat above he was called "Jim" and greatly hugged by Mrs. James Dillingham Young, already introduced to you as Della. Which is all very good.

Della finished her cry and attended to her cheeks with the powder rag. She stood by the window and looked out dully at a gray cat walking a gray fence in a gray backyard. Tomorrow would be Christmas Day, and she had only $1.87 with which to buy Jim a present. She had been saving every penny she could for months, with this result. Twenty dollars a week doesn't go far. Expenses had been greater than she had calculated. They always are. Only $1.87 to buy a present for Jim. Her Jim. Many a happy hour she had spent planning for something nice for him. Something fine and rare and sterling—something just a little bit near to being worthy of the honor of being owned by Jim.

There was a pier-glass between the windows of the room. Perhaps you have seen a pier-glass in an $8 flat. A very thin and very agile person may, by observing his reflection in a rapid sequence of longitudinal strips, obtain a fairly accurate conception of his looks. Della, being slender, had mastered the art.

Suddenly she whirled from the window and stood before the glass. Her eyes were shining brilliantly, but her face had lost its color within twenty seconds. Rapidly she pulled down her hair and let it fall to its full length.

Now, there were two possessions of the James Dillingham Youngs in which they both took a mighty pride. One was Jim's gold watch that had been his father's and his grandfather's. The other was Della's hair. Had the queen of Sheba lived in the flat across the airshaft, Della would have let her hair hang out the window some day to dry just to depreciate Her Majesty's jewels and gifts. Had King Solomon been the janitor, with all his treasures piled up in the basement, Jim would have pulled out his watch every time he passed, just to see him pluck at his beard from envy. So now Della's beautiful hair fell about her rippling and shining like a cascade of brown waters. It reached below her knee and made itself almost a garment for her, but she did it up again nervously and quickly. Once she faltered for a minute and stood still while a tear or two splashed on the worn red carpet.

On went her old brown jacket; on went her old brown hat, and with a whirl of skirts and with the brilliant sparkle still in her eyes, she fluttered out the door and down the stairs to the street.

Where she stopped the sign read: MLLE. SOFRONIE. HAIR GOODS OF ALL KINDS. One flight up Della ran, and collected herself, panting. Madame, large, too white, chilly, hardly looked the "Sofronie."

"Will you buy my hair?" asked Della.

"I buy hair," said Madame. "Take yer hat off and let's have a sight at the looks of it."

Down rippled the brown cascade.

"Twenty dollars," said Madame, lifting the mass with a practiced hand.

"Give it to me quick," said Della.

Oh, and the next two hours tripped by on rosy wings. Forget the hashed metaphor. She was ransacking the stores for Jim's present.

She found it at last. It surely had been made for Jim and no one else. There was no other like it in any of the stores, and she had turned all of them inside out. It was a platinum fob chain simple and chaste in design, properly proclaiming its value by substance alone and not by meretricious ornamentation—as all good things should do. It was even worthy of The Watch. As soon as she saw it she knew that it must be Jim's. It was like him. Quietness and value—the description applied to both.

Twenty-one dollars they took from her for it, and she hurried home with the 87 cents. With that chain on his watch Jim might be properly anxious about the time in any company. Grand as the watch was, he sometimes looked at it on the sly on account of the old leather strap that he used in place of a chain.

When Della reached home her intoxication gave way a little to prudence and reason. She got out her curling irons and lighted the gas and went to work repairing the ravages made by generosity added to love. Which is always a tremendous task, dear friends—a mammoth task.

In forty minutes her head was covered with tiny, close-lying curls that made her look wonderfully like a truant schoolboy. She looked at her reflection in the mirror long, carefully, and critically.

"If Jim doesn't kill me," she said to herself, "before he takes a second look at me, he'll say I look like a Coney Island chorus girl. But what could I do—Oh! what could I do with a dollar and eighty-seven cents?"

By 7 o'clock the coffee was made and the frying pan was on the back of the stove hot and ready to cook the chops.

Jim was never late. Della doubled the fob chain in her hand and sat on the corner of the table near the door that he always entered. Then she heard his step on the stair away down on the first flight, and she turned white for just a moment. She had a habit for saying little silent prayers about the simplest everyday things, and now she whispered: "Please God, make him think I am still pretty."

The door opened and Jim stepped in and closed it. He looked thin and very serious. Poor fellow, he was only twenty-two—and to be burdened with a family! He needed a new overcoat and he was without gloves.

Jim stopped inside the door, as immovable as a setter at the scent of quail. His eyes were fixed upon Della, and there was an expression in them that she could not read, and it terrified her. It was not anger, nor surprise, nor disapproval, nor horror, nor any of the sentiments that she had been prepared for. He simply stared at her fixedly with that peculiar expression on his face.

Della wriggled off the table and went for him.

"Jim, darling," she cried, "don't look at me that way. I had my hair cut off and sold because I couldn't have lived through Christmas without giving you a present. It'll grow out again—you won't mind, will you? I just had to do it. My hair grows awfully fast. Say 'Merry Christmas!' Jim, and let's be happy. You don't know what a nice—what a beautiful, nice gift I've got for you."

"You've cut off your hair?" asked Jim, laboriously, as if he had not arrived at that patent fact yet even after the hardest mental labor.

"Cut it off and sold it," said Della. "Don't you like me just as well, anyhow? I'm me without my hair, ain't I?"

Jim looked about the room curiously.

"You say your hair is gone?" he said, with an air almost of idiocy.

"You needn't look for it," said Della. "It's sold, I tell you—sold and gone, too. It's Christmas Eve, boy. Be good to me, for it went for you. Maybe the hairs of my head were numbered," she went on with sudden serious sweetness, "but nobody could ever count my love for you. Shall I put on the chops, Jim?"

Out of his trance Jim seemed quickly to wake. He enfolded his Della. For ten seconds let us regard with discreet scrutiny some inconsequential object in the other direction. Eight dollars a week or one million in a year—what is the difference? A mathematician or a wit would give you the wrong answer. The magi brought valuable gifts that first Christmas, but that was not among them.

"Don't make any mistake, Dell," he said, "about me. I don't think there's anything in the way of a haircut or a shave or a shampoo that could make me like my girl any less. But if you'll unwrap that package you may see why you had me going a while at first."

White fingers and nimble tore at the string and paper. And then an ecstatic scream of joy; and then, alas! a quick feminine change to hysterical tears and wails, necessitating the immediate employment of all the comforting powers of the lord of the flat.

For there lay The Combs—the set of combs, side and back, that Della had worshipped long in a Broadway window. Beautiful combs, pure tortoise shell, with jeweled rims—just the shade to wear in the beautiful vanished hair. They were expensive combs, she knew, and her heart had simply craved and yearned over them without the least hope of possession. And now, they were hers, but the tresses that should have adorned the coveted adornments were gone.

But she hugged them to her bosom, and at length she was able to look up with dim eyes and a smile and say: "My hair grows so fast, Jim!"

And then Della leaped up like a little singed cat and cried, "Oh, oh!"

Jim had not yet seen his beautiful present. She held it out to him eagerly upon her open palm. The dull precious metal seemed to flash with a reflection of her bright and ardent spirit.

"Isn't it a dandy, Jim? I hunted all over town to find it. You'll have to look at the time a hundred times a day now. Give me your watch. I want to see how it looks on it."

Instead of obeying, Jim tumbled down on the couch and put his hands under the back of his head and smiled.

"Dell," said he, "let's put our Christmas presents away and keep 'em a while. They're too nice to use just at present. I sold the watch to get the money to buy your combs. And now suppose you put the chops on."

The magi, as you know, were wise men—wonderfully wise men—who brought gifts to the Babe in the manger. They invented the art of giving Christmas presents. Being wise, their gifts were no doubt wise ones, possibly bearing the privilege of exchange in case of duplication. And here I have lamely related to you the uneventful chronicle of two foolish children in a flat who most unwisely sacrificed for each other the greatest treasures of their house. But in a last word to the wise of these days let it be said that of all who give gifts these two were the wisest. O all who give and receive gifts such as they are wisest. Everywhere they are wisest. They are the magi.

CHRIST'S JUGGLER

Anatole France

There is hardly a literary genre that Anatole France did not touch
in a writing career that spanned forty-five years. His real name
was Jacques Anatole Thibault and he was a native of Paris where,
rather appropriately, his father was a book dealer. France became
well known for many writings and won the Nobel prize for
literature in 1921.

   The following story, orginally titled "Our Lady's Juggler," is
retold here as "Christ's Juggler." It's the tale of a humble juggler
named Barnaby who learns that he does not have to be a great
preacher or theologian to glorify Christ.

In the days of King Louis there was a poor juggler in France. His name
was Barnaby and he travelled about from town to town performing
feats of skill and strength.

   On fair days he would unfold an old worn-out carpet in the public
square and, by means of a jovial speech (which he had learned from a
very ancient juggler and which he never varied in the least), he would
draw together the children and loafers. Immediately he assumed
extraordinary moves and balanced a tin plate on the tip of his nose.

At first the crowd would feign indifference. Then Barnaby would stand on his hands with face downward. He would throw into the air six copper balls, all glittery in the sunlight, then catch them with his feet. Sometimes he threw himself backward until his heels met the nape of his neck, and he juggled in this posture with a dozen knives. Murmurs of admiration would swell from the spectators and small pieces of money would rain down upon the carpet.

Still, like the majority of those who live by their wits, Barnaby of Compiegne had a great struggle to make a decent living. Earning his bread by the sweat of his brow, he bore rather more than his share of the penalties falling upon the misdoings of his father Adam.

Also he was unable to work constantly, as he would have been willing to do, because he depended on the light of day and pleasantness of season. The warmth of the sun and the broad daylight were as necessary for him to display his brilliance as to trees expected to bear flowers and fruit. In winter he was nothing more than a tree stripped of its leaves and dormant. The frozen ground was too hard, and he suffered both cold and hunger. But being simple-natured, he bore these ills patiently.

He never meditated on the origin of wealth, nor upon the inequality of the human condition. He believed firmly that if this life should prove cruel, the life to come could not fail to redress the balance, and this hope upheld him. He never blasphemed God's name, and though he had no wife, he didn't covet his neighbor's.

Never did he fail upon entering a church to fall upon his knees before the presence of Christ and offer up this prayer to him: "My Lord Christ, keep watch over my life until it shall please God that I die, and when I am dead, ensure to me the possession of the joys of paradise."

Now on a certain evening of a dreary, sodden day, Barnaby sadly walked along a road, lugging under his arm his balls and knives, watching for some barn where he might sleep. He noticed a monk coming behind him and saluted courteously. They walked together and began talking.

"Fellow pilgrim," said the monk, "how is it that you are clothed all in green? Are you a jester in a mystery play?"

"Not at all, good Father," replied Barnaby. "I am called Barnaby and my skill is juggling. There would be no more pleasurable calling in the world if it would always provide one's daily bread."

"Friend Barnaby, be careful what you say. There is no calling more pleasant than the monastic life. Those who lead it are occupied with the praises of Christ and serving the saints. Indeed, the religious life is one ceaseless hymn to the Lord."

Barnaby said, "Father, I spoke ignorantly. Your calling cannot be at all compared with mine. Though there may be some merit in dancing and juggling, it does not come close to your gift. Gladly would I sing and learn the Scriptures. Though I am known in six hundred villages, I would willingly abandon it to serve my Lord Christ."

The monk was touched. "Friend Barnaby, your simplicity of spirit is rare. Come with me and I will have you admitted into the monastery."

It was in this manner that Barnaby became a monk. In the monastery he found many monks who each employed his gifts for Christ with all the knowledge and skill possible: The prior wrote books to help others understand the words of God. Brother Maurice copied the Scriptures beautifully upon sheets of vellum. Brother Alexander painted exquisite works of biblical scenes. Brother Marbode served with the children, leading them to salvation in the Lord Christ and nurturing them in His ways. And Brother Benedict planted healthy vegetables in the monastery field and praised God for his creative works.

Being a witness of the glorious harvest of their labors, Barnaby mourned his own ignorance and simplicity.

"Alas," he murmured as he sat in the restful chapel arbor. "Wretched child that I am, to be unable like my brothers to worthily worship the Lord Christ. I am but a rough man and unskilled in arts and service. I know no edifying sermons, I cannot write theological treatises, nor create magnificent paintings. I have no knowledge of planting or teaching the children."

So Barnaby gave up himself to sorrow. But one evening when the monks were conversing he heard a tale of a religious man who could repeat nothing more than a few stuttered words of praise to his Lord. He was despised for his ignorance, until after death his heart issued a lone rose illustrating the beauty Christ always saw in this man's inner thoughts.

Barnabas marvelled at the kindness and understanding of his Lord, but he still was in great sorrow. Then one morning he awakened with joy. He hastened to the chapel and remained there alone for one hour. After dinner he returned to the chapel. His sad demeanor vanished and he no longer groaned throughout his day.

The other monks could not help their curiosity. They began to whisper among themselves as to what could have changed old Barnaby—and what was he indulging in so persistently? The prior decided to observe him more closely and took two of the older monks with him to the chapel. They spied Barnaby through the chinks in the door. He stood on his hands before the altar with his feet in the air, juggling six balls of copper and a dozen knives. In honor of his Christ he was performing those feats which formerly had won him great fame.

The two old monks exclaimed against the sacrilege. The prior, though aware of the purity of Barnaby's soul, thought perhaps he had been seized with madness. The three monks entered and began to drag the juggler swiftly from the chapel. Suddenly the Lord Christ descended the steps of the altar. A trace of a smile touched his lips, and afterwards the prior always insisted that there was the merest twinkle in his eye. Christ reached out and gently wiped away with his robe the sweat dripping from the juggler's forehead.

Then the prior, falling upon his face on the pavement, called out, "Blessed are the simplehearted, for they shall see God."

"Amen!" said the old brothers, and they kissed the ground for it was holy.

Uncle David's Birthday

Carter Wright
Retold by Stephen Fortosis

The Williams family should have been everlastingly grateful for the uncle who entered their lives just when they were going down for the last time. But time dimmed their love instead of intensifying it. Uncle David became first a savior, then a figurehead, and finally a nuisance.

We Christians also know a person named David—that is, the Son of David. He came to us as Savior. But for some, his birthday may have lost its true significance. Maybe honoring friends and relatives at Christmas has become more important to us than honoring Christ. If so, this year is the right time—not only to give unselfishly to others, but to give our lives afresh to him.

And when they . . . saw the young child with Mary his mother, and fell down and worshipped him; and when they had opened their treasures, they presented unto him gifts; gold, and frankincense, and myrrh.

Matthew 2:11 (KJV)

It was Christmas Eve. The calendar said so. Nature proclaimed it with her dazzling robe of white. The merry face of expectant children reflected it. The piled-up bundles in the arms of belated shoppers testified to it.

A peep into thousands of homes made festive with holly wreaths and Christmas trees would have proved it.

But in the home of Brett Williams, you never could have guessed that the holiday season was here. There were no decorations or happy faces, not even a cheery fire. Shivering before dying embers sat a mother and her three little children. Another child, a small boy of four years, was nestled on the sofa with his father, who just recovered from a long illness.

"Daddy," the child was saying, "why won't Santa Claus come tonight?"

The man's hand trembled slightly as he stroked the child's head. It was several minutes before he spoke. "Well, little man, Daddy has been sick so long and Mama's had to work hard just to buy clothes and medicine and food . . ."

"But, Daddy," argued the baby philosopher, "that's the very reason he should be more good to us! I wrote him about that and asked him to bring me some shoes and toys and candy. And I wrote him not to think we lived in a nice house like we used to, but a 'partment. He's got to come 'cause I told him I'd be looking . . ."

The mother could stand no more. She arose suddenly and went into the small kitchen. She knew empty stockings would mean broken hearts on Christmas morning. As she prepared a simple dinner, she prayed for help.

While the family ate, a Rolls Royce suddenly breezed into their driveway.

"Oh!" cried the youngest. "I bet it's Santa right now."

A knock on the door was answered by all four children. The stranger standing on the threshold did not look like Santa Claus, though he had white hair and the kindest face. "Excuse me," he said, "I'm looking for the home of Brett Williams."

Something in the voice and mannerisms of the stranger seemed familiar to Brett as he replied, "Sir, you're already at the home of Brett Williams."

With arms outstretched, the man hurried across the room. "Brett, don't you recognize me—your brother, David. I'm so glad I've finally found you!"

It would be a long, long story to tell all that was said there that Christmas night, for the brothers hadn't been together in twenty years. When Brett was only fifteen, David, then an adult of thirty-five, had left America for a business venture in mainland China. Somehow, through the years, Brett had stopped replying to David's letters and they'd completely lost contact with each other. In the meantime, one had grown extremely rich and the other extremely poor. The poor brother had a family and nothing else. The rich brother had everything money could buy, but no family; now he was growing older and longed for his old home and loved ones left behind.

Upon his return to America, David knew that his only sibling still living was Brett. Still it required several days just to locate this one brother.

Now, with eager sympathy, David listened to the misfortunes of Brett's family, then generously promised to supply their needs. He merely wanted a home with them—and love.

Often as the adults talked Brett's little boy went to the window and looked out. Uncle David noticed and said, "Little man, I'll give you a ride in that car first thing in the morning."

"I was looking for Santa Claus," he remarked. "Papa said he wouldn't come . . ."

"Stephen," his father said, "God's given us someone a lot better than any Santa Claus this year."

Uncle David just smiled.

Ten and a half years passed, and the Williamses no longer lived on a back street. Theirs was one of the most expensive homes in an exclusive section of the suburbs, surrounded by a terraced lawn and well-manicured gardens. Its furnishings were lavish and in perfect taste.

One morning, a friend from other, darker days came to call.

Mrs. Williams spoke cordially, "You know, we've almost forgotten we were ever poor. Uncle Dave, as we all call him, has been so good to us . . .

"How's Brett? Oh, very well. Uncle Dave sent him to a hospital where he received the best of care and soon regained his health. Now they're in business together. Have you seen their new office building downtown? Uncle Dave furnishes all the capital and has done the bulk of the work, but Brett handles all the accounting.

"How are the girls? Terrific! They're enjoying college life, but, of course, they're on vacation now. They keep me busy buying them clothing and entertaining their friends. They'll be downstairs before long. I'm so glad you stopped by today. We're celebrating Uncle Dave's birthday. He's been so good to us; we owe him everything."

The friend replied, "It's nice to see such gratitude. So many people forget their benefactors. What a good idea to make Uncle David's birthday special each year . . . You know, I really shouldn't stay . . ."

But Mrs. Williams insisted. Soon Brett arrived, and the family and guests assembled. The doors of the spacious dining room swung back and all were ushered in. Now the visitor thought, of course, she'd find dear Uncle David in the seat of honor, but he was nowhere to be seen. Numerous packages were piled on the chairs for family and guests. On each box was a card bearing these words: "Wishing you a merry time on Uncle Dave's birthday."

She could keep quiet no longer: "I'm sorry, I don't quite understand. Where's the guest of honor—the one whose birthday you're celebrating?"

Brett's eyes dropped. His wife's face flushed and she stammered, "Well, you see, um, our table won't seat more than fourteen. Some of our guests are strangers to Uncle Dave, and, well, he never complains, you know. We just let him spend the day in his room. It's so quiet up on the second floor, sort of in the back of the house—it's nice and sunny in late afternoon. As soon as everyone's served, we send him a little tray."

The friend sat dumbfounded as, with exclamations of delight, the family and guests began unwrapping gifts. "Where," the visitor asked presently, "are Uncle Dave's gifts?"

"Oh, we never forget him!" said Mrs. Williams.

"No," chimed in one of the daughters. "I made a special trip to the drugstore yesterday to get his things."

Taking a small box from the serving table, she continued, "See these handkerchiefs? They only cost 50 cents each, but they look just like linen. And this is a $10 tie—I got it for $5 because of one little damaged corner. Uncle Dave will never know the difference."

So they sent Uncle David a tray, together with a few gifts they'd picked up at the last minute. Their benefactor took the food and thanked them for the gifts, but they didn't see his eyes as he softly closed the door.

Then one morning a few weeks later one of the children hammered on Uncle David's door, but there was only silence. The child finally rushed in, only to find the room deserted. None of Uncle David's simple belongings remained. He had moved out.

The Williams family never saw Uncle David again, and Brett and his wife remarked more than once on the ungratefulness of a man to simply move out without any prior notice.

Where Love Is, God Is

Leo Tolstoy

Though the Russian novelist Leo Tolstoy is considered one of the greatest writers of realistic fiction, his beginnings were not especially promising. He was orphaned at age nine and quit formal schooling in 1847 without a degree. Then, in 1852, he completed an autobiographical novel, and its popularity inspired him to continue writing. War and Peace *and* Anna Karenina *are considered his greatest masterpieces.*

Tolstoy's religious faith was a tortured one because of his own perceived hypocrisy, as well as the disparity he saw between biblical Christianity and the practices of government and church. In his story, "Where Love Is, God Is," Tolstoy seeks to illustrate that kindness done from a pure heart is kindness done to Christ himself.

In a little town in Russia there lived a cobbler, Martin Avedeitch by name. He had a tiny room in a basement with one window, which looked onto the street. Through it one could see only the feet of those who passed by, but Martin recognized the people by their boots. He had lived long in the place and had many acquaintances. There was hardly a pair of boots in the neighborhood that had not been through his hands once or twice, so he often saw his own handiwork through the window. Some boots he had soled again and again, some patched, some stitched up, and to some he even made fresh uppers. He had plenty to do, for he worked well, used good material, did not charge too much, and could be relied upon by the people—if he could do a job by the day required, he undertook it, but if not, he told the truth and gave no false promises. So he was well known and never short of work.

Martin had always been a good man, but in his old age he began to think more about his soul and to draw nearer to God. From that time Martin's whole life changed, becoming peaceful and joyful. He sat down to his task in the morning, and when he had finished his day's work he took the lamp down from the wall, stood it on the table, fetched his Bible from the shelf, opened it, and sat down to read. The more he read, the better he understood and the clearer and happier he felt in his mind.

It happened once that Martin sat up late, absorbed in his book. He was reading Luke's Gospel, and in the sixth chapter he came upon the verses:

> To him that smiteth thee on one cheek offer also the other, and from him that taketh away thy cloak withhold not thy coat also. Give to every man that asketh thee; and of him that taketh away thy good ask them not again. And as ye would that men should do to you, do ye also to them likewise.

He thought about this, and was about to go to bed, but was loath to leave his book. So he went on reading the seventh chapter—about the centurion, the widow's son, and the answer to John's disciples—and he came to the part where a rich Pharisee invited the Lord to his house. He read how the woman who was a sinner anointed his feet and washed them with her tears, and how he justified her. Coming to the forty-fourth verse, he read:

> And turning to the woman, he said unto Simon, "Seest thou this woman? I entered into thine house, thou gavest me no water for my feet, but she hath wetted my feet with her tears and wiped them with her hair. Thou

gavest me no kiss, but she, since the time I came in, hath not ceased to kiss my feet. My head with oil thou didst not anoint, but she hath anointed my feet with ointment."

He read these verses again: "He gave me no water for his feet, gave no kiss, his head with oil he did not anoint . . ." And Martin took off his spectacles once more, laid them on his book, and pondered: *He must have been like me, that Pharisee. He too thought only of himself—how to get a cup of tea, how to keep warm and comfortable, never a thought of his guest. He took care of himself, but for his guest he cared nothing at all. Yet who was the guest? The Lord Himself! If He came to me, should I behave like that?*

Then Martin laid his head upon both his arms and fell asleep.

"Martin!" He suddenly heard a voice, as if someone had breathed the word above his ear. He started from his sleep. "Who's there?" he asked.

He turned around and looked at the door. No one was there. He called again, then heard quite distinctly: "Martin, Martin! Look out into the street tomorrow, for I shall come."

Martin roused himself, rose from his chair and rubbed his eyes, but did not know whether he had heard these words in a dream or awake. He put out the lamp and lay down to sleep.

The next morning he rose before daylight, and after saying his prayers lit the fire and prepared his cabbage soup and buckwheat porridge. Then he lit the samovar, put on his apron, and sat down by the window to his work. He looked out into the street more than he worked, and whenever anyone passed in unfamiliar boots he would stoop and look up, so as to see not only the feet but the face of the passerby as well.

A house porter passed in new felt boots, then a water carrier. Presently an old soldier of Nicholas's reign came near the window, spade in hand. Martin knew him by his boots, which were shabby old felt once, galoshed with leather. The old man was called Stepanitch. A neighboring trades- man kept him in his house for charity, and his duty was to help the house porter. He began to clear away the snow before Martin's window, and Martin glanced at him and then went on with his work.

After the cobbler had made a dozen stitches he felt drawn to look out of the window again. He saw that Stepanitch had leaned his spade against the wall, and either was resting himself or trying to get warm. The man was old and broken down, and had evidently not enough strength even to clear away the snow.

What if I called him in and gave him some tea? thought Martin. *The samovar is just on the boil.*

He stuck his awl in its place and rose. Putting the samovar on the table, he made tea. Then he tapped the window with his fingers. Stepanitch turned and came to the window. Martin beckoned to him to come in, and went himself to open the door.

"Come in," he said, "and warm yourself a bit. I'm sure you must be cold."

"May God bless you!" Stepanitch answered. "My bones do ache, to be sure." He came in, first shaking off the snow, and lest he should leave marks on the floor he began wiping his feet. But as he did so, he tottered and nearly fell.

"Don't trouble to wipe your feet," said Martin. "I'll wipe up the floor—it's all in a day's work. Come, friend, sit down and have some tea."

Filling two tumblers, he passed one to his visitor, and pouring his own tea out into the saucer, began to blow on it.

Stepanitch emptied his glass and, turning it upside down, put the remains of his piece of sugar on the top. He began to express his thanks, but it was plain that he would be glad of some more.

"Have another glass," said Martin, refilling the visitor's tumbler and his own. But while he drank his tea, Martin kept looking out into the street.

"Are you expecting anyone?" asked the visitor.

"Am I expecting anyone? Well, now, I'm ashamed to tell you. It isn't that I really expect anyone, but I heard something last night which I can't get out of my mind. Whether it was a vision, or only a fancy, I can't tell. You see, friend, last night I was reading the Gospel about Christ the Lord, how He suffered, and how He walked on earth. You have heard tell of it, I dare say."

"I have heard tell of it," answered Stepanitch. "But I'm an ignorant man and not able to read."

"Well, you see, I was reading and I came to that part, you know, where He went to a Pharisee who did not receive Him well. Friend, as I read about it, I thought how that man did not receive Christ the Lord with proper honor. Suppose such a thing should happen to a man such as myself, I thought, what would I not do to receive Him? But that man gave Him no reception at all. Well, friend, I began to doze, and as I dozed I heard someone call me by name. I got up and thought I heard someone whispering, 'Expect me. I will come tomorrow.' This happened twice.

163

And to tell you the truth, it sank so into my mind that, though I am ashamed of it myself, I keep on expecting Him, the dear Lord!"

Stepanitch shook his head in silence, finished his tumbler, and laid it on its side, but Martin stood it up again and refilled it for him.

"Thank you, Martin Avedeitch," he said. "You have given me food and comfort both for soul and body."

"You're very welcome. Come again another time. I am glad to have a guest," said Martin.

Stepanitch went away, and Martin poured out the last of the tea and drank it. Then he put away the tea things and sat down to work, stitching the back seam of a boot. As he stitched he kept looking out the window. His head was full of Christ's sayings.

Two soldiers went by, one in government boots, the other in boots of his own; then the master of a neighboring house, in shining galoshes; then a baker carrying a basket. All these passed on. Then a woman came up in worsted stockings and peasant-made shoes. She passed the window but stopped by the wall. Martin glanced up at her. She was a stranger, poorly dressed and with a baby in her arms. She stopped with her back to the wind, trying to wrap up the baby, though she had hardly anything for wrapping. The woman had on only summer clothes, and they were shabby and worn. Martin heard the baby crying and the woman trying to soothe it, but unable to do so. Martin rose and, going out the door and up the stairs, he called to her, "My dear, I say, my dear . . ."

The woman heard and turned.

"Why do you stand out there with the baby in the cold? Come inside. You can wrap him up better in a warm place."

The woman was surprised to see he was an old man in an apron with spectacles on his nose, but she followed him. They went down the steps, entered the little room, and the old man led her to the bed.

"There, sit down, my dear, near the stove. Warm yourself, and feed the baby."

"Haven't any milk. I have eaten nothing myself since early morning," said the woman, but still took the baby to her breast. Martin shook his head. He brought out a basin and some bread. Then he opened the oven door and poured some cabbage soup into the basin. He took out the porridge pot, but it was not yet ready. He spread a cloth on the table and served the soup and bread.

"Sit down and eat, my dear, and I'll mind the baby. Why, bless me, I've had children of my own. I know how to manage them."

The woman crossed herself, sat down, and began to eat while Martin put the baby on the bed and sat down by it. Martin sighed. "Haven't you any warmer clothing?" he asked.

"How could I get warm clothing?" she said. "I pawned my last shawl yesterday."

Then the woman came and took the child, and Martin got up. He went and looked among some things that were hanging on the wall and brought back an old cloak.

"Here," he said, "though it's a worn-out thing, it will do to wrap him up in."

The woman looked at the cloak, then at the old man, and taking it, burst into tears. Martin turned away, and groping under the bed brought out a small trunk. He fumbled about in it and again sat down opposite the woman, who cried, "The Lord bless you, friend."

"Take this for Christ's sake," said Martin and gave her sixpence to get her shawl out of pawn. The woman crossed herself and Martin did the same, and then he saw her out.

After a while Martin saw an apple woman stop just in front of his window. She carried her basket of apples and on her back she had a sack full of chips—no doubt gathered someplace under construction.

The sack evidently hurt her, and she wanted to shift it from one shoulder to the other, so she put it down on the footpath and began to shake down the chips in the sack. A boy in a tattered cap ran up, snatched an apple out of the basket and tried to slip away. But the old woman caught the boy by his sleeve. As he began to struggle, the woman held on with both hands, knocked the boy's cap off his head, and seized hold of his hair. The boy screamed and the old woman scolded. Martin dropped his awl, and rushed out of the door. Stumbling up the steps and dropping his spectacles in his hurry, he ran into the street. The old woman was pulling the boy's hair, threatening to take him to the police. The lad struggled, saying, "I did not take it! What are you beating me for? Let me go."

Martin separated them. He took the boy by the hand and said, "Let him go, Granny. Forgive him for Christ's sake."

"I'll pay him out," she said, "so that he won't forget it for a year! I'll take him to the police."

Martin entreated the old woman. "Let him go, Granny. He won't do it again."

The old woman let go and the boy tried to run away, but Martin stopped him.

"Ask the Granny's forgiveness," the cobbler said. "And don't do it another time. I saw you take the apple."

The boy began to cry and to beg pardon.

"That's right, and now here's an apple for you," Martin said, taking one to give to the boy, adding, "I will pay you, Granny."

"You will spoil them that way, the young rascals," said the old woman. "He ought to be whipped so that he will remember it for a week."

"Oh, Granny, Granny," said Martin, "that's our way—but it's not God's way. If he should be whipped for stealing an apple, what should be done to us for our sins?"

The old woman was silent.

Martin told her the parable of the lord who forgave his servant a large debt, and how the servant went out and seized his debtor by the throat. The woman listened to it all, and the boy stood by and listened too.

"God bids us forgive," said Martin, "or else we shall not be forgiven. Forgive everyone and a thoughtless youngster most of all."

The old woman wagged her head and sighed. "It's true enough, but they are getting terribly spoiled."

"Then we old ones must show them better ways," Martin replied.

"That's just what I say," she said. "I have seven of them, myself, and only one daughter is left."

She told how she lived with her daughter and about her grandchildren. "I have but little strength left, yet I work hard for the sake of the grandchildren, and nice children they are. No one comes out to meet me but the children . . ." The old woman completely softened.

"Of course, it was only his childishness," said she, referring to the boy.

As the woman hoisted the sack on her back, the lad sprang forward, saying, "Let me carry it for you, Granny. I'm going that way."

The old woman nodded her head and put the sack on the boy's back and they left, the old woman quite forgetting to ask Martin to pay for the apple. Martin stood and watched as they went along talking.

The cobbler went back to the house. Having found his spectacles unbroken on the steps, he picked up his awl and sat down again to work. He worked a little but soon it grew dark and he could not see to pass the bristle through the holes in the leather. He noticed the lamplighter passing on his way to light street lamps.

"Seems it's time to light up," thought he. So he trimmed the lamp, hung it, and sat again to work. Finishing one boot, he turned it to examine the work. It was all right. He gathered his tools together, swept up the cuttings, put away the thread and awls; taking down the lamp, he placed it on the table. He took the Gospels from the shelf, meaning to open them at the place he had marked with morocco. But the book opened at another place. Martin thought of yesterday's dream, and no sooner had he thought of it than he seemed to hear footsteps behind him. He turned round, and it seemed to him as if people were standing in the dark corner, but he could not make out who they were. And a voice whispered in his ear, "Martin, Martin, don't you know me?"

"Who is it?" muttered Martin.

"It is I," said the voice. And out of the dark corner stepped Stepanitch, who smiled and vanished like a cloud of smoke.

"It is I," said the voice. And out of the darkness stepped the woman with the baby in her arms. The woman smiled and the baby laughed, but they too quickly disappeared.

"It is I," said the voice once more. And the old woman and the boy with the apple stepped out. Both smiled and vanished.

Martin's soul grew glad. He put on his spectacles and began searching the Gospel just where it had opened. At the top of the page he read: "I was hungry and ye gave me meat, I was thirsty and ye gave me drink, I was a stranger, and ye took me in."

At the bottom of the page he read: "Inasmuch as ye did it unto one of the least of these my brethren, ye did it unto me."

Martin understood that his dream had come true. The Savior really had come to him that day, and he had welcomed Him.

THE GOOD THINGS
OF LIFE

Arthur Gordon

Sometimes we get caught up in the great things we intend to do for God. However, in the process, we can lose sight of the greater things he would like to do through us. In the story "The Good Things of Life," Arthur Gordon—author of several books including A Touch of Wonder, *and former editorial director of* Guideposts *magazine—introduces us to a pastor who learns a lesson in humility. Consumed in becoming a well-known preacher, this pastor has forgotten a most crucial principle in ministry—people are more important to God than all our talents, plans, and programs.*

Near the crest of the hill he felt the rear wheels of the car spin for half a second, and he felt a flash of the unreasonable irritability that had been plaguing him lately.

"Good thing it didn't snow more than an inch or two," he said a bit grimly. "We'd be in trouble if it had."

His wife was driving. She often did, so that he could make notes for a sermon or catch up on his endless correspondence by dictating into the tape recorder he had built into the car. Now she looked out at the woods and fields gleaming in the morning sunlight. "It's pretty, though," she said, "and Christmasy. We haven't had a white Christmas like this in years."

He gave her an amused and affectionate glance. "You always see the best side of things, don't you, my love?"

"Well, after hearing you urge umpteen congregations to do precisely that . . ."

Arnold Barclay smiled and some of the lines of tension and fatigue went out of his face. "Remember the bargain we made twenty years ago? I'd do the preaching and you'd do the practicing."

Her mouth curved faintly. "I remember."

They came to a crossroads, and he found that after all these years he still remembered the sign: LITTLEFIELD, 1 MILE. He said, "How's the time?"

She glanced at the diamond watch on her wrist; his present to her this year. "A little after ten."

He leaned forward and switched on the radio. In a moment his own voice, strong and resonant, filled the car, preaching a Christmas sermon prepared and recorded weeks before. He listened to a sentence or two, then smiled sheepishly and turned it off. "Just wanted to hear how I sounded."

"You sound fine," Mary Barclay said. "You always do."

They passed a farmhouse, the new snow sparkling like diamonds on the roof, the Christmas wreath bright against the front door. "Who lived there?" he asked. "Peterson, wasn't it? No, Johannsen."

"That's right," his wife said. "Eric Johannsen. Remember the night he made you hold the lantern while the calf was born?"

"Do I ever!" He rubbed his forehead wearily. "About this new television proposition, Mary. What do you think? It would be an extra load, I know. But I'd be reaching an enormous audience. The biggest—"

She put her hand on his arm. "Darling, it's Christmas Day. Can't we talk about it later?"

"Sure, OK," he said, but something in him was offended all the same. The television proposal was important. Why, in fifteen minutes he would reach ten times as many people as Saint Paul had reached in a lifetime. He said, "How many people did the Littlefield church hold, Mary? About a hundred, wasn't it?"

"Ninety-six," his wife said, "to be exact."

"Ninety-six!" He gave a rueful laugh. "Quite a change of pace."

It was that, all right. It was years since he had preached in anything but metropolitan churches. The Littlefield parish had been the beginning. Now, on Christmas morning, he was going back—back for an hour or two, to stand in the little pulpit where he had preached his first hesitant, fumbling sermon twenty years ago.

He let his head fall back against the seat and closed his eyes. The decision to go back had not been his really. It had been Mary's. She handled all his appointments, screening the continual invitations to preach or speak. A month ago she had come to him. There was a request, she said, for him to preach a sermon at Littlefield on Christmas morning.

"Littlefield?" he had asked, incredulous. "What about that Washington invitation?" He had been asked to preach to a congregation that would, he knew, include senators and cabinet members.

"We haven't answered it yet," she said. "We could drive to Littlefield on Christmas morning, if we got up early enough . . ."

He had stared at her. "You mean, you think we ought to go back there?"

She had looked back at him calmly. "That's up to you, Arnold." But he knew what she wanted him to say.

Making such a decision wasn't so hard at the moment, he thought wearily. Not resenting afterward—that was the difficult part. Maybe it wouldn't be so bad. The church would be horribly overcrowded, the congregation would be mostly farmers, but . . .

The car stopped; he opened his eyes.

They were at the church, all right. There it sat by the side of the road, just as it always had; if anything, it looked smaller than he remembered. Around it the fields stretched, white and unbroken, to neighboring farmhouses. But there was no crowd, no sign of anyone. The church was shuttered and silent.

He looked at Mary, bewildered. She did not seem surprised. She pushed open the car door. "Let's go inside, shall we? I still have a key."

The church was cold. Standing in the icy gloom, he could see his breath steam in the gray light. He said, and his voice sounded strange, "Where is everybody? You said there was a request . . ."

"There was a request," Mary said. "From me."

She moved forward slowly until she was standing by the pulpit. "Arnold," she said, "the finest sermon I ever heard you preach was right here in this church. It was your first Christmas sermon. We hadn't been married long. You didn't know our first baby was on the way, but I did. Maybe that's why I remember so well what you said.

"You said God tried every way possible to get through to people. He tried prophets and miracles and revelations—and nothing worked. So then He said, 'I'll send them something they can't fail to understand. I'll send them the simplest and yet the most wonderful thing in all My creation. I'll send them a Baby . . .' Do you remember that?"

He nodded wordlessly.

"Well," she said, "I heard they had no minister here now, so I knew they wouldn't be having a service this morning. And I thought . . . well, I thought it might be good for . . . for both of us if you could preach that sermon again. Right here, where your ministry began. I just thought . . ."

Her voice trailed off, but he knew what she meant. He knew what she was trying to tell him, although she was too loyal and too kind to say it in words. That he had gotten away from the sources of his strength. That as success had come to him, as his reputation had grown larger, some things in him had grown smaller. The selflessness. The humility. The most important things of all.

He stood there, silent, seeing himself with a terrifying clarity: the pride, the ambition, the hunger for larger and larger audiences. Not for the glory of God. For the glory of Arnold Barclay.

He clenched his fists, feeling panic grip him, a sense of terror and guilt unlike anything he had ever known. Then faintly, underneath the panic, something else stirred. He glanced around the little church. She was right, Mary was right, and perhaps it wasn't too late. Perhaps here, now, he could rededicate himself . . .

Abruptly he stripped off his overcoat, tossed it across the back of a pew. He reached out and took both of Mary's hands. He heard himself laugh, an eager, boyish laugh. "We'll do it! We'll do it just the way we used to. You open the shutters. That was your job, remember? I'll start the furnace. We'll have a Christmas service just for the two of us. I'll preach that sermon, all for you!"

She turned quickly to the nearest window, raised it, began fumbling with the catch that held the shutters. He opened the door that led to the cellar steps. Down in the frigid basement he found the furnace squatting, as black and malevolent as ever. He flung open the iron door. No fire was laid, but along the wall wood was stacked, and kindling, and newspapers.

He began to crumple papers and thrust them into the furnace, heedless of the soot that blackened his fingers. Overhead he heard the sound that made him pause. Mary was trying the wheezy old melodeon. "Ring

171

the bell, too," he shouted up the stairs. "We might as well do the job right."

He heard her laugh. A moment later, high in the belfry, the bell began to ring. Its tone was as clear and resonant as ever, and the sound brought back a flood of memories: the baptisms, the burials, the Sunday dinners at the old farmhouses, the honesty and brusqueness and simple goodness of the people.

He stood there, listening, until the bell was silent. Then he struck a match and held it to the newspapers. Smoke curled reluctantly. He reached up, adjusted the old damper, tried again. This time a tongue of flame flickered. For perhaps five minutes he watched it, hovering over it, blowing on it. When he was sure that it was kindled, he went back up the cellar steps.

The church was a blaze of sunlight. Where the window glass was clear, millions of dust motes whirled and danced. Where there were panes of stained glass, the rays fell on the old floor in pools of ruby and topaz and amethyst. Mary was standing at the church door. "Arnold," she said, "come here."

He went and stood beside her. After the darkness of the cellar, the sun on the snow was so bright he couldn't see anything.

"Look," she said in a whisper. "They're coming."

Cupping his hands round his eyes, he stared out across the glistening whiteness, and he saw that she was right. They were coming. Across the fields. Down the roads. Some on foot. Some in cars. They were coming, he knew, not to hear him, not to hear any preacher, however great. They were coming because it was Christmas Day, and this was their church and its bell was calling them. They were coming because they wanted someone to give them the ancient message—to tell them the good news.

He stood there with his arm around his wife's shoulders and the soot black on his face and the overflowing happiness in his heart.

"Merry Christmas," he said. "Merry Christmas, and thank you, darling."

DEATH'S VICTORY

Tamar's Touch

Diane Komp

Diane Komp's dual career as a medical doctor and writer has been featured in Life, *the* New York Times, Family Circle, Guideposts, Christianity Today, *and* Today's Christian Woman. *She is the author of five books; the story included in this collection was drawn from* Hope Springs from Mended Places.

In this story, Komp draws a poignant parallel between the wounded Tamar of the Bible and a woman she met in her medical practice named Tamara Lowell. Your heart will be moved as you see an abused mother struggling to love a son who faces life-threatening illness.

Tamar put ashes on her head and tore the ornamented robe she was wearing. She put her hand on her head and went away, weeping aloud as she went. . . . Tamar lived in her brother Absalom's house, a desolate woman.

2 Samuel 13:19–20

Today some might call Carter Lowell a nerd. A longish mane spilled over his horn-rimmed glasses when he concentrated, forming a blond blind. Significant passages of his textbooks were punctuated by a sideways whiplash, a toss of head and neck to clear his vision. Book-bent was the common posture of this passionate scholar I knew years ago.

Although his school did not encourage accelerated progression, Carter had already skipped two grades by the time he reached the seventh. He was intrigued by the physical sciences. There was a lab in the corner of his bedroom filled with beakers and Bunsen burners, flasks and flames. He continued to experiment long past school hours.

Excellent! That was one of Carter's favorite phrases.

The boy was not one of those family surprises, more brilliant than his forebears. Both his parents had earned advanced degrees from prestigious institutions. He was clearly their child.

Carter was conceived when his mother was in graduate school. The boy's father was a post-doctorate who was one of the laboratory teaching assistants. Married to another woman, he returned to England with his wife when the boy was born.

When the nurse first handed the newborn baby to her, Tamara was afraid to touch him for fear that he would break. He was so tiny! She was so inexperienced. Tamara dropped out of graduate school to move back with her parents and care for the child. Carter never knew his father.

Eventually she went back to complete her degree, and by the time I met her, Tamara Lowell was a well-established research scientist. The boy grew up mostly in the care of his grandparents.

There was a spirit in the lad that seemed alien in that particular family. He often felt as if he was a disapppointment to them, especially to his mother. He didn't know how to please her. There was a warmth in Carter that was missing in his mother, an anticipation that something exciting might happen when you meet ordinary people.

Carter Lowell followed a solitary path. He walked alone to school each day. He ate alone in the lunchroom; he joined the math team rather than take up a sport. He didn't have a girlfriend, nor had he ever attended a school dance. Carter excelled in academics, but lived on the fringes of teenage society. Younger than his classmates by two years, he had no real chums at school. To them, Carter seemed somewhat pompous. The poor kid simply was so enthusiastic about learning that he had no discernment of when to remain silent in the presence of dolts. At sixteen, his passion was for Bach, not rock.

It was a distracting pain in his shoulder that brought Carter to my office. The X-rays confirmed his family doctor's suspicion of a bone tumor. In all my years of practice, I've never had a conversation with a mother like that first session when I told Dr. Tamara Lowell that Carter had cancer.

With anger flashing in her eyes, she raged, "We don't believe in God!" At that point in my life, neither did I, but there was such a hatred in her voice that I took sharp notice. I disbelieved quietly. There was a chilling intonation to Tamara's denunciation. This was her first thought when I told her that her son had cancer.

In those days few teenagers with Ewing's sarcoma survived. Yet there were patients outliving our gloom-and-doom talk every day. I wanted to talk about treatment. Tamara wanted to talk about her son's death, there in that first meeting.

"How do patients with this tumor usually die?" she asked as her son listened, tears running down his face. I could not believe what I was hearing.

"It's possible that Carter may not die from this at all," I said. "We have treatment to offer. He may kick it rather than succumb to it."

"There won't be a service," his mother continued. "Not even an obituary in the papers. There is no life after death." It was at that point that I realized that I had never before met a parent of a child with cancer who actually claimed to be an atheist.

I asked about the boy's father, if he would be coming to see his son. The father, she said, was not a factor in his life and would hardly be a help in his death.

Months into his treatment, Carter's English teacher noticed a constant sadness and asked if he would like to talk to a counselor. In a brief conversation, the school psychologist learned enough to alarm him. He called Tamara to suggest formal therapy. The notion was hostilely rejected.

Eventually, Carter's sadness worked its way to the surface. He stole a car and crashed it into a telephone pole, nearly killing himself in the process. The juvenile court set psychotherapy as a condition for probation. Tamara had no other choice.

I liked Carter very much. He was quite pleasant, downright fun, and intrigued by everything to do with his treatment. As a future scientist, he had to know all the technical points. He made me draw a schematic of all the metabolic pathways, showing him the mechanism of action of every drug he would receive. He would study my charts for hours and then propose a new type of chemotherapy that might work better.

As independent as teenagers are, they treasure the comfort of a mother's hand or hug. They are rarely too proud in such circumstances to relinquish their hard-won control. Carter would have done the same. But his mother rarely came into the treatment room while he was having a painful test or treatment. Tamara would not touch him.

Once he cried for her, and she fled the room. I held him in my arms as he wept silently for half an hour. When his tears were spent, he thanked me and left with Tamara, walking together down the hallway without exchanging a word.

I must admit I didn't spend as much time with Carter as with other patients; I struggled to treat this family in a nonjudgmental fashion. Over time this became overwhelmingly difficult. I could not steel myself to spend any more attention on them than absolutely necessary. Carter sensed this, I think, and for that I've always had regret.

What got to me was something in his mother's attitude that I could not understand. She seemed unable to affirm him as other mothers cherish their cancer-afflicted children. I wanted Carter to cry out, "Deliver me from this woman!" But of course, he didn't. He was her son and loved her dearly.

One day a minor surgical procedure caused him a great deal of pain. Carter cried for his mother. She raged at him and told him to act like a man. But she called him "Robbie," then left the room. I asked Carter, "Is 'Robbie' your middle name?"

"No," he said. "Robbie was my uncle. I never met him. He died before I was born."

The foreboding I had about this family would not go away. It was not for many years after Carter died that I learned Tamara's story.

She was a beautiful child with a distant father—the only girl in the family, and the youngest. As a three-year-old, she passed long hours standing before her mirrored closet, choosing her dress for the day, and longing for her father to notice her.

It was her oldest brother who paid her the most attention. He became her hero, playing with her when the others told the little kid to take off. He liked war games, tommy guns, and such; on his wall was a poster of Attila the Hun. When Tammy got into fights, Robbie fought her battles. She loved to come to his room to play.

She was six and he was fourteen when it started, one of those times she came to his room. No one else was home. She was pleased when he drew her close and set her on his lap. He rocked her and closed his eyes, rubbing her against him.

The first time he took her hand and asked her to touch him, she drew away. That's where boys were different from girls, what Mommy called their private parts.

"It's OK, Tammy," he said, taking her hand again. "Don't I take care of you? I wouldn't do anything to hurt you. It will just be our secret. If you want to come to my room and play, then we will have our little secret."

The child loved her brother more than anyone in the world. The thought that he might not play with her was more than she could bear, and so she touched him where he asked. He held her hand, showed her how to please him. She was frightened when he groaned and seemed to be in another world. She tried to let go, but he held her hand tightly and kissed her.

That first night she had a nightmare and cried out in her sleep. As her mother came to comfort her, she found Robbie already in the hallway. "That's OK, Mom. I'll take care of her. I'll stay with her until she falls back asleep." And so, he held her and rocked her, and she was glad that he was there.

These trysts continued for three years. It was their secret, and he never hurt her, just showed her how to make him happy. And yet, the child had a sense of guilt and abandonment. Sometimes she wished that her parents would find out so that it would end. She felt dirty, yet she loved Robbie so much that she could not say no when he asked her to touch him in that special way.

It ended one night when Robbie came to her room. Their mother heard noise and, checking on the children, screamed at what she saw. She was quickly joined by her husband, who throttled Robbie and slapped him hard in the face. Tammy pleaded for them not to hurt him, that it was her fault, not his. Robbie ran out of the house, grabbing the car keys on the way as his father screamed, "You're not my son. I disown you, you little piece of filth!"

The police did not identify Robbie until the next morning. Two patrol cars pursued him in a high-speed chase after they saw him driving 120 miles per hour down the highway.

The car caught fire as soon as it hit the telephone pole. They had to wait for the wreckage to cool before they could check the motor number against vehicle records. No identification was found on the body or in the car. The police considered it fortunate that it was a single-car accident, that no one but the driver was killed.

There was no service for Robbie, no obituary in the newspaper. The small-town headlines had already said more than enough. The parents explained to friends that the body was burned beyond recognition. It was simpler to have a private graveside service. They just set him in the ground without a marker.

Tammy was not there to see her brother committed to earth. She was sobbing in her room, blaming herself for her brother's death. If she had not touched him, Robbie never would have died.

When her son was three years old, Tamara first noticed that Carter looked like her brother. By the time he was six, she found the likeness intolerable. From that time on, she never touched her son. That is, until the week of his death.

I suppose it was inevitable that Carter never did get well. To help with his pain, to try for another remission, we gave him more powerful chemotherapy. His pain was controlled, but an infection developed that caused his fever to climb.

Two teary-eyed nurses tried to restrain the boy onto a cooling blanket as his temperature and his body soared. They held his outstretched arms as I heard him cry out, "Oh God, tell me if You exist." Seven lasting words.

Can a woman forget her nursing child or show no compassion for the child of her womb? Somehow, there had to be an answer for this almost motherless child's needs. I remember thinking: *If there was a God, surely He would reach out in mercy to this young man.*

I never knew what brought the change in Tamara and most likely never will. It was simply that all of a sudden she seemed free to meet her son's needs. She took Carter home.

I visited them as often as possible. Although his body was deteriorating, the boy was at peace. I sat on his bed one day, still holding his hand after I finished checking his pulse, extending a medical touch into a more human one.

From his bed we could see some ducks climbing out of a pond and padding onto the tennis court. Two neighbor boys volleyed with more vigor than skill that day. There was longing in Carter's face, a tiny benign spark of envy, but then he closed his eyes as if to blink them away and himself back to his room.

Carter thought that his temperature was going up again, and he was right. Tamara came quietly into the room, laid her hand on his forehead, and confirmed his suspicion. Then she took a cool cloth and wiped her son's face. I moved away from the bed as she took a basin of water and a cloth, began to wash his body, and then spread baby oil on his shoulders. The muscles relaxed, the body did not arch. Carter fell asleep, gently holding his mother's hand to his lips. Her own lips met her son's hand gently before releasing it.

Tamara walked with me to my car. I could think of nothing to say. There was not much to discuss, medically speaking; all my unanswered questions were far too personal to pursue. So I took my questions home with me, leaving Carter in his own bed, with his own family.

On the way back to the hospital, I remembered Carter's prayer to the God in whom his mother did not believe. Then I remembered an ancient promise as well: *Even if a mother were to forget, I will not forget you.*

Perhaps, I thought, *there is a God who hears the prayers of the poor and afflicted. Maybe the Creator of this universe is generous enough to tell one dying boy, "Yes, I exist. And I love you."*

Later, I would find this to be true for myself. In the meantime, after Carter's death, there was a notice in the local newspaper. A memorial service would take place by the duck pond he had watched from his window. Carter deserved to be honored and remembered, it said. He was Tamara Lowell's beloved son.

The Making of a Minister

Walter Wangerin Jr.

Master storyteller Walter Wangerin Jr. has been captivating both reading and listening audiences for several decades with tales that are timeless. His books have won many honors, including the American Book Award, Gold Medallion awards, and the New York Times' *Best Children's Book of the Year.*

In "The Making of a Minister," Wangerin describes one of the most important growing experiences he had as a young pastor, and how an unlikely old man named Arthur Forte taught some hard lessons never forgotten.

I wish to memorialize Arthur Forte, dead the third year of my ministry, poor before he died, unkempt, obscene, sardonic, arrogant, old, lonely, black, and bitter—but one whose soul has never ceased to teach me. From Arthur, from the things this man demanded of me, and from my restless probing of that experience, I grow. This is absolutely true. My pastoral hands are tenderized. My perceptions into age and pain are daily sharpened. My humility is kept soft, unhardened. And by old, dead Arthur I remember the more profound meaning of my title, minister.

It is certainly time now to memorialize teachers, those undegreed, unasked, ungentle, and unforgettable.

In memoriam, then: Arthur Forte.

Arthur lived in a shotgun house, so-called because it was three rooms in a dead straight line, built narrowly on half a city lot.

More properly, Arthur lived in the front room of his house. Or rather, to speak the cold, disturbing truth, Arthur lived in a rotting stuffed chair in that room, from which he seldom stirred the last year of his life.

Nor, during that year, did anyone mourn his absence from church and worship. I think most folks were grateful that he had turned reclusive, for the man had a walk and manner like the toad, a high-backed slouch and a burping contempt for fellow parishioners. Arthur's mind, though mostly uneducated, was excellent. He had written poetry in his day, both serious and sly, but now he used words to shiv Christians in their pews. Neither time nor circumstance protected the people, but their holiness caught on the hooks of his observations, and pain could spread across their countenance even in the middle of an Easter melody, while Arthur sat lumpish beside them, triumphant.

No, none felt moved to visit the man when he became housebound.

Except me.

I was the pastor, so sweetly young and dutiful. It was my job, and Arthur phoned to remind me of my job.

But to visit Arthur was grimly sacrificial.

After several months of chair-sitting, both Arthur and his room were filthy. I do not exaggerate: roaches flowed from my step like puddles stomped in; they dropped casually from the walls. I stood very still. The TV flickered constantly. There were newspapers strewn all over the floor. There lay a damp film on every solid object in the room, from which arose a close, moldy odor, as though it were alive and sweating. But the dampness was a blessing, because Arthur smoked.

He had a bottom lip like a shelf. Upon that shelf he placed lit cigarettes, and then he did not remove them again until they had burned quite down, at which moment he blew them toward the television set. Burning, they hit the newspapers on the floor. But it is impossible to ignite a fine, moist mildew. Blessedly, they went out.

Then the old man would sharpen the sacrifice of my visit. Motioning toward a foul and oily sofa, winking as though he knew what mortal damage such a compost could do to my linens and my dignity, he said in hostly tones: "Have a seat, why don't you, Reverend?"

From the beginning, I did not like to visit Arthur Forte. Nor did he make my job ("My ministry!" you cry. "My service! My discipleship!" No, just my job) any easier. He did not wish a quick psalm, a professional prayer, or devotions. Rather, he wanted acutely to dispute a young clergyman's faith.

Seventy years a churchgoer, the old man narrowed his eye at me and debated the goodness of God. With incontrovertible proofs, he delivered shattering damnations of hospitals (at which he had worked) and doctors (whom he had closely observed): "Twenty dollars a strolling visit when they come to a patient's room," he said. "For what? Two minute's time is what, and no particular news to the patient. A squeeze, a punch, a scribble on their charts, and they leave that sucker feeling low and worthless." *Wuhthless*, he said, hollowing the word at the center. "God-in-a-smock had listened to the heart, then didn't even tell what he heard. Ho, ho!" said Arthur, "I'll never go to a hospital. That cock-a-roach is more truthful of what he's about. Ho, ho! I'll never lie in a hospital bed, ho, ho!" And then, somehow he wove the failure of doctors into his intense argument against the goodness of the Deity, and he slammed me with facts, and I was a fumbling, lubberly sort to be defending the Almighty—

When I left him, I was empty in my soul and close to tears, and testy, my own faith seeming more stale, flat, and unprofitable at the moment. I didn't like to visit Arthur.

Then came the days of his incontinence, both physical and religious.

The man was, by late summer, failing. He did not remove himself from the chair to let me in (I entered an unlocked door), nor even to pass urine (which entered a chair impossibly seamy). The August heat was unbearable and dangerous to one in his condition; therefore, I argued that Arthur go to the hospital despite his criticism of the place.

But he had a better idea, ho, ho! He took off all his clothes. Naked, Arthur greeted me. Naked, finally, the old man asked my prayers and the devout performance of private worship—and we prayed. Naked, too, he demanded Communion. Oh, these were not the conditions I had imagined. It is an embarrassing thing, to put bread into the mouth of a naked man: "My body, my blood," and Arthur's belly and his groin. He'd raised the level of my sacrifice to anguish. I was mortified.

And still he was not finished.

For in those latter days, the naked Arthur Forte asked me, his pastor, to come forward and put on his slippers, his undershorts, and his pants.

I did. His feet had begun to swell, so it caused him (and me) terrible pain in those personal moments when I took his hard heel in my hands and worked a split-backed slipper round it. He groaned out loud when he stood to take the clothing one leg at a time, then leaned on me. I put my arm around his naked back and drew up his naked leg and groaned too—deep, deep in my soul I groaned. We hurt, he and I. But his was the sacrifice beyond my telling. In those moments I came to know a certain wordless affection for Arthur Forte.

(Now read me your words, "ministry" and "service" and "discipleship," for then I began to understand them: then, at the touching of Arthur's feet, when that and nothing else was all that Arthur yearned for, one human being to touch him, physically to touch his old flesh, and not to judge. Holy Communion. In the most dramatic terms available, the old man had said, "Love me.")

When I came to him in the last week of August, I found Arthur prone on the floor. He'd fallen from his chair during the night, but his legs were too swollen and his arms too weak for climbing in again.

I said, "This is it, Arthur. You're going to the hospital."

He was tired. He didn't argue anymore. He let me call two other members of the congregation. While they came, I dressed him—and he groaned profoundly. He groaned when we carried him out to the car. He groaned even during the transfer from cart to wheelchair when Douglas and Clarence and I had brought him to emergency.

But once inside the shining building, his groaning took new meaning.

"I'm thirsty," he said.

"He's thirsty," I said to a nurse. "Would you get him a drink of water?"

"No," she said.

"What?"

"No," she said. "He can ingest nothing until his doctor is contacted."

"But, water—?"

"Nothing."

"Would you contact his doctor, then?"

185

"That will be done once he's in a room and by the unit nurse."

Arthur, slumped in his chair and hurting, said again, "I'm thirsty."

I said, "Well, then, can I wheel him to his room?"

"I'm sorry, no," the nurse said.

"Please," I said. "I'm his pastor. I'll take responsibility for him."

"In this place he is our responsibility, not yours," she said. "Be patient. An aide will get him up in good time."

O Arthur, forgive me not getting you water at home. Forgive us the "good time," twenty minutes waiting without a drink. Forgive us our rules, our irresponsibility!

Even in his room they took the time to wash him, to take away the stink.

"Please—call his doctor," I pleaded.

"We're about to change shifts," they said. "The next nurse will call his doctor, sir. All in good time."

So, Arthur, whose smell had triggered much discussion in the halls, finally did not stink. But Arthur still was thirsty. He said two things before I left.

He mumbled, "Bloody, but unbowed."

Poetry!

"Good, Arthur!" I praised him with all my might. Even a malicious wit was better than lethargy. Perhaps I could get him to shiv a nurse or two.

But he turned an eye toward me, gazing on this fool for the first time since we entered the hospital. "Bloody," he said, "and bowed."

He slept an hour. I sat, bedside, my face in my hands.

Then, suddenly, Arthur started awake and stared about himself. "Where am I? Where am I?" he called.

"In the hospital," I answered.

And he groaned horribly. "Why am I?"

In all my ministry I have wept uncontrollably for the death of only one parishioner.

The hospital knew no relative for Arthur Forte. Therefore, at 11 that same Saturday night, they telephoned me. Then I laid the receiver aside and cried as though it were my father dead. My father. Indeed, it was my father. Anger, failure, and want of a simple glass of water: I sat in the kitchen and cried.

But that failure has since nurtured a certain calm success. I do not suppose that Arthur consciously gave me the last year of his life, nor that he chose to teach me. Yet, by his mere being; by forcing me to take that life real, unsweetened, bare-naked, hurting, and critical; by demanding that I serve him altogether unrewarded; by wringing from me first mere gestures of loving and then the love itself—but a sacrificial love, a Christlike love, being love for one so indisputably unlovable—he did prepare me for my ministry.

My tears were my diploma, his death my benediction, and failure my ordination. For the Lord did not say, "Blessed are you if you know" or "teach" or "preach these things." He said, rather, "Blessed are you if you do them."

When, on the night on which He was betrayed, Jesus had washed His disciples' feet, He sat and said, "If I then, your Lord and Teacher, have washed your feet, you also ought to wash one another's feet. For I have given you an example that you also should do as I have done to you. Truly, truly I say to you, a servant is not greater than his master; nor is he who is sent greater than he who sent him. If you know these things," said Jesus, "blessed are you if you do them."

Again and again the Lord expanded on this theme: "Drink to the stinking is drink to Me!"

One might have learned by reading it . . . but it is a theme made real in experience alone, by doing it. And the first flush of that experience is, generally, a sense of failure, for this sort of ministry severely diminishes the minister, makes him insignificant, the merest servant, the least in the transaction. To feel so small is to feel somehow failing, weak, unable.

But there, right there, begins true servanthood: the disciple who has, despite himself, denied himself.

And then, for perhaps the first time, one is loving not out of his own bowels, merit, ability, superiority, but out of Christ: for he has discovered himself to be nothing and Christ everything.

In the terrible, terrible doing of ministry is the minister born. Curiously, the best teachers of that nascent minister are sometimes the neediest people, foul to touch, unworthy, ungiving, unlovely, yet haughty in demanding—and then miraculously receiving—love. These poor, forever with us, are our riches.

Arthur, my father, my father! So seeming empty your death, it was not empty at all. There is no monument above your pauper's grave—but here, it is here in me and in my ministry. However could I make little of the godly wonder that I love you?

FATHER ZOSSIMA'S BROTHER

Fyodor Dostoevsky

As a young intellectual, Dostoevsky was arrested in czarist Russia for openly discussing French socialist theories. After a last minute reprieve from a firing squad, he was sentenced to four years hard labor in Siberia. While imprisoned, his reading was limited to the Bible, and this study convinced him to forsake atheism and embrace Christianity. Though Dostoevsky's writings became increasingly popular in Russia, he lived in chronic poverty for most of his life.

Dostoevsky treasured his faith in Christ and this is reflected in his writings, especially his masterpiece, Brothers Karamazov. *The following excerpt is taken from this novel, where Dostoevsky portrays brothers who are starkly different in their outlook and worldview. One minor character is named Father Zossima, a godly monk who, as he is dying, recalls how his older brother rejected a bitter agnosticism and came to faith in Christ.*

Beloved fathers and teachers, I was born in a distant province in the north, in the town of V. My father was a gentleman by birth, but of no great consequence or position. He died when I was only two years old, and I don't remember him at all. He left my mother a small house built of wood, and a fortune—not large, but sufficient to keep her and her children in comfort.

There were two of us, my elder brother Markel and I. He was eight years older than I, and of hasty, irritable temperament, yet kind-hearted and never teasing. He was remarkably silent, especially at home with me, our mother, and the servants. He did well at school, but did not get on with his schoolfellows, though he never fought—at least so my mother has told me.

Six months before his death, when he was seventeen, Markel made friends with a political exile who had been banished from Moscow to our town for freethinking. The exile led a solitary existence there, and was a good scholar who had gained distinction in the university. Something made him take a fancy to Markel, so he used to ask my brother to see him. Markel would spend whole evenings with this man during that winter, until one day the exile was summoned to return to Petersburg and resume his post. This was at his own request, as he had powerful friends.

But the "freethinking" influence stuck with Markel, for it was the beginning of Lent and he would not fast. He was rude and laughed at it. "That's all silly twaddle and there is no God," he said, horrifying my mother, the servants, and me too. For though I was only nine, I was aghast at hearing such words.

In the sixth week in Lent, my brother, who was never strong and had a tendency for consumption, took ill. He was tall, but thin and delicate-looking, and of a very pleasing countenance. I suppose he caught cold. Anyway the doctor who came soon whispered that it was galloping consumption, and that Markel would not live through the spring. My mother began to weep privately. Careful not to alarm my brother, she entreated him to go to church, to confess, and to take the sacrament, as he still was able to move about. This made him angry, and he said something profane about the church.

He grew thoughtful, however. He guessed at once that he was seriously ill, and that this was why our mother had begged him to confess and take the sacrament. He had been aware for a long time that he was far from well, and had a year before coolly observed at dinner to our mother and me, "My life won't be long among you. I may not live another year," which seemed now like a prophecy.

189

So three days passed when Holy Week came. That Tuesday morning my brother began going to church. "I am doing this simply for your sake, mother, to please and comfort you," he said.

My mother wept with joy and grief. *But,* she worried, *his end must be near if there's such a change in him.*

Indeed, Markel was not able to go to church long. He took to his bed and had to confess and take the sacrament at home.

It was a late Easter and the days were bright, fine, and full of fragrance. I remember how Markel coughed all night and slept badly. But in the morning he dressed and tried to sit up in an armchair. That's how I remember him most vividly: sitting, sweet and gentle, smiling, his face bright and joyous in spite of the illness. A marvelous change passed over him, and his spirit seemed transformed.

The old nurse would come in and say, "Let me light the lamp before the holy image, my dear."

Once he would not have allowed it and would have blown it out. Now, however, he would say, "Light it, light it, dear. I was a wretch to have prevented you doing it. You are praying when you light the lamp, and I am praying when I rejoice seeing you. We are praying to the same God."

Markel's words seemed strange to us, and mother would go to her room and weep, but when she went to him, she wiped her eyes and looked cheerful.

"Mother, don't weep, darling," he would say. "I've long to live yet, long to rejoice with you, and life is glad and joyful."

"Ah, dear boy, how can you talk of joy when you lie feverish at night, coughing as though you would tear yourself to pieces."

"Don't cry, Mother," he would answer. "Life is paradise and we are all in paradise, but don't see it. If we would, we should have heaven on earth the next day."

Everyone wondered at his words. He spoke so strangely and positively, and we were all touched and wept.

When friends came to see us, he would say to them, "Dear ones, what have I done that you should love me so? How can you love anyone like me? And how was it I did not know—I did not appreciate it before?"

When the servants came in to him he would say continually, "Dear, kind people, why are you doing so much for me? Do I deserve to be waited on? If it were God's will for me to live, I would wait on you, for all men should wait on one another."

Mother shook her head as she listened. "My darling, it's your illness that makes you talk like that."

"Mother, darling," he would say, "there must be servants and masters, but, if so, I will be the servant of my servants, the same as they are to me. And another thing, Mother, every one of us has sinned against all men, and I more than any."

Mother positively smiled at that, smiled through her tears. "Why, how could you have sinned against all men more than all? Robbers and murderers have done that, but what sin have you committed yet, that you hold yourself more guilty than all?"

"Mother, little heart of mine," he said (he had begun using such strange caressing words at that time), "my joy, believe me, everyone is really responsible to all men, for all men, and for everything. I don't know how to explain it to you, but I feel it so—painfully even. And how is it we went on then living, getting angry and not knowing?"

So he would get up every day, more and more sweet and full of love. Then the doctor came.

"Well, doctor, have I another day in this world?" Markel would ask, joking.

"You'll live many days yet," the doctor would answer, "and months and years too."

"Months and years!" Markel would exclaim. "Why reckon the days? One day is enough for a man to know all happiness. My dear ones, why do we quarrel, try to outshine each other, and keep grudges against each other? Let's go straight into the garden, walk and play there—love, appreciate, kiss each other, and glorify life."

"Your son cannot last long," the doctor then whispered to my mother, as she accompanied him to the door. "The disease is affecting his brain."

The windows of Markel's room looked out into the garden—a shady one, with old trees coming into bud. The first birds of spring were flitting in the branches, chirruping and singing at the windows. Looking at them and admiring them, Markel suddenly began begging their forgiveness too.

"Birds of heaven, happy birds, forgive me, for I have sinned against you."

None of us could understand at the time, but he shed tears of joy.

"Yes," he said, "there was such a glory of God all about me—birds, trees, meadows, sky—only I lived in shame and dishonored it all and did not notice the beauty and glory."

"You take too many sins on yourself," Mother used to say, weeping.

"Mother, darling, it's for joy, not for grief I am crying. Though I can't explain it to you, I like to humble myself before them, for I don't know how to love them enough. If I have sinned against every one, yet all forgive me, that's heaven. So am I not in heaven now?"

Now there is a great deal more I don't remember, but once when I went into his room, there was no one else there. It was a bright evening. The sun was setting, lighting up the whole room. Markel beckoned me and I went to him. He put his hands on my shoulders and looked into my face tenderly, lovingly. He said nothing for a minute, only looked at me like that.

"Well," he said, "run and play now, enjoy life for me too."

I went out then to run and play, and many times in my life afterwards I remembered even with tears how he told me to enjoy life for him too. There were many other marvelous and beautiful sayings of his, though we did not understand them at the time.

My brother died the third week after Easter, fully conscious, though he could not talk. He looked happy, his eyes beamed and sought us; he smiled at us and beckoned us.

There was a great deal of talk, even in the town, about his death. I was impressed by all this at the time, but not too much (though I cried a great deal at his funeral) as I was young then, a child. Still, a lasting impression, a hidden feeling of it all, has remained in my heart, ready to rise up and respond when the time came.

THE EXECUTIONER

Ruth Bell Graham

Ruth Bell Graham, the daughter of missionaries, is well qualified to write a story about world missions. She's also extremely qualified as a writer. From her busy pen have come autobiographical works, children's stories, books of poetry, and more. Though some may know her as the wife of Billy Graham, she has more than distinguished herself independently in ministry.

In this story, Ruth tells of another Graham whom God used to begin a great spiritual harvest following the Boxer Rebellion.

In 1900 in China, the Boxer Rebellion erupted with the blessing of the Dowager Empress, Tz'u-his.

Orders went out from the American Consul that all missionaries were to proceed quickly to places of safety. As many as possible were to go to Shanghai or Peking. The rest were to go to their provincial capitals and seek political asylum from the governor of the province until things calmed.

The Reverend James R. Graham hurried his wife, Sophie, and their three children down to Shanghai. There, daily reports arrived of a missionary killed here, a family there, and some faithful Chinese Christians

193

brutally murdered by the Boxers in another town. The missionaries, gathered in safety, lived from report to report with heavy hearts.

Graham wondered about his friend of the Bible Society, Mr. Whitehouse and his young bride of two weeks. They had been in Shansi Province. Were they safe?

Then came the blackest day of all. Between forty-six and one hundred missionaries from the northern provinces had sought refuge in the governor's courtyard at the provincial capital, Taiyuanfu in Shansi. Not knowing the governor was a leader of the Boxer uprising, they had all been executed.

The question "why?" trembled on the lips of more than one brave missionary. The need had been so great, and now this waste. Numb with grief they awaited details. But the only news was filtered by word of mouth from someone who had been told by someone, who had been told by someone . . .

Weeks dragged past. Gradually the fury of the storm spent itself, and in the grim stillness that followed, Graham returned alone to Tsingkiang, nearly three hundred miles north on the Grand Canal, to see if it was safe enough for the others to return.

Shortly after his arrival Graham had a visitor. Few stopped to notice the stranger making his way down the narrow streets, carefully avoiding the puddles. It was night and lamps had been lit in the little shops. Rickshaws and wheelbarrows, dogs and people were everywhere. At the little tea shop overlooking the canal, the visitor stopped to inquire his way. Was there a foreigner in the town? No. He with his family had moved to Shanghai when the trouble broke out.

Someone spoke up. The foreigner had returned a few days ago, alone. Where did he live? Up the street a little way—turn here, turn there. At the end of the little alley is a gate. Bang loudly. The gateman is deaf. The stranger thanked them briefly, and those in the tea shop speculated after he had gone: from the north, by his speech, most likely. Then they went back to sucking in their boiling tea.

"Coming," mumbled the gateman, pulling on his jacket and shuffling out of his room. Then louder, as the knocking continued insistently, "Coming! Coming! Who is it?"

He received no reply. An imperious voice demanded, "Open the gate!" He slid back the heavy wooden bolt and peered through the crack. "Who is it?"

"Is the foreigner at home?"

"Wait a minute . . ."

Bolting the door in the stranger's face, the gateman hurried within.

"I do not like his looks. He has an evil face," he informed the missionary. "I do not like his way. He is from the north. If you tell me, I will say it is late and you do not wish to be disturbed."

"No," the missionary said. "Let him in and pour some tea."

Grumbling, the gateman obeyed. Shortly, he ushered the stranger into the simple living quarters. He was an ordinary-looking man with an extraordinarily hard face. In spite of his authoritative bearing, he appeared nervous. The preliminary greetings over, he inquired what lay behind the door to the right. "The bedroom," replied the missionary.

"What lies in there?" he asked, pointing his chin to the adjoining door.

"The kitchen."

"What is in there?" his chin jerked toward the next door.

"Just a minute," replied the missionary, beginning to feel irritated. "This is my home and you are my guest. It is none of your affair what lies beyond these doors."

Hastily the stranger apologized for his rudeness, adding that he was only wanting to make sure they were alone as he had some business of a very private nature to discuss.

Assured they were absolutely alone, he proceeded.

"Do you remember the foreigners who sought protection at Taiyuanfu with Yu Hsien, Governor of the Shansi Province?"

"I have heard."

"You have heard." The stranger sat silent a few minutes. "I was there," he added.

"You saw them die?"

"I am captain of Yu Hsien's bodyguard. I was in charge."

"You were responsible?" But something in the man's face—so hard, so hopeless—stopped him. He could have told him what he thought. He could have lashed out at him with all the grief and indignation in him. But something sealed his lips and kept him silently waiting for the captain to proceed.

"I was following instruction," he continued. "To me, at the time, it was nothing. I am a man accustomed to killing. Another life—ten, twenty, one hundred. It was nothing.

"Yu Hsien, Governor of the Shansi Province—he does not like foreigners. He does not like them nor their ways, nor their doctrine. When they began to gather at this door asking for protection in the name of their government, his soul rankled within him. 'Protection? I can only protect you by putting you in the prison,' he replied harshly.

"So he put them in prison. For several days he kept them there while his hatred grew. Then he called me in and gave me my orders. I am a man trained to obey, and I am a man accustomed to killing. These foreigners—I cared not one way or the other."

The missionary flinched and shook his head.

"We led them out into the prison courtyard and lined them up. Yu Hsien was there and berated them loudly and angrily. 'I do not like you foreigners,' he shouted. 'I do not like you, or your ways or your foreign teaching.' Then he told them they were all to be killed."

The stranger paused again—struggling for words. The missionary was sitting forward, scarcely breathing. "Go on. Go on," he whispered. "What happened next?"

"Then happened the strangest sight I have ever witnessed. There was no fear. Husbands and wives turned and kissed one another. When the little children, sensing something terrible about to happen, began to cry, their parents put their arms about them and spoke to them of 'Yiesu,' pointing up toward the heavens and smiling.

"Then they turned to face their executioners, calmly as though this thing did not concern them. They began singing, and singing they died. When I saw how they faced death," he hurried on, "I knew this 'Yiesu' of whom they spoke was truly God.

"But tell me. Can God forgive my so-great sin?"

The missionary thought of his close friend, Whitehouse, and his bride of a few weeks, who had been among those killed. He thought of others and felt the anger.

The captain was speaking again. "I am at present on my way escorting Yu Hsien's wife to the northeast. Tonight we rest in this city. Tomorrow we continue our journey. I sought you out, foreigner, to ask you—is there nothing, nothing I might do to atone for my wrong? Is there nothing?"

A hand was on the missionary's heart as he thought to himself: *Can God forgive? What of Christ on the cross praying, "Father, forgive"? What of Saul of Tarsus who kept the clothes of those who stoned young Stephen and persecuted those of the Way beyond measure? What of him?*

The officer sat silent, waiting. The missionary reached for his worn Chinese Bible. "Listen," he found himself saying, "our God, whom we serve, is a merciful God. True, your sin was great. Very great. But His mercy is even greater. This Yiesu is His Son who came to earth to die for sinners like you. I, too, am a sinner. All men are sinners. And because Yiesu died for you—for this Son's sake—God can forgive you."

The captain listened closely. Foreign words these, to a mind schooled to hate and kill, but not to forgive. He drank in every strange word. "Love . . . Forgiveness . . . Life." He listened. The little he could understand, he accepted simply, asking an occasional question and again listening closely.

It was late when the missionary escorted the captain to the gate and bowed farewell. It was the last he saw or heard of him.

The missionary sat for a long while thinking. Fresh in his mind were hundreds of new graves strewn across China like wheat sown at random. No more the anguished, "Lord, why this great waste?"

The harvest had begun.

OUR MYSTERIOUS PASSENGER

Ira Spector

Ira Spector is the author of the novel Last Chance *as well as other writings. In "Our Mysterious Passenger," Spector reveals how links in a chain prove kindness begets kindness, and how the good we do often comes back to us, sometimes in mysterious ways.*

Life is short and we have never too much time for gladdening the hearts of those who are travelling the dark journey with us. Oh be swift to love, make haste to be kind.

Henri Frederic Amiel

The midday sun beat down on my wife, Barbara, and me as we walked across the tarmac to the terminal at Loreto International Airport on Mexico's Baja peninsula. We were flying our single-engine plane home to Calexico, California, later that day, ending a week's vacation.

A tall man stood near the terminal, nervously dabbing at his face and neck with a handkerchief. I had noticed him earlier, watching us as we readied our plane.

Suddenly he approached, blocking the doorway. He was in his forties and looked as if he had spent the night in the terminal. "Excuse me," he said, removing his Panama hat. "Can you help me out? I'm an American and I got bumped from the flight to Los Angeles. I need to catch my connecting flight to Florida."

Trying to muster an authoritative tone, I said, "I'm sorry, but I've already filed my flight plan with the airport commandant. It only allows me to take my wife out of the country. Why don't you get a later flight?"

"There isn't another flight until tomorrow, and I've got to leave today," he said.

"Well, we're only going to Calexico, at the border."

"That's OK," the stranger said. "Let's go to the commandant's office and ask if I can leave with you." He turned to enter the building.

"Wait a minute," I said uneasily. "I don't have an oxygen mask for you, and we're flying at 14,500 feet. You'd feel altitude sickness."

"That's OK. I'm in good shape."

"And there's no room for additional luggage," I added, glancing at his suitcase. "The plane's full."

"I'll hold the bag in my lap."

At this point Barbara asked, "Would you excuse us for a second? I need to talk to my husband."

"Sure." The stranger stood aside to let us enter the terminal. Barbara, a trial lawyer and the voice of reason in the family, whispered, "Are you crazy? You want to risk our lives by giving a ride to some strange person who could be a fugitive or a terrorist?" Her voice was rising. "What if he hijacks us?"

"Something tells me he's legitimate," I said. "Maybe it's payback time." I was thinking of when Barbara and I had flown to Mexico ten years earlier. We had ridden a little motorcycle into the desert and lost our way. We were sweaty, sunburned, and covered with dust when we finally made it into a town. We met some American pilots and asked if they could take us to our plane, but they walked away. Finally, some California college students got us back to our plane.

"Remember being down here years ago?" I asked. "Let's go to the commandant's office and see what he says. I doubt he'll allow him to go with us, but I'd feel better if we at least asked."

The commandant listened to the stranger's story, glanced at his tickets and quickly changed our passenger registry from a "1" to a "2." The entire transaction took about one minute.

Now I had to take the stranger with us. Not knowing what else to do, I wandered off in the direction of our plane. Barbara walked beside me, glaring straight ahead. To break the tension I turned to the stranger following us and asked his name. "Virgil," he said.

Cruising northwesterly at 14,500 feet, Barbara and I sat in silence, breathing oxygen from our masks. I looked back at Virgil, seated behind her. Strangely, the lack of supplemental oxygen didn't seem to bother him. He nodded back at me and smiled. I was beginning to think things might work out. The drone of the engine had a soothing effect, and an unusually strong tail wind promised to put us in Calexico well ahead of schedule. Virgil's chances of making it to Los Angeles were improving by the minute. Yes, maybe things would work out after all.

Barbara didn't necessarily agree. She sat, arms folded across her chest, head hunched down, as if she expected a hatchet blow from behind.

Just north of the border, I became more concerned with the weather than with Virgil. The ride grew turbulent, with wind gusts causing our plane, a Mooney 231, to rattle.

Suddenly, we plunged 100 feet in a downdraft. Barbara glanced nervously at me. The radio warned of strong, gusting winds with blowing dust and sand throughout California's Imperial Valley. Visual flight was not recommended.

Looking toward Calexico, I could see a strange, dark brown cloud spanning the horizon. A sandstorm! In my twenty-three years of flying, I had never witnessed anything like it.

Calexico is a small field unequipped for instrument approaches. If we couldn't land visually, our depleted fuel and the increasingly choppy ride would mean flying back to Mexicali on the Mexican side of the border. I shivered as I imagined the air filter clogging up and the engine quitting.

Even if we made it, our unexpected arrival at Mexicali would surely get the attention of some savvy border official. We could be held up for days while our passenger, whom we knew nothing about, was being investigated. Virgil wasn't the only one who had to get back to work.

Whack! Turbulent air jolted me out of my musings, causing the plane to pitch up. Whap! Now the nose pitched down, spilling my maps on the floor. I decided that we were going to Mexicali and probably to jail.

Just as I retrieved the maps from the floor, Barbara exclaimed, "I see Calexico!"

There it was, only five miles in front of us. The sandstorm was swirling all around the airport, but the runway was in the clear. I banked the plane toward the runway, praying that the hole over the airport would remain open a bit longer. As I eased into our final turn, we encountered wind shear, setting off a wail from the stall-warning alarm. I jockeyed the throttle back and forth. Barbara was frightened, yet her look told me: *You can do it.*

Suddenly the air smoothed out, and we were down. As we turned off the runway, the sandstorm closed in around us. In all my years of flying, this was my closest call.

I looked back at Virgil, and couldn't believe how calm he was. He was sitting there reading, and of all things, he was reading a Bible. He smiled as he put it away.

Inside Calexico's airport, Barbara sipped coffee and watched the sand blowing across the landscape. Finally she said, "Well, what do you make of him?" I still wasn't sure.

Just then Virgil came to the table. I asked him about his prospects for getting to Los Angeles. People weren't even driving in this weather.

"I found a commuter flight leaving for Imperial Valley Airport, a few miles from here. Unfortunately, they don't know when it will take off. On top of that, the flight is sold out. But just in case, I called a cab. Maybe someone will cancel."

I knew the time had come to learn more about this stranger. "What were you doing in Loreto?" I asked.

Virgil stared into his coffee cup. "My wife and I were in a terrible accident in Loreto ten years ago. We were with another couple on vacation, touring Baja in a rented motor home. The other couple was in the front, and we were in the back. Suddenly the right tire went off the road, and we rolled down an embankment. We were carrying 160 gallons of fuel. The butane tank for the stove exploded. There was a horrible fire. I managed to escape out the back window, and my wife squeezed through the door. The other couple was trapped inside, screaming for help. I tried to pull them out the front window, but I couldn't. It was too late.

"My wife and I were burned pretty badly," he continued, "and my spleen had ruptured. We were several miles from Loreto. We crawled up the embankment to try and flag down someone to help us. Finally a Mexican fellow pulled over and rushed us to Loreto's health center. The staff saved our lives, but the clinic was poorly equipped. The operating table looked like an old ironing board. I spent the night in a dental chair because there was no bed. We were transferred to a burn unit in California; I vowed that I would come back and give the clinic money to buy proper equipment and medical supplies."

"And your wife?" I asked.

"She had skin grafts and she's doing fine. I guess I buried the whole experience in the back of my mind. I'm starting my own business—a boat sales company. I hadn't thought about the accident until last Saturday."

Virgil took a deep breath. "I awoke with a start. Something told me I needed to act on that vow I made ten years ago. I arrived in Loreto yesterday. The health center was still in bad shape—the paint was peeling, the bedsheets were torn, and broken windows were covered with tinfoil. I wrote them a check. It wasn't a large sum, but they were extremely grateful. You should have seen the looks on their faces."

"I'll bet," I said.

"This morning, the flight to Los Angeles was full, and I was left stranded. Then I saw you folks."

We sat in silence for a moment. Then a man approached our table. It was the cab driver Virgil had called, so Virgil hurriedly picked up his hat and bag. "Thanks again, folks," he said.

"Wait." I handed Virgil a business card. "Let us know if you make it aboard that flight."

Still thinking about Virgil, Barbara and I returned home and settled into routine. Virgil had reminded us that there were links in a growing chain of kindness, and each kindness you do always comes back to you, sometimes in mysterious ways. So it was no surprise when one day we received a letter from Virgil, written on the letterhead of his boat sales company:

Just a short note to say thanks once again. I made my flight out of Imperial Valley. The plane was loading as I arrived at the gate. I got the last seat.
Love, Virgil

Tim

Philip Gulley

Once a Quaker minister, Philip Gulley began writing essays about lessons learned in his life and his experiences among a small body of country parishioners. After newscaster Paul Harvey read some of Gulley's work on his daily broadcast, people began asking to hear more from this inexperienced young writer. As a result of this demand several books of short stories have been published, including Front Porch Tales, *out of which this selection was drawn. It's a tale where Gulley explains the inner struggle he experienced when his closest childhood friend was killed by a drunk driver.*

Why do the wicked live on, growing old and increasing in power? . . . One man dies in full vigor, completely secure and at ease, his body well nourished, his bones rich with marrow. Another man dies in bitterness of soul, never having enjoyed anything good.

Job 21:7, 23–25

I first met Tim in the second grade, where we sat together in Mrs. Worrel's class. We became friends when we discovered no other group

203

would have us. We weren't athletic enough to be jocks. The girls didn't like us because we looked funny. Even the Scouts, who had pledged solemnly to be kind and charitable, steered clear of us.

Tim lived on a farm. I lived in town. When we hit fourth grade, our parents let us ride our bikes back and forth to each other's houses. Our social life increased exponentially. On Fridays Tim would ride in to my house to spend the night. We'd go to the movies up at the Royal Rathole. The jocks would sit near the back and neck with the girls, and we'd sit behind them and make kissing noises.

On Saturdays I'd ride my Schwinn Varsity out to Tim's, and we'd stay up late to watch *Planet of the Apes*. His mom was a night-shift nurse at the county hospital. She'd bring us a tray of Cokes and Pringles, give us both a good-night kiss, and head in to work. She was real nice. A lot of mothers don't like having extra kids around, but she never seemed to mind and I always felt welcome. I'm going to try and remember that when my boys start bringing their friends home.

When Tim and I were in the eighth grade, I invited a girl named Amy to the spring dance. Of course, Tim came along. We wore plaid leisure suits and drank a lot of punch. Amy spent most of her time in the bathroom.

Then we went to high school. We took all the same classes so we could be together. We were both girl crazy. Unfortunately, our feelings weren't reciprocated. The prettiest girl in the school—a cheerleader— was named Laura, and Tim loved her. She was a friend of my brother's, a jock, so I asked her for her picture. She signed it "to someone I really admire." I think it's because she didn't remember my name. I sold it to Tim for two bucks. Friendship had its limits.

When we graduated from high school, we got jobs. I worked in an office for an electric utility; Tim was a mechanic at Logan's Mobil. I'd stop by every morning on my way to work for a dollar's worth of gas and conversation. Then at night we'd get in his car and drive to McDonald's in the next town over.

Flush with money from our jobs, we decided to buy motorcycles. Tim bought one that had a custom paint job. It didn't run well, but it looked good. We'd ride every Sunday afternoon and most nights. A lot of times we'd end up at the Dairy Queen, where we'd sit on our bikes and talk about stuff that doesn't seem too important now, and was incredibly so then.

One night, at 2 A.M., I got a phone call from the sheriff's chaplain, Joe Stump. He told me that my best friend since Mrs. Worrel's second grade class had been hit by a drunken driver and was dead. They were afraid I had been hit too, so they were calling to check on me.

Tim's funeral was three days later. I was a pallbearer and sat in the front row. His parents sat across from me. His mother was a knot of grief; his dad was bent and weighed. We buried him at the South Cemetery. All I remember now is the crying.

There are a lot of things about Tim I've forgotten. I do remember that he liked *The Dukes of Hazzard* and that he was taking a correspondence course on how to be a diesel mechanic. I remember his laugh. And I remember that in the fourteen years of our friendship, I never once heard him ridicule anyone.

When Tim died a lot of people took it upon themselves to explain to me why it happened. I would listen and smile and nod my head, mostly so they'd go away and leave me alone.

There are some things about this life I'll never understand. One of them is why a drunken driver dies of old age when a never-hurt-a-flea young man barely sees twenty. Someday I'm going to see God face to face. And when I do, I'm going to ask Him why that is.

THE VOLUNTEER AT AUSCHWITZ

Charles Colson

During the Second World War, several million people were murdered at the Nazi concentration camp at Auschwitz and the neighboring camp of Treblinka in central Poland. Countless acts of faith and bravery occurred amid the horror. This is one of the stories as told to the founder of Prison Fellowship, one of America's largest ministries bringing the gospel to the incarcerated.

Maximilian Kolbe was forty-five years old in the early autumn of 1939 when the Nazis invaded his homeland. He was a Polish friar in Niepkalanow, a village near Warsaw, where 762 priests and lay brothers lived in the largest friary in the world. Father Kolbe presided over Niepkalanow with a combination of industry, joy, love, and humor that made him beloved by the plainspoken brethren there.

In his simple room he sat each morning at a pigeonhole desk, a large globe before him, praying over the world. He did so tortured by the fact that a pale man with arresting blue eyes and a terrifying power of manipulation had whipped the people of Germany into a frenzy. Whole nations had already fallen to the evil Adolf Hitler and his Nazis.

"An atrocious conflict is brewing," Father Kolbe told a group of friars one day after he had finished prayers. "We do not know what will develop. In our beloved Poland, we must expect the worst." Father Kolbe was right. His country was next.

On September 1, 1939, the Nazi blitzkrieg broke over Poland. Within several weeks a group of Germans arrived at Niepkalanow on motorcycles and arrested Father Kolbe and all but two of his friars who had remained behind. They were loaded on trucks, then into livestock wagons, and two days later arrived at Amtitz, a prison camp.

Conditions were horrible, but not horrific. Prisoners were hungry, but no one died of starvation. Strangely, within a few weeks the brothers were released from prison. Back at the friary they found the buildings vandalized and the Nazis in control, using the facility as a deportation camp for political prisoners, refugees, and Jews.

The situation was an opportunity for ministry, and Father Kolbe took advantage of it, helping the sick and comforting the fearful.

While Kolbe and the friars used their time to serve others, the Nazis used theirs to decide just how to impose their will on the rest of Europe. To Adolf Hitler the Jews and Slavic people were the *untermenschen,* or subhumans. Their cultures and cities were to be erased and their industry appropriated for Germany. On October 2, Hitler outlined a secret memorandum to Hans Frank, the governor general of Poland. In a few phrases he determined the grim outcome for millions: "The [ordinary] Poles are especially born for low labor . . . the Polish gentry must cease to exist . . . all representatives of the Polish intelligentsia are to be exterminated . . . There should be one master for the Poles—the Germans."

As for Poland's hundreds of thousands of priests?

"They will preach what we want them to preach," said Hitler's memo. "If any priest acts differently, we will make short work of him. The task of the priest is to keep the Poles quiet, stupid, and dull-witted."

Maximilian Kolbe was clearly a priest who would "act differently" from the Nazis' designs.

In early February 1941, the Polish underground smuggled word to Kolbe that his name was on a Gestapo list: He was about to be arrested. Kolbe knew what happened to loved ones of those who tried to elude the Nazi grasp: Their friends and colleagues were taken instead. He had no wife or children; his church was his family. He could not risk the loss of any of his brothers in Christ. So he stayed at Niepkalanow.

At nine o'clock on the morning of February 17, Father Kolbe was sitting at his pigeonhole desk, his eyes and prayers on the globe before him, when he heard the sound of heavy vehicles outside the thick panes of his green-painted windows. He knew it was the Nazis, but he remained at his desk. He would wait for them to come to him.

After being held in Nazi prisons for several months, Father Kolbe was found guilty of the crime of publishing unapproved materials and sentenced to Auschwitz. Upon his arrival at the camp in May 1941, an SS officer informed him that the life expectancy of priests there was about a month. Kolbe was assigned to the timber detail; he was to carry felled tree trunks from one place to another. Guards stood by to ensure that the exhausted prisoners did so at a quick trot.

Years of slim rations and overwork at Niepkalanow had already weakened Kolbe. Now, under the load of wood, he staggered and collapsed. Officers converged on him, kicking him with their shiny leather boots and beating him with their whips. He was stretched out on a pile of wood, dealt fifty lashes, then shoved into a ditch, covered with branches, and left for dead.

Later, having been picked up by some brave prisoners, he awoke in a camp hospital bed alongside several near-dead inmates. There, miraculously, he revived.

"No need to waste gas or a bullet on that one," chuckled one SS officer to another. "He'll be dead soon."

Kolbe was switched to other work and transferred to Barracks 14, where he continued to minister to fellow prisoners so tortured by hunger that they could not sleep.

By the end of July 1941, Auschwitz was working like a well-organized killing machine, and the Nazis congratulated themselves on their efficiency. The camp's five chimneys never stopped smoking. The stench was terrible, but the results were excellent: Eight thousand Jews could be stripped, their possessions appropriated for the Reich, and their bodies gassed and cremated—all in twenty-four hours. Every twenty-four hours.

About the only problem was the occasional prisoner from the work side of the camp who would figure out a way to escape. When these escapees were caught, as they usually were, they would be hanged with special nooses that slowly choked out their miserable lives—a grave warning to others who might be tempted to try.

Then one July night as the frogs and insects in the marshy land surrounding the camp began their evening chorus, the air suddenly was filled with the baying of dogs, the curses of soldiers, and the roar of motorcycles. A man had escaped from Barracks 14.

The next morning there was a peculiar tension as the ranks of phantom-like prisoners lined up for morning roll call in the central square, their eyes on the large gallows before them. But there was no condemned man standing there, his hands bound behind him, his face bloodied from blows and dog bites. That meant the prisoner had made it out of Auschwitz. And that meant death for some of those who remained.

After the roll call Camp Commandant Fritsch ordered the dismissal of all but Barracks 14. While the rest of the camp went about its duties, the prisoners from Barracks 14 stood motionless in line. They waited. Hours passed. The summer sun beat down. Some fainted and were dragged away. Some swayed in place but held on—until they were beaten down by the SS officers using the butts of their guns. Father Kolbe, by some miracle, stayed on his feet, his posture as straight as his resolve.

By evening roll call the commandant was ready to levy sentence. The other prisoners had returned from their day of slave labor; now he could make a lesson out of the fate of this miserable barracks.

Fritsch began to speak, the veins in his thick neck standing out with rage. "The fugitive has not been found," he screamed. "Ten of you will die for him in the starvation bunker. Next time, twenty will be condemned."

The rows of exhausted prisoners began to sway as they heard the sentence. The guards let them. Terror was part of their punishment.

The starvation bunker! Anything was better: death on the gallows, a bullet in the head at the Wall of Death, or even the gas in the chambers. All those were quick, even humane, compared to Nazi starvation, for they denied you water as well as food.

The prisoners had heard the stories from the starvation bunker in the basement of Barracks 11. They said the condemned didn't even look like human beings after a day or two. They frightened even the guards. Their throats turned to paper, their brains turned to fire, their intestines dried up and shriveled like dessicated worms.

Commandant Fritsch walked the rows of prisoners. When he stopped before a man, he would command in bad Polish, "Open your mouth! Put out your tongue! Show your teeth!" And so he went, choosing victims like horses.

His dreary assistant, Palitsch, followed behind. As Fritsch chose a man, Palitsch noted the number stamped on the prisoner's filthy shirt. The Nazis, as always, were methodical. Soon there were ten men—ten numbers neatly listed on the death roll. The chosen groaned, sweating with fear. "My poor wife," one man cried. "My poor children. What will they do?"

"Take off your shoes," the commandant barked at the ten men. This was one of his rituals. They must march to their deaths barefoot. A pile of twenty wooden clogs made a small heap at the front of the grassy square.

Suddenly there was a commotion in the ranks. A prisoner had broken out of line, calling for the commandant. It was unheard of to leave the ranks, let alone address a Nazi officer. It was cause for execution.

Fritsch had his hand on his revolver, as did the officers behind him. But he broke precedent. Instead of shooting the prisoner, he shouted at him.

"Halt! What does this Polish pig want of me?"

The prisoners gasped. It was their beloved Father Kolbe, the priest who shared his last crust, who comforted the dying, and nourished their souls. Not Father Kolbe! The frail priest spoke softly, even calmly, to the Nazi butcher. "I would like to die in place of one of the men you condemned."

Fritsch stared at the prisoner, No. 16670. He never considered them as individuals; they were just a gray blur. But he looked now. No. 16670 didn't appear to be insane.

"Why?" snapped the commandant.

Father Kolbe sensed the need for exacting diplomacy. The Nazis never reversed an order; he must not seem to be asking the commandant to do so. Kolbe knew the Nazi dictum of destruction: the weak and elderly first. He would play on this well-ingrained principle.

"I am an old man, sir, and good for nothing. My life will serve no purpose."

His ploy triggered the response Kolbe wanted. "In whose place do you want to die?" asked Fritsch.

210

"For that one," Kolbe responded, pointing to the weeping prisoner who had bemoaned his wife and children.

Fritsch glanced at the weeping prisoner. He did look stronger than this tattered No. 16670 before him. For the first and last time, the commandant looked Kolbe in the eye. "Who are you?" he asked.

The prisoner looked back at him, a strange fire in his dark eyes. "I am a priest."

"*Ein Pfaffe!*" the commandant snorted. He looked at his assistant and nodded. Palitsch drew a line through No. 5659 and wrote down No. 16670. Kolbe's place on the death ledger was set.

Father Kolbe bent down to take off his clogs, then joined the group to be marched to Barracks 11. As he did so, No. 5659 passed by him at a distance—and on the man's face was an expression so astonished that it had not yet become gratitude.

But Kolbe wasn't looking for gratitude. If he was to lay down his life for another, the fulfillment had to be in the act of obedience itself. The joy must be found in submitting his small will to that of one more grand.

As the condemned men entered Barracks 11, guards roughly pushed them down the stairs to the basement.

"Remove your clothes," shouted an officer. *Christ died on the cross naked*, Father Kolbe thought as he took off his pants and thin shirt. *It is only fitting that I suffer as He suffered.*

In the basement the ten men were herded into a dark, windowless cell.

"You will dry up like tulips," sneered one jailer. Then he swung shut the heavy door.

As the hours and days passed, however, the camp became aware of something extraordinary happening in that death cell. Past prisoners had spent their dying days howling, attacking one another, and clawing the walls in a frenzy of despair.

But now those outside the death box heard the faint sounds of singing. This time the prisoners had someone to gently lead them through the shadows of the valley of death, pointing them to the Great Shepherd. Perhaps for that reason Father Kolbe was the last to die.

On August 14, 1941, there were four prisoners still alive in the bunker, and it was needed for new occupants. A German doctor named Boch descended the steps of Barracks 11, four syringes in his hand. Several SS troopers and a prisoner named Brono Borgowiec (who would survive Auschwitz) were with him—the former to observe, and the latter to carry out the bodies.

211

When they swung the bunker door open, there, in the light of a flashlight, they saw Father Maximilian Kolbe, a living skeleton, propped against one wall. His head was inclined a bit to the left. He had the ghost of a smile on his lips and his eyes were wide open, fixed on some faraway vision. He did not move.

The other three prisoners on the floor were unconscious but alive. The doctor took care of them first: a jab of the needle into the bony left arm, the push of the piston in the syringe. It seemed a waste of the drug, but he had his orders. Then he approached No. 16670 and repeated the action.

In a moment Father Kolbe was dead.

ONLY THE BEGINNING

Mark Littleton

Have you ever imagined, as a Christian, what it will be like when you encounter Christ face to face and he evaluates the way you've invested your life? In this story, Mark Littleton seeks to do just that. He pictures himself before Christ, and hypothesizes what might be said of an ordinary believer like him who hardly realized what importance even his small efforts for God's kingdom would take in light of eternity.

I remembered everything. We met Him in the air, as it had been written. At the time it had seemed impossible that such a prophecy could be fulfilled so exactly. But once it happened everything became clear—in an instant, as it had been written, nothing left to chance or misinterpretation.

Now we were to stand before Him. This moment, this day, had always seemed so distant, so far away. But now here I was. All of us, gathered. White robes like light. Faces beautiful and young. Everyone delighted, ebullient, secure.

But I was afraid. What would He say about me? What could He say?

All my life I'd known the words. "He will repay everyone according to his deeds." "We must all stand before the judgment seat." "He will recompense us for our deeds in the body, according to what we have done, whether good or bad."

I'd always thought . . .

What does it matter what I'd thought? This was reality. The real thing. There was no hiding now, no going back, no changes to make.

I knew very well what would happen, or, should I say, could happen. That passage in Corinthians—he shall escape "as through fire." That was me. I might as well not try to hide it. Everything would be burned up, nothing left worthy of reward.

After all, what is a salesman? What is the machinery industry? What is being a husband and father? Anybody can do those things.

But deep down I wished I'd done something grand, like those early fathers. "The golden-throated one." Who was he? Chrysostom? Or one of the great monks. Or Augustine, Thomas Aquinas, Luther, Calvin, Zwingli, Wesley, Whitefield, Spurgeon. I had heard about them. Pastors I had sat under referred to them all the time. Joan of Arc, Tyndale, Hus—history blazed with them like great bolts of lightning upon the pages of writ.

Next to them, who was I?

I tried not to feel sorry for myself. In fact, I couldn't. All I could feel was a vague sense of regret. At one time I had sensed a call, at least I thought I had. But circumstances had prevented . . .

No, I couldn't even use that excuse. Things just never had worked out the way I'd hoped. I had been afraid mainly, and young. Then middle-aged. Then old. Then too late.

I tried to do things. But I hadn't been good at them. Teaching in the Sunday school, what good was that? None of my students went on to be great pastors or teachers. At least none that I knew.

Serving on the deacon board? I had been asked several times. But I'd never quite qualified. Who was I? Just a salesman. I knew I did things I didn't like. I always confessed them and tried to make them right. But it never endeared me to the board of deacons.

Please understand. I'm not trying to make you feel sorry for me. I just didn't see what I'd amounted to. I did decent work. I had tried to be honest. When I hedged, I always tried to make it right. I sold a good product: printing machinery. I advanced in my company. I gave people a fair shake.

But who didn't try to do that? It had little to do with being a Christian. I guess in a way I'd done it just to make sure nothing came back to me. In that industry, things had a way of hitting you over the head a year to two down the road, if you weren't straight with people. But there had been lots of salespeople who had nothing to do with Jesus who had done the same. What did that merit?

I hadn't been anything but a very average guy. Man, I hated saying it. It sounded so stupid. "Pretty average guy." Maybe "less than average" was a better description.

But here it was now. The judgment. Everything accounted for. Standing before Him. What was I supposed to say: "Hey, I can't wait till You make me Your right-hand man, Lord?" I didn't even lead many people to Christ. I could count on my left hand the number of people I knew that had stuck with Him.

That bothered me a lot too. I had passed out tracts at times. I told people what I believed. I "witnessed," as we had called it in my age. But I never saw much fruit. Certainly not the "thirty-fold, sixty-fold, or one-hundred-fold" that Jesus spoke about. I could remember one, maybe two folks. But I'd lost touch with them. I didn't even know where they ended up.

I was beginning to feel worse and worse. Even with a new body and a sense of perfection, I felt a little sick. What was He going to say? "Glad to have you here, Mr. Colter. Have a good eternity!"

How much could He sugarcoat a below-average life? Well, maybe it hadn't been below average. Was that mock humility? I mean, I had a good life. A decent life. I had enjoyed it—enjoyed things like church, worship, visiting people, and trying to teach. I had even liked reading the Bible and praying. I wasn't any Holy Joe, but I did have something of a spiritual walk, as we called it.

In a way, though, I almost wished He simply would pass over me, like when the whole team wins the trophy, but no one is singled out for special mention. Now all I really hoped for were no reprimands, no angry exposures.

But everyone would have a chance to stand up here.

It was almost funny. Remember how we used to try to "say something nice" about someone? I remember my dad telling us kids, "If you don't have something good to say, don't say anything." A lot of times, though, you'd exaggerate or make up something so a friend would feel good, even though you knew what you said was only half true.

But I knew He wouldn't do that. He was holy, perfect, just. He couldn't make up things about me or anyone else just to make us feel good. Doing that always had a negative kickback anyway. Sooner or later you realized it was all just flattery, and you lost respect for the person who did it. I knew one thing: He wouldn't make me lose respect for Him.

What would He come up with? Frankly, I couldn't think of a thing. I never had got my name in the paper, except once as a Little League manager of my son's team. I never wrote a book, sang a solo, preached a great sermon, or even discipled someone who went on to serve the Lord in great and significant ways. The people I had discipled, . . . well, they never did much better than me. They just lived, so far as I could tell, decent, quiet lives with few or no big moments. Anyway, what was the point of flagellating myself? I'd just have to take what came. "Chin up," my mom always said.

She was here, you know. Honestly, I hadn't thought she would be, but I was overjoyed. All those years of lambasting her with the gospel, and all along she'd believed. Not quite like me, but she had believed, and that satisfied Him.

Dad, too; and my sister and brother and members of their families. I never had thought it could be true. I always had been caught up in certain narrow interpretations of things. But they all believed, even though they hadn't experienced the kind of "lightning bolt" born-again experience I had, so I'd thought maybe that meant they didn't really have faith in Christ. But they did.

My three kids were here, too, and my wife. I don't know what I would have done if they hadn't made it. I had been confident they would, of course, because I knew they believed. But there were always doubts.

And I was here! Even if He couldn't honestly say, "Well done," I was still here. I was part of His kingdom forever and ever. My loved ones were here. Most of them. And it would never end. There was plenty of rejoicing in that.

And then it began. He called us by name and each one came forward. It was astonishing. I wasn't bored or tired for a moment. He stood each one before the rest of us. We could see right into that person; his heart was revealed before us. We saw all he or she had done. We went right on through the ages, from the beginning of time.

In this place there was no sense of time. You could concentrate completely on what had gone before, of what was coming after. I'm sure it would have taken several years in earth time, although there was no way to tell. It didn't matter.

I was looking forward to the review of the twentieth century. I had some things to say about people I had known. I had already had opportunities to talk about people throughout history who had special ministries in my life. I got to thank Habakkuk and Elijah and Abraham—all of them. Paul, Peter, James. I was able to tell them how reading things from their writings had influenced me. I remarked on things I'd read from Martin Luther and Calvin and Wesley. It was marvelous, thanking and praising those people in person. All of them were rewarded.

He Himself spoke. So many "well dones." So many accolades.

I almost wished I had been some of those people. They'd done so much. But I would be content, I knew, with whatever happened to me, even if it were little. There were a few, yes, a few, who seemed to "escape so as through fire." But even in their cases . . .

It choked me up to think of it because I knew I might be one of them, so I didn't want to sound hard or disappointed when it happened to me. I just wished . . .

I had to make myself stop saying that! Whatever happened to me would happen. It was a strange feeling. On the one hand, I longed that everyone be rewarded well. Yet, when it came to myself, I had no idea what He might say. The suspense was almost murderous.

Each time before He spoke, He gave the whole group a chance to tell and bear witness to what the person at the judgment seat had done. It was amazing, the things that were said. Words, kindnesses, good deeds, thanks, praise. Everything was remembered. For some of them—such as Paul and Peter—the talk went on and on until He Himself pronounced a judgment and gave the reward. So many received rewards similar to both Paul's and Peter's.

He took each of us by order of birth and gave everyone a chance to speak. Then He opened the book—the book on each person's life. He passed it through the fire, and whatever gold, silver, and precious stones were upon it He gave to the subject as part of his or her spiritual reward. There were all sorts of crowns, the hidden manna, the white stone, and many other honors. Each one was individual and complete. Everyone agreed that His judgment was perfect.

I never wanted it to end. Everyone was excited and happy. You just wanted the person up there to do well and to receive a reward. You were rooting for everyone. When He did pronounce His judgment, you knew it was right and exact, and you took in everything. I trusted Him. I knew He'd bring it all out right.

It was a blur, yet everyone's face and deeds were imprinted on my mind. When I met them personally later, I knew I'd remember everything they'd been commended for and even praise them for it.

Then He came to the year of my birth, 1950.

It would be my turn soon. What would He say? What could He say? I was practically jumping in place. I felt like a schoolkid waiting for his report card and not being sure whether he'd get an F, an A, or something in between. Why was I so unsure?

Then He spoke my name.

I wove my way through the crowd. He motioned me to stand before Him. He was so august, like infinite light. There was a warmth about Him, a kindness. He loved me! I could feel His love holding me and strengthening me.

He asked the crowd if anyone wanted to speak. My son stepped forward first. "There are so many things, Lord."

"Tell them all," He said.

I was astonished. We had some bitter times on earth. But he began. "I remember his playing with me, Lord. Piggyback rides. Singing songs in the car. Fun. He made life fun. And he told me about You." My boy recounted all sorts of deeds. I was amazed and grateful. These were the things he remembered?

My wife said she had always loved the way I held her, even when I was tired and wanted to go to sleep. She spoke of how I gave her money to buy groceries and clothing with a smile and no resentment. She seemed to go on and on. A lump formed in my throat, and I fought to control my tears. Her face shone like the sun. I was so thankful He had given her to me.

There were others who told of my teaching them in church, a Bible story that had stuck in their minds and influenced them later in life. One boy said, "He told a story one time in Sunday school about Zaccheus giving his money back to the poor. Later in life it motivated me to help some homeless people."

My mouth dropped open. He remembered that? I didn't even remember it.

Johnny Martin told how I'd taught him to throw a ball. Bill Briggs, a fellow salesman I'd patiently trained, said he'd come to Christ years after he left our company. Doris Liston told how my strong singing in church one Sunday had encouraged her. It went on and on; most of the time I was in tears. I couldn't believe it.

A lady named Grace Schwartz told about once, driving her car, that it had broken down on the road with a flat tire, and how I had fixed it. I hadn't even known she was a Christian. I had witnessed to her, sort of, but she was bitter at the time about problems in her marriage and didn't tell me. She said my words had reminded her of the need to walk with Jesus again.

There was a boy, now a man, from my Little League team—Casey Szabo—who said I had encouraged him and given him a Bible verse. Even though he wasn't a believer at the time, it had come into his mind years later when he did believe.

The time I'd prayed for a friend during a funeral. The time I'd fixed a leaky faucet in the company bathroom because no one else would do it. The time I talked in church about the need to give sacrificially.

I'd forgotten them all. They seemed so insignificant. But He had said that anything done in His name would last, and it did.

Then the Lord Himself put the book in the fire. And suddenly gold, silver, and jewels appeared. So many pieces I couldn't count them. Each one a remembrance of a deed, a word, a thought, a prayer. They were all remembered. Every one.

He spoke then. He reminded me that I had practiced biblical principles in my work. He recounted that nearly every time I had refused to lie or cheat or steal; that I had been honest, worked hard, and given a good day's work to my employer. I hadn't even known if it mattered.

He spoke of how I had worked to be a good husband, listening to my wife, changing, growing, learning, and responding to her needs. He pointed out that I had stuck by her even when there were problems that could have ended in divorce. He remembered that I had tried to teach the family the Bible and had applied its principles. Even though He had not given me gifts in the area of teaching or speaking, He said I had tried and done well.

He reminded me of how I labored to be a good father. He brought out deeds of gentleness and patience that even my children didn't recall. Every time I had prayed in the car for someone, He pointed out the answer, and sometimes people stood and thanked me for my deed.

He showed me the accounting books of my giving to organizations and to the church. Missionaries, pastors, people all over the world stood—from Nigeria and China and Israel, places I knew little about and had never visited—and praised me for my deeds to them, although neither they nor I had known anything about them.

It went on and on. He moved on through my life, picking out each episode of good, showing who had benefited. There were people who had become Christians partly through the smallest particles of my influence—a kind word, a tract, a prayer in passing.

There were people who I'd prayed for while standing in supermarket lines. They'd become Christians, sometimes years later. He had them all stand. They thanked me and acknowledged my small part.

He spoke of others who were simply touched by my presence. He showed how many people in the gathering had been influenced by my family's saying grace in restaurants. Often, at the time, I had been vaguely uneasy. But He showed that some of the people were moved toward faith by those small acts.

Then He asked all the people to stand who had been in some way influenced by something I had done—whether it was a prayer for a missionary in Europe or a small gift to an organization in Los Angeles. All of it was connected. I could not count the number of people who stood, cheered, and thanked me.

I couldn't stop feeling choked up. The things I had done—the little things I considered so small and unimportant—had achieved far-reaching effects?

Finally, after it was all done, He stood to speak. "John," He said, "look at Me."

I looked into His eyes. It was the most hallowed, cleansing, thrilling moment of my life. As I looked at Him, I saw His heart. It was revealed in that blinding instant. I saw who He was and how He had loved me. I knew then that my God had loved me from all eternity and that I had been in His heart before I was even conceived in my mother's womb. I knew that He would never leave me and had been with me through every experience. I knew that He had ordered every detail of my life to bring me to this moment of triumph, and I saw that long ago He had planned every opportunity for a good deed in advance so that when I came to this moment there would be much reward.

I knew it all in that instant. And in that instant I loved Him as I had never loved Him. He spoke, His eyes shining and true, "John, you have

done what I planned. You have done many good works in My name. You have touched the lives of thousands. Well done, good and faithful servant. You will sit with me and rule with Me on My throne. I welcome you into the joy of your Father."

He embraced me, and in that moment the fear and doubt fell away forever. Then He presented me to the gathering. "Welcome John Colter into the eternal bliss and reward of his Lord."

The cheering never seemed to stop. And it was only the beginning.

PERMISSIONS
AND ACKNOWLEDGMENTS

"The Lion, the Witch, and the Wardrobe" excerpted from *The Lion, the Witch, and the Wardrobe,* bk. 2 of *The Chronicles of Narnia* series by C. S. Lewis, © 1950. Used by permission of C. S. Lewis Pte. Ltd.

"The Lesson of the Sweeter Day," and "The Lesson of the Broken Crayons" excerpted from *All I Really Need to Know I Learned in Sunday School* by Cliff Schimmels, © 1991. Used by permission of Cook Communications Ministries.

"The Best Christmas Pageant Ever" condensed from *The Best Christmas Christmas Pageant Ever* by Barbara Robinson, © 1972. Used by permission of HarperCollins Publishers.

"Lost Tooth," "Concerning Rest," "Concerning Lemons," and "The Millionaire and the Scrub Lady" all excerpted from *The Millionaire and the Scrub Lady and Other Parables* by William Barton, © 1990. Used by permission of Hendrickson Publishers, Inc.

"Sacraments" excerpted from *O Ye Jigs and Juleps* by Virginia Cary Hudson, © 1990 by Beverly Cary Mayne Kienzie. Used by permission of Scribner, a division of Simon & Schuster.

"In Search of a Proper Mate," and "Only the Beginning" excerpted from *Tales of the Neverending* by Mark Littleton, © 1990. Used by permission of Moody Press.

"The Good Bishop" adapted from *Les Miserables* by Victor Hugo.

"I Saw Gooley Fly," and "A Small Happening at Andover" excerpted from *How Silently, How Silently and Other Stories* by Joseph Bayly, © 1973. Used by permission of Timothy Bayly.

"Pilgrim's Progress" condensed and retold by Stephen Fortosis from *Pilgrim's Progress* by John Bunyan.

"My Salvation and Yours" excerpted from *The Carpenter and the Unbuilder: Stories for the Spiritual Quest* by David M. Griebner, © 1996. Used by permission of Upper Room Books.

About the Editor

Stephen Fortosis grew up in the mountains of North Carolina, loving the wildlife, tree houses, endless hiking, and stories his father would read to his three sons. The first story Fortosis remembers being mesmerized by is the one beginning this collection: C. S. Lewis's "The Lion, the Witch, and the Wardrobe."

The author's love for story-telling and reading continued after graduating from Columbia Bible College, serving as a youth pastor for six years, earning his master's degree from Talbot School of Theology, and earning a doctorate from Biola University. He's taught everything from critical thinking and writing, to interpersonal communication and Bible interpretation at Western Seminary in Portland, Oregon, and then across country at Trinity International University in Miami, Florida. Along the way he's written more than seventy stories in eight genres, including six books on topics that range from Bible characters (such as in his book *Great Men and Women of the Bible*) to biblical fiction. On the side, he paints murals for hospitals, schools, and private and model homes; and for fun he watches Duke basketball, oil paints, and—of course—reads, reads, reads.

A long-time bachelor, Fortosis, at 45, met and married his life partner in 2000. "Debra," he says, "was worth the wait." They live in Boca Raton, Florida, where he says he hopes to live happily ever after, reading fine books and publishing good stories in every genre until he's too arthritic to type.